And Thee

is one of Agatha Christie's greatest tales of mystery. A taut drama of a small group of people at the mercy of a vindictive, almost pathological killer, this novel has become a modern classic of the criminal story and has been made into a highly popular motion picture and successful Broadway play.

The Reader's Supplement to this ENRICHED CLASSICS edition appears in the center insert. It has been prepared under the supervision of an editorial committee directed by Harry Shefter, Professor of English, New York University, and author of many books used extensively for the improvement of skills in the language arts. The contributing editor for this edition was Leonard R.N. Ashley, Professor of English, Brooklyn College. Grateful acknowledgment is made to the Picture Collection Division of the New York Public Library, which provided much of the illustrative material.

Titles available in the
ENRICHED CLASSICS SERIES

Most Washington Square Press Books are available at special quantity discounts for bulk purchases for sales promotions, premiums or fund raising. Special books or book excerpts can also be created to fit specific needs.

For details write the office of the Vice President of Special Markets, Pocket Books, 1230 Avenue of the Americas, New York, New York 10020.

And Then There Were None

Agatha Christie

Previously published as
TEN LITTLE INDIANS

WASHINGTON SQUARE PRESS
PUBLISHED BY POCKET BOOKS

New York   London   Toronto   Sydney   Tokyo   Singapore

A Washington Square Press Publication of
POCKET BOOKS, a division of Simon & Schuster Inc.
1230 Avenue of the Americas, New York, NY 10020

ISBN: 0-671-70466-4

First Pocket Books printing July 1973

23 22 21 20 19 18 17 16

WASHINGTON SQUARE PRESS and WSP colophon are
registered trademarks of Simon & Schuster Inc.

Printed in the U.S.A.

CAST OF CHARACTERS

AND THEN
THERE WERE NONE

1

IN THE CORNER of a first-class smoking carriage, Mr. Justice Wargrave, lately retired from the bench, puffed at a cigar and ran an interested eye through the political news in the *Times*. He laid the paper down and glanced out of the window. They were running now through Somerset. He glanced at his watch—another two hours to go.

He went over in his mind all that had appeared in the papers about Indian Island. There had been its original purchase by an American millionaire who was crazy about yachting—and an account of the luxurious modern house he had built on this little island off the Devon coast. The unfortunate fact that the new third wife of the American millionaire was a bad sailor had led to the subsequent putting up of the house and island for sale. Various glowing advertisements of it had appeared in the papers. Then came the first bald statement that it had been bought—by a Mr. Owen. After that the rumors of the gossip writers had started. Indian Island had really been bought by Miss Gabrielle Turl, the Hollywood film star! She wanted to spend some months there free from all publicity! *Busy Bee* had hinted delicately that it was to be an abode for Royalty??! *Mr. Merryweather* had had it whispered to him that it had been bought for a honeymoon—Young Lord L—— had surrendered to Cupid at last! *Jonas* knew for a *fact* that it had been purchased by the Admiralty with a view to carrying out some very hush-hush experiments! Definitely, Indian Island was news!

From his pocket Mr. Justice Wargrave drew out a letter. The handwriting was practically illegible but words here and there stood out with unexpected clarity. *Dearest Lawrence . . . such years since I heard anything of you . . . must come to Indian Island . . . the most enchanting*

9

place . . . so much to talk over . . . old days . . . communion with Nature . . . bask in sunshine . . . 12:40 from Paddington . . . meet you at Oakbridge . . . and his correspondent signed herself with a flourish his *ever Constance Culmington.*

Mr. Justice Wargrave cast back in his mind to remember when exactly he had last seen Lady Constance Culmington. It must be seven—no, eight years ago. She had then been going to Italy to bask in the sun and be at one with Nature and the *contadini.* Later, he had heard, she had proceeded to Syria where she proposed to bask in yet stronger sun and live at one with Nature and the Bedouin.

Constance Culmington, he reflected to himself, was exactly the sort of woman who *would* buy an island and surround herself with mystery! Nodding his head in gentle approval of his logic, Mr. Justice Wargrave allowed his head to nod. . . . He slept. . . .

ii.

Vera Claythorne, in a third-class carriage with five other travelers in it, leaned her head back and shut her eyes. How hot it was traveling by train today! It would be nice to get to the sea! Really a great piece of luck getting this job. When you wanted a holiday post it nearly always meant looking after a swarm of children—secretarial holiday posts were much more difficult to get. Even the agency hadn't held out much hope.

And then the letter had come.

I have received your name from the Skilled Women's Agency together with their recommendation. I understand they know you personally. I shall be glad to pay you the salary you ask and shall expect you to take up your duties on August 8th. The train is the 12:40 from Paddington and you will be met at Oakbridge station. I enclose five pound notes for expenses.

Yours truly,
Una Nancy Owen

And at the top was the stamped address INDIAN ISLAND, STICKLEHAVEN, DEVON. . . .

Indian Island! Why, there had been nothing else in the papers lately! All sorts of hints and interesting rumors. Though probably that was mostly untrue. But the house had certainly been built by a millionaire and was said to be absolutely the last word in luxury.

Vera Claythorne, tired by a recent strenuous term at school, thought to herself: Being a games mistress in a third-class school isn't much of a catch. . . . If only I could get a job at some *decent* school. And then, with a cold feeling round her heart, she thought: But I'm lucky to have even this. After all, people don't like a Coroner's Inquest, even if the Coroner *did* acquit me of all blame!

He had even complimented her on her presence of mind and courage, she remembered. For an inquest it couldn't have gone better. And Mrs. Hamilton had been kindness itself to her. Only Hugo (*but she wouldn't think of Hugo!*).

Suddenly, in spite of the heat in the carriage she shivered and wished she wasn't going to the sea. A picture rose clearly before her mind. *Cyril's head, bobbing up and down, swimming to the rock.* . . . Up and down—up and down. . . . And herself, swimming in easy, practiced strokes after him—cleaving her way through the water but knowing, only too surely, that she wouldn't be in time. . . .

The sea—its deep, warm blue—mornings spent lying out on the sands—Hugo—Hugo who had said he loved her. . . . She must *not* think of Hugo. . . .

She opened her eyes and frowned across at the man opposite her. A tall man with a brown face, light eyes set rather close together and an arrogant, almost cruel mouth. She thought to herself: I bet he's been to some interesting parts of the world and seen some interesting things. . . .

iii.

Philip Lombard, summing up the girl opposite in a mere flash of his quick-moving eyes, thought to himself: Quite attractive—a bit schoolmistressy perhaps. . . . A cool customer, he should imagine—and one who could hold her own—in love or war. He'd rather like to take her on. . . .

He frowned. No, cut out all that kind of stuff. This was business. He'd got to keep his mind on the job.

What exactly was up? he wondered. Morris had been damned mysterious. "Take it or leave it, Captain Lombard."

He had said thoughtfully, "A hundred guineas, eh?"

He had said it in a casual way as though a hundred guineas were nothing to him. *A hundred guineas* when he was literally down to his last square meal! He had fancied, though that Morris had not been deceived—that was the damnable part about Morris, you couldn't deceive him about money—he *knew!*

He had said in the same casual tone, "And you can't give me any further information?"

Mr. Isaac Morris had shaken his little bald head very positively. "No, Captain Lombard, the matter rests there. It is understood by my client that your reputation is that of a good man in a tight place. I am empowered to hand you one hundred guineas in return for which you will travel to Sticklehaven, Devon. The nearest station is Oakbridge. You will be met there and motored to Sticklehaven where a motor launch will convey you to Indian Island. There you will hold yourself at the disposal of my client."

Lombard had said abruptly, "For how long?"

"Not longer than a week at most."

Fingering his small mustache, Captain Lombard said, "You understand I can't undertake anything—illegal?"

He had darted a very sharp glance at the other as he had spoken. There had been a very faint smile on the thick lips of Mr. Morris as he answered gravely, "If anything illegal is proposed, you will, of course, be at perfect liberty to withdraw."

Damn the smooth little brute, he had smiled! It was as though he knew very well that in Lombard's past actions legality had not always been a *sine qua non.* . . .

Lombard's own lips parted in a grin. By Jove, he'd sailed pretty near the wind once or twice! But he'd always got away with it! There wasn't much he drew the line at really. . . . No, there wasn't much he'd draw the line at. He fancied that he was going to enjoy himself at Indian Island. . . .

iv.

In a non-smoking carriage Miss Emily Brent sat very upright as was her custom. She was sixty-five and she did not approve of lounging. Her father, a Colonel of the old school, had been particular about deportment. The present generation was shamelessly lax—in their carriage, *and in every other way.* . . .

Enveloped in an aura of righteousness and unyielding principles, Miss Brent sat in her crowded third-class carriage and triumphed over its discomfort and its heat. Everyone made such a fuss over things nowadays! They wanted injections before they had teeth pulled—they took drugs if they couldn't sleep—they wanted easy chairs and cushions and the girls allowed their figures to slop about anyhow and lay about half-naked on the beaches in summer. Miss Brent's lips set closely. She would like to make an example of certain people.

She remembered last year's summer holiday. This year, however, it would be quite different. Indian Island. . . . Mentally she reread the letter which she had already read so many times.

Dear Miss Brent,

I do hope you remember me? We were together at Bellhaven Guest House in August some years ago, and we seemed to have so much in common.

I am starting a guest house of my own on an island off the coast of Devon. I think there is really an opening for a place where there is good plain cooking and a nice old-fashioned type of person. None of this nudity and gramophones half the night. I shall be very glad if you could see your way to spending your summer holiday on Indian Island—quite free

13

—as my guest. Would early in August suit you? Perhaps the 8th.

Yours sincerely,

U. N.——

What was the name? The signature was rather difficult to read. Emily Brent thought impatiently: So many people write their signatures quite illegibly.

She let her mind run back over the people at Bellhaven. She had been there two summers running. There had been that nice middle-aged woman— Mrs.—Mrs.— now what *was* her name?—her father had been a Canon. And there had been a Miss Olton—Ormen— No, surely it was *Oliver!* Yes—Oliver.

Indian Island! There had been things in the paper about Indian Island—something about a film star—or was it an American millionaire? Of course often those places went very cheap—islands didn't suit everybody. They thought the idea was romantic but when they came to live there they realized the disadvantages and were only too glad to sell.

Emily Brent thought to herself: I shall be getting a free holiday at any rate. With her income so much reduced and so many dividends not being paid, that was indeed something to take into consideration. If only she could remember a little more about Mrs.—or was it Miss— Oliver?

v.

General Macarthur looked out of the carriage window. The train was just coming into Exeter where he had to change. Damnable, these slow branch-line trains! This place, Indian Island, was really no distance at all as the crow flies.

He hadn't got it clear who this fellow Owen was. A friend of Spoof Leggard's, apparently—and of Johnny Dyer's.

—*One or two of your old cronies are coming—would like to have a talk over old times.*

Well, he'd enjoy a chat about old times. He'd had a fancy lately that fellows were rather fighting shy of him. All owing to that damned rumor! By God, it was pretty hard—nearly thirty years ago now! Armstrong had talked, he supposed. Damned young pup! What did *he* know about it? Oh, well, no good brooding about these things! One fancied things sometimes—fancied a fellow was looking at you queerly.

This Indian Island now, he'd be interested to see it. A lot of gossip flying about. Looked as though there might be something in the rumor that the Admiralty or the War Office or the Air Force had got hold of it. . . .

Young Elmer Robson, the American millionaire, had actually built the place. Spent thousands on it, so it was said. Every mortal luxury . . .

Exeter! And an hour to wait! And he didn't want to wait. He wanted to get on. . . .

vi.

Dr. Armstrong was driving his Morris across Salisbury Plain. He was very tired. . . . Success had its penalties. There had been a time when he had sat in his consulting room in Harley Street, correctly appareled, surrounded with the most up-to-date appliances and the most luxurious furnishings and waited—waited through the empty days for his venture to succeed or fail. . . .

Well, it had succeeded! He'd been lucky! Lucky *and* skillful, of course. He was a good man at his job—but that wasn't enough for success. You had to have luck as well. And he'd had it! An accurate diagnosis, a couple of grateful women patients—women with money and position—and word had got about. "You ought to try Armstrong— *quite* a young man—but *so* clever— Pam had been to all sorts of people for *years* and he put his finger on the trouble at once!" The ball had started rolling.

And now Dr. Armstrong had definitely arrived. His days were full. He had little leisure. And so, on this August morning, he was glad that he was leaving London and going to be for some days on an island off the Devon coast. Not that it was exactly a holiday. The letter he had received had been rather vague in its terms, but there was nothing vague about the accompanying check. A whacking fee. These Owens must be rolling in money. Some little difficulty, it seemed, a husband who was worried about his wife's health and wanted a report on it without her being alarmed. She wouldn't hear of seeing a doctor. Her nerves—

Nerves! The doctor's eyebrows went up. These women and their nerves! Well, it was good for business, after all. Half the women who consulted him had nothing the matter with them but boredom, but they wouldn't thank you for telling them so! And one could usually find something.

"A slightly uncommon condition of the—some long word—nothing at all serious—but it just needs putting right. A simple treatment."

Well, medicine was mostly faith-healing when it came to it. And he had a good manner—he could inspire hope and belief.

Lucky that he'd managed to pull himself together in time after that business ten—no, fifteen years ago. It had been a near thing, that! He'd been going to pieces. The shock had pulled him together. He'd cut out drink altogether. By Jove, it had been a near thing though. . . .

With a devastating, ear-splitting blast on the horn an enormous Super Sports Dalmain car rushed past him at eighty miles an hour. Dr. Armstrong nearly went into the hedge. One of these young fools who tore around the country. He hated them! That had been a near shave, too. Damned young fool!

vii.

Tony Marston, roaring down into Mere, thought to himself: The amount of cars crawling about the roads is frightful. Always something blocking your way. *And* they will drive in the middle of the road! Pretty hopeless

16

driving in England, anyway. . . . Not like France where you really *could* let out. . . .

Should he stop here for a drink, or push on? Heaps of time! Only another hundred miles and a bit to go. He'd have a gin and ginger beer. Fizzing hot day!

This island place ought to be rather good fun—if the weather lasted. Who *were* these Owens, he wondered? Rich and stinking, probably. Badger was rather good at nosing people like that out. Of course, he *had* to, poor old chap, with no money of his own. . . .

Hope they'd do one well in drinks. Never knew with these fellows who'd made their money and weren't born to it. Pity that story about Gabrielle Turl having bought Indian Island wasn't true. He'd like to have been in with that film-star crowd. Oh, well, he supposed there'd be a few girls there. . . .

Coming out of the hotel, he stretched himself, yawned, looked up at the blue sky and climbed into the Dalmain. Several young women looked at him admiringly—his six feet of well-proportioned body, his crisp hair, tanned face, and intensely blue eyes.

He let in the clutch with a roar and leapt up the narrow street. Old men and errand boys jumped for safety. The latter looked after the car admiringly.

Anthony Marston proceeded on his triumphal progress.

viii.

Mr. Blore was in the slow train from Plymouth. There was only one other person in his carriage, an elderly seafaring gentleman with a bleary eye. At the present moment he had dropped off to sleep. Mr. Blore was writing carefully in a little notebook.

"That's the lot," he muttered to himself. "Emily Brent, Vera Claythorne, Dr. Armstrong, Anthony Marston, old Justice Wargrave, Philip Lombard, General Macarthur, C.M.G., D.S.O. Manservant and wife: Mr. and Mrs. Rogers."

He closed the notebook and put it back in his pocket.

He glanced over at the corner and the slumbering man. "Had one over the eight," diagnosed Mr. Blore accurately.

He went over things carefully and conscientiously in his mind. "Job ought to be easy enough," he ruminated. "Don't see how I can slip up on it. Hope I look all right."

He stood up and scrutinized himself anxiously in the glass. The face reflected there was of a slightly military cast with a mustache. There was very little expression in it. The eyes were gray and set rather close together. "Might be a major," said Mr. Blore. "No, I forgot. There's that old military gent. He'd spot me at once. South Africa," said Mr. Blore, "that's my line! None of these people have anything to do with South Africa, and I've just been reading that travel folder so I can talk about it all right."

Fortunately there were all sorts and types of colonials. As a man of means from South Africa, Mr. Blore felt that he could enter into any society unchallenged.

Indian Island. He remembered Indian Island as a boy. . . . Smelly sort of rock covered with gulls—stood about a mile from the coast. It had got its name from its resemblance to a man's head—an American Indian profile.

Funny idea to go and build a house on it! Awful in bad weather! But millionaires were full of whims!

The old man in the corner woke up and said, "You can't never tell at sea—never!"

Mr. Blore said soothingly, "That's right. You can't."

The old man hiccuped twice and said plaintiv'ly, "There's a squall coming."

Mr. Blore said, "No, no, mate, it's a lovely day."

The old man said angrily, "There's a squall ahead. I can *smell* it."

"Maybe you're right," said Mr. Blore pacifically.

The train stopped at a station and the old fellow rose unsteadily. "Thish where I get out." He fumbled with the window. Mr. Blore helped him.

The old man stood in the doorway. He raised a solemn hand and blinked his bleary eyes. "Watch and pray," he said. "Watch and pray. The day of judgment is at hand."

He collapsed through the doorway onto the platform. From a recumbent position he looked up at Mr. Blore and said with immense dignity, "I'm talking to *you*, young man. The day of judgment is very close at hand."

Subsiding into his seat Mr. Blore thought to himself: He's nearer the day of judgment than I am!

But there, as it happens, he was wrong. . . .

2

OUTSIDE OAKBRIDGE STATION a little group of people stood in momentary uncertainy. Behind them stood porters with suitcases. One of these called "Jim!" The driver of one of the taxis stepped forward. "You'm for Indian Island, maybe?" he asked in a soft Devon voice. Four voices gave assent—and then immediately afterwards gave quick surreptitious glances at each other.

The driver said, addressing his remarks to Mr. Justice Wargrave as the senior member of the party: "There are two taxis here, sir. One of them must wait till the slow train from Exeter gets in—a matter of five minutes—there's one gentleman coming by that. Perhaps one of you wouldn't mind waiting? You'd be more comfortable that way."

Vera Claythorne, her own secretarial position clear in her mind, spoke at once. "I'll wait," she said, "if you will go on." She looked at the other three; her glance and voice had that slight suggestion of command in them that comes from having occupied a position of authority. She might have been directing which tennis sets the girls were to play in.

Miss Brent said stiffly, "Thank you," bent her head and entered one of the taxis, the door of which the driver was holding open. Mr. Justice Wargrave followed her.

Captain Lombard said, "I'll wait with Miss—"

"Claythorne," said Vera.

"My name is Lombard, Philip Lombard."

The porters were piling luggage on the taxi. Inside, Mr.

Justice Wargrave said with due legal caution, "Beautiful weather we are having."

Miss Brent said, "Yes, indeed."

A very distinguished old gentleman, she thought to herself. Quite unlike the usual type of man in seaside guest houses. Evidently Mrs. or Miss Oliver had good connections. . . .

Mr. Justice Wargrave inquired, "Do you know this part of the world well?"

"I have been to Cornwall and to Torquay, but this is my first visit to this part of Devon."

The judge said, "I also am unacquainted with this part of the world."

The taxi drove off. The driver of the second taxi said, "Like to sit inside while you're waiting?"

Vera said decisively, "Not at all."

Captain Lombard smiled. He said, "That sunny wall looks more attractive. Unless you'd rather go inside the station?"

"No, indeed. It's so delightful to get out of that stuffy train."

He answered, "Yes, traveling by train *is* rather trying in this weather."

Vera said conventionally, "I do hope it lasts—the weather, I mean. Our English summers are so treacherous."

With a slight lack of originality Lombard asked, "Do you know this part of the world well?"

"No, I've never been here before." She added quickly, conscientiously determined to make her position clear at once, "I haven't even seen my employer yet."

"Your employer?"

"Yes, I'm Mrs. Owen's secretary."

"Oh, I see." Just imperceptibly his manner changed. It was slightly more assured—easier in tone. He said, "Isn't that rather unusual?"

Vera laughed. "Oh, no, I don't think so. Her own secretary was suddenly taken ill and she wired to an agency for a substitute and they sent me."

"So that was it. And suppose you don't like the post when you've got there?"

Vera laughed again. "Oh, it's only temporary—a holiday post. I've got a permanent job at a girls' school. As a matter of fact, I'm frightfully thrilled at the prospect of seeing Indian Island. There's been such a lot about it in the papers. Is it really very fascinating?"

Lombard said, "I don't know. I haven't seen it."

"Oh, really? The Owens are frightfully keen on it, I suppose. What are they like? Do tell me."

Lombard thought: Awkward, this—am I supposed to have met them or not? He said quickly, "There's a wasp crawling up your arm. No—keep quite still." He made a convincing pounce. "There. It's gone!"

"Oh, thank you. There are a lot of wasps about this summer."

"Yes, I suppose it's the heat. Who are we waiting for, do you know?"

"I haven't the least idea."

The loud, drawn-out scream of an approaching train was heard. Lombard said, "That will be the train now."

ii.

It was a tall, soldierly old man who appeared at the exit from the platform. His gray hair was clipped close and he had a neatly trimmed white mustache. His porter, staggering slightly under the weight of the solid leather suitcase, indicated Vera and Lombard.

Vera came forward in a competent manner. She said, "I am Mrs. Owen's secretary. There is a car here waiting." She added, "This is Mr. Lombard."

The faded blue eyes, shrewd in spite of their age, sized up Lombard. For a moment a judgment showed in them—had there been anyone to read it.

Good-looking fellow. Something just a little wrong about him. . . .

The three of them got into the waiting taxi. They drove through the sleepy streets of little Oakbridge and continued about a mile on the main Plymouth road. Then they plunged into a maze of cross-country lanes, steep, green and narrow.

General Macarthur said, "Don't know this part of Devon at all. My little place is in East Devon—just on the borderline of Dorset."

Vera said, "It really is lovely here. The hills and the red earth and everything so green and luscious looking."

Philip Lombard said critically, "It's a bit shut in. . . . I like open country myself. Where you can see what's coming. . . ."

General Macarthur said to him, "You've seen a bit of the world, I fancy?"

Lombard shrugged his shoulders disparagingly. "I've knocked about here and there, sir."

He thought to himself: He'll ask me now if I was old enough to be in the War. These old boys always do.

But General Macarthur did not mention the War.

iii.

They came up over a steep hill and down a zigzag track to Sticklehaven—a mere cluster of cottages with a fishing boat or two drawn up on the beach. Illuminated by the setting sun, they had their first glimpse of Indian Island jutting up out of the sea to the south.

Vera said, surprised, "It's a long way out."

She had pictured it differently, close to shore, crowned with a beautiful white house. But there was no house visible, only the boldly silhouetted rock with its faint resemblance to a giant Indian's head. There was something sinister about it. She shivered faintly.

Outside a little inn, the Seven Stars, three people were sitting. There was the hunched elderly figure of the judge, the upright form of Miss Brent, and a third man—a big, bluff man who came forward and introduced himself. "Thought we might as well wait for you," he said. "Make one trip of it. Allow me to introduce myself. Name's Davis. Natal, South Africa's, my natal spot, ha, ha!" He laughed.

Mr. Justice Wagrave looked at him with active malevolence. He seemed to be wishing that he could order the court to be cleared. Miss Emily Brent was clearly not sure if she liked Colonials.

"Anyone care for a little nip before we embark?" asked Mr. Davis hospitably.

Nobody assenting to his proposition, Mr. Davis turned and held up a finger. "Mustn't delay, then. Our good host and hostess will be expecting us," he said. He might have noticed that a curious constraint came over the other members of the party. It was as though the mention of their host and hostess had a curiously paralyzing effect upon the guests.

In response to Davis' beckoning finger, a man detached himself from a nearby wall against which he was leaning and came up to them. His rolling gait proclaimed him a man of the sea. He had a weather-beaten face and dark eyes with a slightly evasive expression. He spoke in a soft Devon voice. "Will you be ready to be starting for the island, ladies and gentlemen? The boat's waiting. There's two gentlemen coming by car, but Mr. Owen's orders was not to wait for them as they might arrive at any time."

The party got up. Their guide led them along a small stone jetty. Alongside it a motor boat was lying. Emily Brent said, "That's a very small boat."

The boat's owner said persuasively, "She's a fine boat, that, ma'am. You could go to Plymouth in her as easy as winking."

Mr. Justice Wargrave said sharply, "There are a good many of us."

"She'd take double the number, sir."

Philip Lombard said in his pleasant, easy voice, "It's quite all right. Glorious weather—no swell."

Rather doubtfully, Miss Brent permitted herself to be helped into the boat. The others followed suit. There was as yet no fraternizing among the party. It was as though each member of it was puzzled by the other members.

They were just about to cast loose when their guide paused, boat hook in hand. Down the steep track into the village a car was coming. A car so fantastically powerful, so superlatively beautiful that it had all the nature of an apparition. At the wheel sat a young man, his hair blown back by the wind. In the blaze of the evening light he looked, not a man, but a young god, a Hero God out of some Northern Saga. He touched the horn and a great roar of sound echoed from the rocks of the bay. It was a fantastic moment. In it, Anthony Marston seemed to be something more than mortal. Afterwards, more than one of those present remembered that moment.

iv.

Fred Narracott sat by the engine thinking to himself that this was a queer lot. Not at all his idea of what Mr. Owen's guests were likely to be. He'd expected something altogether more classy. Togged-up women and gentlemen in yachting costume and all very rich and important looking.

Not at all like Mr. Elmer Robson's parties. A faint grin came to Fred Narracott's lips as he remembered the millionaire's guests. That had been a party if you like—and the drink they'd got through!

This Mr. Owen must be a very different sort of gentleman. Funny it was, thought Fred, that he'd never yet set eyes on Owen—or his Missus either. Never been down here yet, he hadn't. Everything ordered and paid for by that Mr. Morris. Instructions always very clear and payment prompt, but it was odd, all the same. The papers said there was some mystery about Owen. Mr. Narracott agreed with them.

Perhaps, after all, it *was* Miss Gabrielle Turl who had bought the island. But that theory departed from him as he surveyed his passengers. Not this lot—none of them looked likely to have anything to do with a film star.

He summed them up dispassionately. One old maid—the sour kind—he knew them well enough. She was a tartar, he could bet. Old military gentleman—real Army by the look of him. Nice-looking young lady—but the ordinary kind, not glamorous—no Hollywood touch about her. That bluff, cheery gent—*he* wasn't a real gentleman. Retired tradesman, that's what he is, thought Fred Narracott. The other gentleman, the lean, hungry-looking gentleman with the quick eyes, he was a queer one, he was. Just possible *he* might have something to do with the pictures.

No, there was only one satisfactory passenger in the boat. The last gentleman, the one who had arrived in the car (and what a car! A car such as had never been seen in Sticklehaven before. Must have cost hundreds and hundreds, a car like that.). He was the right kind. Born to money, he was. If the party had been all like him, he'd understand it. . . .

Queer business when you came to think of it—the whole thing was queer—very queer. . . .

v.

The boat churned its way round the rock. Now at last the house came into view. The south side of the island was quite different. It shelved gently down to the sea. The house was there facing south—low and square and modern-looking with rounded windows letting in all the light. An exciting house—a house that lived up to expectation!

Fred Narracott shut off the engine; they nosed their way gently into a little natural inlet between rocks.

Philip Lombard said sharply, "Must be difficult to land here in dirty weather."

Fred Narracott said cheerfully, "Can't land on Indian Island when there's a southeasterly. Sometimes 'tis cut off for a week or more."

Vera Claythorne thought: The catering must be very difficult. That's the worst of an island. All the domestic problems are so worrying.

The boat grated against the rocks. Fred Narracott jumped out and he and Lombard helped the others to alight. Narracott made the boat fast to a ring in the rock. Then he led the way up steps cut in the rock.

General Macarthur said, "Ha, delightful spot!" But he felt uneasy. Damned odd sort of place.

As the party ascended the steps, and came out on a terrace above, their spirits revived. In the open doorway of the house a correct butler was awaiting them, and something about his gravity reassured them. And then the house itself was really most attractive, the view from the terrace magnificent. . . .

The butler came forward, bowing slightly. He was a tall, lank man, gray-haired and very respectable. He said, "Will you come this way, please?"

In the wide hall drinks stood ready. Rows of bottles. Anthony Marston's spirits cheered up a little. He'd just been thinking this was a rum kind of show. None of *his* lot! What could old Badger have been thinking about to let him in for this? However the drinks were all right. Plenty of ice, too.

What was it the butler chap was saying? Mr. Owen—unfortunately delayed—unable to get here till tomorrow. Instructions—everything they wanted—if they would like to go to their rooms? Dinner would be at 8 o'clock.

vi.

Vera had followed Mrs. Rogers upstairs. The woman had thrown open a door at the end of a passage and Vera had walked into a delightful bedroom with a big window that opened wide upon the sea and another looking east. She uttered a quick exclamation of pleasure.

Mrs. Rogers was saying, "I hope you've got everything you want, miss?"

Vera looked round. Her luggage had been brought up and had been unpacked. At one side of the room a door stood open into a pale-blue tiled bathroom. She said quickly, "Yes, everything, I think."

"You'll ring the bell if you want anything, miss?"

Mrs. Rogers had a flat, monotonous voice. Vera looked at her curiously. What a white, bloodless ghost of a woman! Very respectable looking, with her hair dragged back from her face and her black dress. Queer light eyes that shifted the whole time from place to place.

Vera thought: She looks frightened of her own shadow. Yes, that was it—frightened! She looked like a woman who walked in mortal fear. . . . A little shiver passed down Vera's back. What on earth was the woman afraid of? She said pleasantly, "I'm Mrs. Owen's new secretary. I expect you know that."

Mrs. Rogers said, "No, miss, I don't know anything. Just a list of the ladies and gentlemen and what rooms they were to have."

Vera said, "Mrs. Owen didn't mention me?"

Mrs. Rogers' eyelashes flickered. "I haven't seen Mrs. Owen—not yet. We only came here two days ago."

Extraordinary people, these Owens, thought Vera. Aloud she said, "What staff is there here?"

"Just me and Rogers, miss."

Vera frowned. Eight people in the house—ten with the host and hostess—and only one married couple to do for them.

Mrs. Rogers said, "I'm a good cook and Rogers is handy about the house. I didn't know, of course, that there was to be such a large party."

Vera said, "But you can manage?"

"Oh, yes, miss, I can manage. If there's to be large parties often perhaps Mrs. Owen could get extra help in."

Vera said, "I expect so."

Mrs. Rogers turned to go. Her feet moved noiselessly over the ground. She drifted from the room like a shadow.

Vera went over to the window and sat down on the window seat. She was faintly disturbed. Everything—somehow—was a little queer. The absence of the Owens, the pale, ghostlike Mrs. Rogers. And the guests! Yes, the guests were queer too. An oddly assorted party. Vera thought: I wish I'd seen the Owens. . . . I wish I knew what they were like.

She got up and walked restlessly about the room. A perfect bedroom decorated throughout in the modern style. Offwhite rugs on the gleaming parquet floor—faintly tinted walls—a long mirror surrounded by lights. A mantelpiece bare of ornaments save for an enormous block of white marble shaped like a bear, a piece of modern sculpture in which was inset a clock. Over it, in a gleaming chromium frame, was a big square of parchment—a poem.

She stood in front of the fireplace and read it. It was

27

the old nursery rhyme that she remembered from her childhood days.

Ten little Indian boys went out to dine;
One choked his little self and then there were nine.

Nine little Indian boys sat up very late;
One overslept himself and then there were eight.

Eight little Indian boys traveling in Devon;
One said he'd stay there and then there were seven.

Seven little Indian boys chopping up sticks;
One chopped himself in halves and then there were six.

Six little Indian boys playing with a hive;
A bumblebee stung one and then there were five.

Five little Indian boys going in for law;
One got in Chancery and then there were four.

Four little Indian boys going out to sea;
A red herring swallowed one and then there were three.

Three little Indian boys walking in the Zoo;
A big bear hugged one and then there were two.

Two little Indian boys sitting in the sun;
One got frizzled up and then there was one.

One little Indian boy left all alone;
He went and hanged himself and then there were none.

Vera smiled. Of course! This was Indian Island! She went and sat again by the window looking out to sea. How big the sea was! From here there was no land to be seen anywhere—just a vast expanse of blue water rippling in the evening sun.

The sea . . . So peaceful today—sometimes so cruel . . . The sea that dragged you down to its depths. Drowned . . . Found drowned . . . Drowned at sea . . . Drowned—drowned—drowned . . . No, she wouldn't remember. . . . She would *not* think of it! All that was over.

vii.

Dr. Armstrong came to Indian Island just as the sun was sinking into the sea. On the way across he had chatted to the boatman—a local man. He was anxious to find out a little about these people who owned Indian Island, but the man Narracott seemed curiously ill informed, or perhaps unwilling to talk. So Dr. Armstrong chatted instead of the weather and of fishing.

He was tired after his long motor drive. His eyeballs ached. Driving west you were driving against the sun. Yes, he was very tired. The sea and perfect peace—that was what he needed. He would like, really, to take a long holiday. But he couldn't afford to do that. He could afford it financially, of course, but he couldn't afford to drop out. You were soon forgotten nowadays. No, now that he had arrived, he must keep his nose to the grindstone. He thought: All the same, this evening, I'll imagine to myself that I'm not going back—that I've done with London and Harley Street and all the rest of it.

There was something magical about an island—the mere word suggested fantasy. You lost touch with the world—an island was a world of its own. A world, perhaps, from which you might never return. He thought: I'm leaving my ordinary life behind me.

And, smiling to himself, he began to make plans, fantastic plans for the future. He was still smiling when he walked up the rock-cut steps.

In a chair on the terrace an old gentleman was sitting and the sight of him was vaguely familiar to Dr. Armstrong. Where had he seen that froglike face, that tortoiselike neck, that hunched-up attitude—yes, and those pale, shrewd little eyes? Of course—old Wargrave. He'd given evidence once before him. Always looked half-asleep, but was shrewd as could be when it came to a point of law. Had great power with a jury—it was said he could make their minds up for them any day of the week. He'd got one or two unlikely convictions out of them. A hanging judge, some people said.

Funny place to meet him . . . here—out of the world.

viii.

Mr. Justice Wargrave thought to himself: Armstrong? Remember him in the witness box. Very correct and cautious. All doctors are damned fools. Harley Street ones are the worst of the lot. And his mind dwelt malevolently on a recent interview he had had with a suave personage in that very street.

Aloud he grunted, "Drinks are in the hall."

Dr. Armstrong said, "I must go and pay my respects to my host and hostess."

Mr. Justice Wargrave closed his eyes again, looking decidedly reptilian, and said, "You can't do that."

Dr. Armstrong was startled. "Why not?"

The judge said, "No host and hostess. Very curious state of affairs. Don't understand this place."

Dr. Armstrong stared at him for a minute. When he thought the old gentleman had actually gone to sleep, Wargrave said suddenly, "D'you know Constance Culmington?"

"Er—no, I'm afraid I don't."

"It's of no consequence," said the judge. "Very vague woman—and practically unreadable handwriting. I was just wondering if I'd come to the wrong house."

Dr. Armstrong shook his head and went on up to the house.

Mr. Justice Wargrave reflected on the subject of Constance Culmington. Undependable like all women.

His mind went on to the two women in the house, the tight-lipped old maid and the girl. He didn't care for the girl, cold-blooded young hussy. No, three women, if you counted the Rogers woman. Odd creature, she looked scared to death. Respectable pair and knew their job.

Rogers coming out on the terrace that minute, the judge asked him, "Is Lady Constance Culmington expected, do you know?"

Rogers stared at him. "No, sir, not to my knowledge."

The judge's eyebrows rose. But he only grunted. He thought: Indian Island, eh? There's a nigger in the wood-pile.

ix.

Anthony Marston was in his bath. He luxuriated in the steaming water. His limbs had felt cramped after his long drive. Very few thoughts passed through his head. Anthony was a creature of sensation—and of action. He thought to himself: Must go through with it, I suppose, and thereafter dismissed everything from his mind.

Warm steaming water—tired limbs—presently a shave —a cocktail—dinner.... And after—?

x.

Mr. Blore was tying his tie. He wasn't very good at this sort of thing. Did he look all right? He supposed so. Nobody had been exactly cordial to him.... Funny the way they all eyed each other—as though they *knew*.... Well, it was up to him.

He didn't mean to bungle his job. He glanced up at the framed nursery rhyme over the mantelpiece. Neat touch, having that there!

He thought: Remember this island when I was a kid. Never thought I'd be doing this sort of a job in a house here. Good thing, perhaps, that one can't foresee the future....

xi.

General Macarthur was frowning to himself.

Damn it all, the whole thing was deuced odd! Not at

all what he'd been led to expect. . . . For two pins he'd make an excuse and get away. . . . Throw up the whole business. . . . But the motor boat had gone back to the mainland. He'd have to stay.

That fellow Lombard now, he was a queer chap.

Not straight. He'd swear the man wasn't straight.

xii.

As the gong sounded, Philip Lombard came out of his room and walked to the head of the stairs. He moved like a panther, smoothly and noiselessly. There was something of the panther about him altogether. A beast of prey—pleasant to the eye.

He was smiling to himself. A week—eh?

He was going to enjoy that week.

xiii.

In her bedroom, Emily Brent, dressed in black silk ready for dinner, was reading her Bible. Her lips moved as she followed the words:

"The heathen are sunk down in the pit that they made: in the net which they hid is their own foot taken. The Lord is known by the judgment which he executeth: the wicked is snared in the work of his own hands. The wicked shall be turned into hell."

Her tight lips closed. She shut the Bible.

Rising, she pinned a cairngorm brooch at her neck, and went down to dinner.

3

■

DINNER WAS DRAWING to a close. The food had been good, the wine perfect. Rogers waited well.

Everyone was in better spirits. They had begun to talk to each other with more freedom and intimacy. Mr. Justice Wargrave, mellowed by the excellent port, was being amusing in a caustic fashion; Dr. Armstrong and Tony Marston were listening to him. Miss Brent chatted to General Macarthur; they had discovered some mutual friends. Vera Claythorne was asking Mr. Davis intelligent questions about South Africa. Mr. Davis was quite fluent on the subject. Lombard listened to the conversation. Once or twice he looked up quickly, and his eyes narrowed. Now and then his eyes played round the table, studying the others.

Anthony Marston said suddenly, "Quaint, these things, aren't they?"

In the center of the round table, on a circular glass stand, were some little china figures. "Indians," said Tony. "Indian Island. I suppose that's the idea."

Vera leaned forward. "I wonder. How many are there? Ten?"

"Yes—ten there are."

Vera cried, "What fun! They're the ten little Indian boys of the nursery rhyme, I suppose. In my bedroom the rhyme is framed and hung up over the mantelpiece."

Lombard said, "In my room, too."

"And mine."

"And mine."

Everybody joined the chorus. Vera said, "It's an amusing idea, isn't it?"

Mr. Justice Wargrave grunted, "Remarkably childish," and helped himself to port.

Emily Brent looked at Vera Claythorne. Vera Claythorne looked at Miss Brent. The two women rose. In the drawing room, the French windows were open onto the terrace and the sound of the sea murmuring against the rocks came up to them. Emily Brent said, "Pleasant sound."

Vera said sharply, "I hate it."

Miss Brent's eyes looked at her in surprise. Vera flushed. She said, more composedly, "I don't think this place would be very agreeable in a storm."

Emily Brent agreed. "I've no doubt the house is shut up in winter," she said. "You'd never get servants to stay here for one thing."

Vera murmured, "It must be difficult to get servants anyway."

Emily Brent said, "Mrs. Oliver has been lucky to get these two. The woman's a good cook."

Vera thought: Funny how elderly people always get names wrong. She said, "Yes, I think Mrs. Owen has been very lucky indeed."

Emily Brent had brought a small piece of embroidery out of her bag. Now, as she was about to thread her needle, she paused. She said sharply, "Owen? Did you say Owen?"

"Yes."

Emily Brent said sharply, "I've never met anyone called Owen in my life."

Vera stared. "But surely—" She did not finish her sentence. The door opened and the men joined them. Rogers followed them into the room with the coffee tray.

The judge came and sat down by Emily Brent. Armstrong came up to Vera. Tony Marston strolled to the open window. Blore studied with naïve surprise a statuette in brass—wondering perhaps if its bizarre angularities were really supposed to be the female figure. General Macarthur stood with his back to the mantelpiece. He pulled at his little white mustache. That had been a damned good dinner! His spirits were rising. Lombard turned over the pages of *Punch* that lay with other papers on a table by the wall.

Rogers went round with the coffee tray. The coffee was good—really black and very hot.

The whole party had dined well. They were satisfied

with themselves and with life. The hands of the clock pointed to twenty minutes past nine. There was a silence—a comfortable, replete silence. Into that silence came The Voice. Without warning, inhuman, penetrating . . .

"*Ladies and gentlemen! Silence, please!*"

Everyone was startled. They looked round—at each other, at the walls. Who was speaking?

The Voice went on—a high clear voice.

You are charged with the following indictments:

Edward George Armstrong, that you did upon the 14th day of March, 1925, cause the death of Louisa Mary Clees.

Emily Caroline Brent, that upon the 5th of November, 1931, you were responsible for the death of Beatrice Taylor.

William Henry Blore, that you brought about the death of James Stephen Landor on October 10th, 1928.

Vera Elizabeth Claythorne, that on the 11th day of August, 1935, you killed Cyril Ogilvie Hamilton.

Philip Lombard, that upon a date in February, 1932, you were guilty of the death of twenty-one men, members of an East African tribe.

John Gordon Macarthur, that on the 4th of January, 1917, you deliberately sent your wife's lover, Arthur Richmond, to his death.

Anthony James Marston, that upon the 14th day of November last, you were guilty of the murder of John and Lucy Combes.

Thomas Rogers and Ethel Rogers, that on the 6th of May, 1929, you brought about the death of Jennifer Brady.

Lawrence John Wargrave, that upon the 10th day of June, 1930, you were guilty of the murder of Edward Seton.

Prisoners at the bar, have you anything to say in your defense?

The Voice had stopped. There was a moment's petrified silence and then a resounding crash! Rogers had dropped the coffee tray! At the same moment, from somewhere outside the room there came a scream and the sound of a thud.

Lombard was the first to move. He leapt to the door and flung it open. Outside, lying in a huddled mass, was Mrs. Rogers. Lombard called, "Marston."

Anthony sprang to help him. Between them, they lifted up the woman and carried her into the drawing room. Dr. Armstrong came across quickly. He helped them to lift her onto the sofa and bent over her. He said quickly, "It's nothing. She's fainted, that's all. She'll be round in a minute."

Lombard said to Rogers, "Get some brandy."

Rogers, his face white, his hands shaking, murmured, "Yes, sir," and slipped quickly out of the room.

Vera cried out, *"Who was that speaking?* Where was he? It sounded—it sounded—"

General Macarthur spluttered out, "What's going on here? What kind of a practical joke was that?" His hand was shaking. His shoulders sagged. He looked suddenly ten years older.

Blore was mopping his face with a handkerchief. Only Mr. Justice Wargrave and Miss Brent seemed comparatively unmoved. Emily Brent sat upright, her head held high. In both cheeks was a spot of hard color. The judge sat in his habitual pose, his head sunk down into his neck. With one hand he gently scratched his ear. Only his eyes were active, darting round and round the room, puzzled, alert with intelligence.

Again it was Lombard who acted. Armstrong being busy with the collapsed woman, Lombard was free once more to take the initiative. He said, "That voice? It sounded as though it were in the room."

Vera cried, *"Who was it?* Who was it? It wasn't one of us."

Like the judge, Lombard's eyes wandered slowly round

the room. They rested a minute on the open window, then he shook his head decisively. Suddenly his eyes lighted up He moved forward swiftly to where a door near the fireplace led into an adjoining room.

With a swift gesture, he caught the handle and flung the door open. He passed through and immediately uttered an exclamation of satisfaction. He said, "Ah, here we are."

The others crowded after him. Only Miss Brent remained alone sitting erect in her chair.

Inside the second room a table had been brought up close to the wall which adjoined the drawing room. On the table was a gramophone—an old-fashioned type with a large trumpet attached. The mouth of the trumpet was against the wall, and Lombard, pushing it aside, indicated where two or three small holes had been unobtrusively bored through the wall. Adjusting the gramophone he replaced the needle on the record and immediately they heard again: *"You are charged with the following indictments—"*

Vera cried, "Turn it off! Turn it off! It's horrible!" Lombard obeyed.

Dr. Armstrong said, with a sigh of relief, "A disgraceful and heartless practical joke, I suppose."

The small, clear voice of Mr. Justice Wargrave murmured, "So you think it's a joke, do you?"

The doctor stared at him. "What else could it be?"

The hand of the judge gently stroked his upper lip. He said, "At the moment I'm not prepared to give an opinion."

Anthony Marston broke in. He said, "Look here, there's one thing you've forgotten. Who the devil turned the thing on and set it going?"

Wargrave murmured, "Yes, I think we must inquire into that." He led the way back into the drawing room. The others followed.

Rogers had just come in with a glass of brandy. Miss Brent was bending over the moaning form of Mrs. Rogers. Adroitly Rogers slipped between the two women. "Allow me, madam, I'll speak to her. Ethel—Ethel—it's all right. All right, do you hear? Pull yourself together."

Mrs. Rogers' breath came in quick gasps. Her eyes, staring frightened eyes, went round and round the ring of faces. There was urgency in Rogers' tone. "Pull yourself together, Ethel."

Dr. Armstrong spoke to her soothingly. "You'll be all right now, Mrs. Rogers. Just a nasty turn."

She said, "Did I faint, sir?"

"Yes."

"It was The Voice—that awful voice—*like a judgment*—" Her face turned green again, her eyelids fluttered.

Dr. Armstrong said sharply, "Where's that brandy?"

Rogers had put it down on a little table. Someone handed it to the doctor and he bent over the gasping woman with it. "Drink this, Mrs. Rogers."

She drank, choking a little and gasping. The spirit did her good. The color returned to her face. She said, "I'm all right now. It just—gave me a turn."

Rogers said quickly, "Of course it did. It gave me a turn too. Fair made me drop that tray. Wicked lies, it was! I'd like to know—"

He was interrupted. It was only a cough—a dry little cough but it had the effect of stopping him in full cry. He stared at Mr. Justice Wargrave and the latter coughed again. Then he said, "Who put that record on the gramophone? Was it you, Rogers?"

Rogers cried, "I didn't know what it was. Before God, I didn't know what it was, sir. If I had I'd never have done it."

The judge said dryly, "That is probably true. But I think you'd better explain, Rogers."

The butler wiped his face with a handkerchief. He said earnestly, "I was just obeying orders, sir, that's all."

"Whose orders?"

"Mr. Owen's."

Mr. Justice Wargrave said, "Let me get this quite clear. Mr. Owen's orders were—what exactly?"

Rogers said, "I was to put a record on the gramophone. I'd find the record in the drawer and my wife was to start the gramophone when I'd gone into the drawing room with the coffee tray."

The judge murmured, "A very remarkable story."

Rogers cried, "It's the truth, sir. I swear to God it's the truth. I didn't know what it was—not for a moment. It had a name on it—I thought it was just a piece of music."

Wargrave looked at Lombard. "Was there a title on it?"

Lombard nodded. He grinned suddenly, showing his white, pointed teeth. He said, "Quite right, sir. It was entitled 'Swan Song.'"

iii.

General Macarthur broke out suddenly. He exclaimed, "The whole thing is preposterous—preposterous! Slinging accusations about like this! Something must be done about it. This fellow Owen, whoever he is—"

Emily Brent interrupted. She said sharply, "That's just it, who is he?"

The judge interposed. He spoke with the authority that a lifetime in the courts had given him. He said, "That is exactly what we must go into very carefully. I should suggest that you get your wife to bed first of all, Rogers. Then come back here."

"Yes, sir."

Dr. Armstrong said, "I'll give you a hand, Rogers."

Leaning on the two men, Mrs. Rogers tottered out of the room. When they had gone Tony Marston said, "Don't know about you, sir, but I could do with a drink."

Lombard said, "I agree."

Tony said, "I'll go and forage."

He went out of the room. He returned a second or two later. "Found them all waiting on a tray outside ready to be brought in."

He set down his burden carefully. The next minute or two was spent in dispensing drinks. General Macarthur had a stiff whisky and so did the judge. Everyone felt the need of a stimulant. Only Emily Brent demanded and obtained a glass of water.

Dr. Armstrong re-entered the room. "She's all right,"

he said. "I've given her a sedative to take. What's that, a drink? I could do with one."

Several of the men refilled their glasses. A moment or two later Rogers re-entered the room. Mr. Justice Wargrave took charge of the proceedings. The room became an impromptu court of law. The judge said, "Now then, Rogers, we must get to the bottom of this. Who is this Mr. Owen?"

Rogers stared. "He owns this place, sir."

"I am aware of that fact. What I want you to tell me is what you yourself know about the man."

Rogers shook his head. "I can't say, sir. You see, I've never seen him."

There was a faint stir in the room. General Macarthur said, "You've never seen him? What d'yer mean?"

"We've only been here just under a week, sir, my wife and I. We were engaged by letter, through an agency. The Regina Agency in Plymouth."

Blore nodded. "Old established firm," he volunteered.

Wargrave said, "Have you got that letter?"

"The letter engaging us? No, sir. I didn't keep it."

"Go on with your story. You were engaged, as you say, by letter."

"Yes, sir. We were to arrive on a certain day. We did. Everything was in order here. Plenty of food in stock and everything very nice. Just needed dusting and that."

"What next?"

"Nothing, sir. We got orders—by letter again—to prepare the rooms for a house party and then yesterday by the afternoon post I got another letter from Mr. Owen. It said he and Mrs. Owen were detained and to do the best we could and it gave the instructions about dinner and coffee and putting on the gramophone record."

The judge said sharply, "Surely you've got *that* letter?"

"Yes, sir, I've got it here."

He produced it from a pocket. The judge took it. "H'm," he said. "Headed Ritz Hotel and typewritten."

With a quick movement Blore was beside him. He said, "If you'll just let me have a look." He twitched it out of the other's hand, and ran his eye over it. He murmured, "Coronation machine. Quite new—no defects.

Ensign paper—the most widely used make. You won't get anything out of that. Might be fingerprints, but I doubt it."

Wargrave stared at him with sudden attention. Anthony Marston was standing beside Blore looking over his shoulder. He said, "Got some fancy Christian names, hasn't he? Ulick Norman Owen. Quite a mouthful."

The old judge said with a slight start, "I am obliged to you, Mr. Marston. You have drawn my attention to a curious and suggestive point." He looked round at the others, and thrusting his neck forward like an angry tortoise, he said, "I think the time has come for us all to pool our information. It would be well, I think, for everybody to come forward with all the information they have regarding the owner of this house." He paused and then went on. "We are all his guests. I think it would be profitable if each one of us were to explain exactly how that came about."

There was a moment's pause and then Emily Brent spoke with decision. "There's something very peculiar about all this," she said. "I received a letter with a signature that was not very easy to read. It purported to be from a woman I had met at a certain summer resort two or three years ago. I took the name to be either Ogden or Oliver. I am acquainted with a Mrs. Oliver and also with a Miss Ogden. I am quite certain that I have never met, or become friendly with, anyone of the name of Owen."

Mr. Justice Wargrave said, "You have that letter, Miss Brent?"

"Yes, I will fetch it for you."

She went away and returned a minute later with the letter. The judge read it. He said, "I begin to understand. . . . Miss Claythorne?"

Vera explained the circumstances of her secretarial engagement. The judge said, "Marston?"

Anthony said, "Got a wire. From a pal of mine. Badger Berkeley. Surprised me at the time because I had an idea the old horse had gone to Norway. Told me to roll up here."

Again Wargrave nodded. He said, "Dr. Armstrong?"

"I was called in professionally."

"I see. You had no previous acquaintanceship with the family?"

"No. A colleague of mine was mentioned in the letter."

The judge said, "To give verisimilitude . . . Yes, and that colleague, I presume, was momentarily out of touch with you?"

"Well—er—yes."

Lombard, who had been staring at Blore, said suddenly, "Look here, I've just thought of something—"

The judge lifted a hand. "In a minute—"

"But I—"

"We will take one thing at a time, Mr. Lombard. We are at present inquiring into the causes which have resulted in our being assembled here tonight. General Macarthur?"

Pulling at his mustache, the General muttered, "Got a letter—from this fellow Owen—mentioned some old pals of mine who were to be here—hoped I'd excuse informal invitation. Haven't kept the letter, I'm afraid."

Wargrave said, "Mr. Lombard?"

Lombard's brain had been active. Was he to come out in the open, or not? He made up his mind. "Same sort of thing," he said. "Invitation, mention of mutual friends —I fell for it, all right. I've torn up the letter."

Mr. Justice Wargrave turned his attention to Mr. Blore. His forefinger stroked his upper lip and his voice was dangerously polite. He said, "Just now we had a somewhat disturbing experience. An apparently disembodied voice spoke to us all by name, uttering certain precise accusations against us. We will deal with those accusations presently. At the moment I am interested in a minor point. Amongst the names recited was that of William Henry Blore. But as far as we know there is no one named Blore amongst us. The name of Davis was *not* mentioned. What have you to say about that, Mr. Davis?"

Blore said sulkily, "Cat's out of the bag, it seems. I suppose I'd better admit that my name isn't Davis."

"You are William Henry Blore?"

"That's right."

"I will add something," said Lombard. "Not only are

you here under a false name, Mr. Blore, but in addition I've noticed this evening that you're a first-class liar. You claim to have come from Natal, South Africa. I know South Africa and Natal and I'm prepared to swear that you've never set foot in South Africa in your life."

All eyes were turned on Blore. Angry, suspicious eyes. Anthony Marston moved a step nearer to him. His fists clenched themselves. "Now then, you swine," he said. "Any explanation?"

Blore flung back his head and set his square jaw. "You gentlemen have got me wrong," he said. "I've got my credentials and you can see them. I'm an ex-C.I.D. man. I run a detective agency in Plymouth. I was put on this job."

Mr. Justice Wargrave asked, "By whom?"

"This man Owen. Enclosed a handsome money order for expenses and instructed me as to what he wanted done. I was to join the house party, posing as a guest. I was given all your names. I was to watch you all."

"Any reason given?"

Blore said bitterly, "Mrs. Owen's jewels. Mrs. Owen, my foot! I don't believe there's any such person."

Again the forefinger of the judge stroked his lip, this time appreciatively.

"Your conclusions are, I think, justified," he said. "Ulick Norman Owen! In Miss Brent's letter, though the signature of the surname is a mere scrawl the Christian names are reasonably clear—Una Nancy—in either case, you notice, the same initials. Ulick Norman Owen—Una Nancy Owen—each time, that is to say, U. N. Owen. Or by a slight stretch of fancy, UNKNOWN!"

Vera cried, "But this is fantastic—mad!"

The judge nodded gently. He said, "Oh, yes. I've no doubt in my own mind that we have been invited here by a madman—probably a dangerous homicidal lunatic."

4

THERE WAS a moment's silence—a silence of dismay and bewilderment. Then the judge's small, clear voice took up the thread once more. "We will now proceed to the next stage of our inquiry. First, however, I will just add my own credentials to the list."

He took a letter from his pocket and tossed it onto the table. "This purports to be from an old friend of mine, Lady Constance Culmington. I have not seen her for some years. She went to the East. It is exactly the kind of vague, incoherent letter she would write, urging me to join her here and referring to her host and hostess in the vaguest of terms. The same technique, you will observe. I only mention it because it agrees with the other evidence—from all of which emerges one interesting point. *Whoever it was who enticed us here, that person knows or has taken the trouble to find out a good deal about us all.* He, whoever he may be, is aware of my friendship for Lady Constance—and is familiar with her epistolary style. He knows something about Dr. Armstrong's colleagues and their present whereabouts. He knows the nickname of Mr. Marston's friend and the kind of telegrams he sends. He knows exactly where Miss Brent was two years ago for her holiday and the kind of people she met there. He knows all about General Macarthur's old cronies." He paused. Then he said, *"He knows, you see, a good deal.* And out of his knowledge concerning us, he has made certain definite accusations."

Immediately a babel broke out. General Macarthur shouted, "A pack of damn lies! Slander!"

Vera cried out, "It's iniquitous!" Her breath came fast. "Wicked!"

Rogers said hoarsely, "A lie—a wicked lie . . . we never did—neither of us. . . ."

Anthony Marston growled, "Don't know what the damned fool was getting at!"

The upraised hand of Mr. Justice Wargrave calmed the tumult. He said, picking his words with care, "I wish to say this. Our unknown friend accuses me of the murder of one Edward Seton. I remember Seton perfectly well. He came up before me for trial in June of the year 1930. He was charged with the murder of an elderly woman. He was very ably defended and made a good impression on the jury in the witness box. Nevertheless, on the evidence, he was certainly guilty. I summed up accordingly, and the jury brought in a verdict of Guilty. In passing sentence of death I concurred with the verdict. An appeal was lodged on the grounds of misdirection. The appeal was rejected and the man was duly executed. I wish to say before you all that my conscience is perfectly clear on the matter. I did my duty and nothing more. I passed sentence on a rightly convicted murderer."

Armstrong was remembering now. The Seton case! The verdict had come as a great surprise. He had met Matthews, K.C., on one of the days of the trail dining at a restaurant. Matthews had been confident. "Not a doubt of the verdict. Acquittal practically certain." And then afterwards he had heard comments: Judge was dead against him. Turned the jury right round and they brought him in guilty. Quite legal, though. Old Wargrave knows his law. It was almost as though he had a private down on the fellow. All these memories rushed through the doctor's mind. Before he could consider the wisdom of the question he had asked impulsively, "Did you know Seton at all? I mean previous to the case."

The hooded reptilian eyes met his. In a clear, cold voice the judge said, "I knew nothing of Seton previous to the case."

Armstrong said to himself, "The fellow's lying—I know he's lying."

Vera Claythorne spoke in a trembling voice. She said, "I'd like to tell you. About that child—Cyril Hamilton. I was nursery governess to him. He was forbidden to swim out far. One day, when my attention was distracted, he started off. I swam after him . . . I couldn't get there in time. . . . It was awful. . . . But it wasn't my fault. At the inquest the Coroner exonerated me. And his mother—she was so kind. If even she didn't blame me, why should—why should this awful thing be said? It's not fair—not fair. . . ." She broke down, weeping bitterly.

General Macarthur patted her shoulder. He said, "There, there, my dear. Of course it's not true. Fellow's a madman. A madman! Got a bee in his bonnet! Got hold of the wrong end of the stick all round."

He stood erect, squaring his shoulders. He barked out, "Best really to leave this sort of thing unanswered. However, feel I ought to say—no truth—no truth whatever in what he said about—er—young Arthur Richmond. Richmond was one of my officers. I sent him on a reconnaissance. He was killed. Natural course of events in war time. Wish to say resent very much—slur on my wife. Best woman in the world. Absolutely—Caesar's wife!"

General Macarthur sat down. His shaking hand pulled at his mustache. The effort to speak had cost him a good deal.

Lombard spoke. His eyes were amused. He said, "About those natives—"

Marston said, "What about them?"

Philip Lombard grinned. "Story's quite true! I left 'em! Matter of self-preservation. We were lost in the bush. I and a couple of other fellows took what food there was and cleared out."

General Macarthur said sternly, "You abandoned your men—left them to starve?"

Lombard said, "Not quite the act of a *pukka sahib,* I'm afraid. But self-preservation's a man's first duty. And natives don't mind dying, you know. They don't feel about it as Europeans do."

Vera lifted her face from her hands. She said, staring at him, "You left them—to *die?*"

Lombard answered, "I left them to die." His amused eyes looked into her horrified ones.

Anthony Marston said in a slow puzzled voice, "I've just been thinking—John and Lucy Combes. Must have been a couple of kids I ran over near Cambridge. Beastly bad luck."

Mr. Justice Wargrave said acidly, "For them, or for you?"

Anthony said, "Well, I was thinking—for me—but of course, you're right, sir, it was damned bad luck on them. Of course it was a pure accident. They rushed out of some cottage or other. I had my license endorsed for a year. Beastly nuisance."

Dr. Armstrong said warmly, "This speeding's all wrong —all wrong! Young men like you are a danger to the community."

Anthony shrugged his shoulders. He said, "Speed's come to stay. English roads are hopeless, of course. Can't get up a decent pace on them." He looked round vaguely for his glass, picked it up off a table and went over to the side table and helped himself to another whisky and soda. He said over his shoulder, "Well, anyway, it wasn't my fault. Just an accident!"

iii.

The manservant, Rogers, had been moistening his lips and twisting his hands. He said now in a low, deferential voice, "If I might just say a word, sir."

Lombard said, "Go ahead, Rogers."

Rogers cleared his throat and passed his tongue once more over his dry lips. "There was a mention, sir, of me and Mrs. Rogers. And of Miss Brady. There isn't a word of truth in it, sir. My wife and I were with Miss Brady till she died. She was always in poor health, sir, always from the time we came to her. There was a storm, sir, that night —the night she was taken bad. The telephone was out of order. We couldn't get the doctor to her. I went for him,

47

sir, on foot. But he got there too late. We'd done everything possible for her, sir. Devoted to her, we were. Anyone will tell you the same. There was never a word said against us. Not a word."

Lombard looked thoughtfully at the man's twitching face, his dry lips, the fright in his eyes. He remembered the crash of the falling coffee tray. He thought, but did not say, "Oh, yeah?"

Blore spoke—spoke in his hearty, bullying, official manner. He said, "Came into a little something at her death, though? Eh?"

Rogers drew himself up. He said stiffly, "Miss Brady left us a legacy in recognition of our faithful services. And why not, I'd like to know?"

Lombard said, "What about yourself, Mr. Blore?"

"What about me?"

"Your name was included in the list."

Blore went purple. "Landor, you mean? That was the bank robbery—London and Commercial."

Mr. Justice Wargrave stirred. He said, "I remember. It didn't come before me, but I remember the case. Landor was convicted on your evidence. You were the police officer in charge of the case?"

Blore said, "I was."

"Landor got penal servitude for life and died in Dartmoor a year later. He was a delicate man."

Blore said, "He was a crook. It was he who knocked out the night watchman. The case was quite clear against him."

Wargrave said slowly, "You were complimented, I think, on your able handling of the case."

Blore said sulkily, "I got my promotion." He added in a thick voice, "I was only doing my duty."

Lombard laughed—a sudden, ringing laugh. He said, "What a duty-loving, law-abiding lot we all seem to be! Myself excepted. What about you, doctor—and your little professional mistake? Illegal operation, was it?"

Emily Brent glanced at him in sharp distaste and drew herself away a little.

Dr. Armstrong, very much master of himself, shook his head good-humoredly. "I'm at a loss to understand the matter," he said. "The name meant nothing to me when it was spoken. What was it—Clees? Close? I really can't remember having a patient of that name, or being connected with a death in any way. The thing's a complete mystery to me. Of course, it's a long time ago. It might possibly be one of my operation cases in hospital. They come too late, so many of these people. Then, when the patient dies, they always consider it's the surgeon's fault." He sighed, shaking his head.

He thought: Drunk—that's what it was—drunk . . . And I operated! Nerves all to pieces—hands shaking. I killed her, all right. Poor devil—elderly woman—simple job if I'd been sober. Lucky for me there's loyalty in our profession. The Sister knew, of course—but she held her tongue. God, it gave me a shock! Pulled me up. But who could have known about it—after all these years?

iv.

There was a silence in the room. Everybody was looking, covertly or openly, at Emily Brent. It was a minute or two before she became aware of the expectation. Her eyebrows rose on her narrow forehead. She said, "Are you waiting for me to say something? I have nothing to say."

The judge said, "Nothing, Miss Brent?"

"Nothing." Her lips closed tightly.

The judge stroked his face. He said mildly, "You reserve your defense?"

Miss Brent said coldly, "There is no question of defense. I have always acted in accordance with the dictates of my conscience. I have nothing with which to reproach myself."

There was an unsatisfied feeling in the air. But Emily Brent was not one to be swayed by public opinion. She sat unyielding.

The judge cleared his throat once or twice. Then he said, "Our inquiry rests there. Now, Rogers, who else is there on this island besides ourselves and you and your wife?"

"Nobody, sir. Nobody at all."

"You're sure of that?"

"Quite sure, sir."

Wargrave said, "I am not yet clear as to the purpose of our Unknown host in getting us to assemble here. But in my opinion this person, whoever he may be, is not sane in the accepted sense of the word. He may be dangerous. In my opinion it would be well for us to leave this place as soon as possible. I suggest that we leave tonight."

Rogers said, "I beg your pardon, sir, but there's no boat on the island."

"No boat at all?"

"No, sir."

"How do you communicate with the mainland?"

"Fred Narracott, he comes over every morning, sir. He brings the bread and the milk and the post, and takes the orders."

Mr. Justice Wargrave said, "Then in my opinion it would be well if we all left tomorrow morning as soon as Narracott's boat arrives."

There was a chorus of agreement with only one dissentient voice. It was Anthony Marston who disagreed with the majority. "A bit unsporting, what?" he said. "Ought to ferret out the mystery before we go. Whole thing's like a detective story. Positively thrilling."

The judge said acidly, "At my time of life, I have no desire for 'thrills,' as you call them."

Anthony said with a grin, "The legal life's narrowing! I'm all for crime! Here's to it." He picked up his drink and drank it off at a gulp. Too quickly, perhaps. He choked—choked badly. His face contorted, turned purple. He gasped for breath—then slid down off his chair, the glass falling from his hand.

5

■

IT WAS so sudden and so unexpected that it took every-one's breath away. They remained stupidly staring at the crumpled figure on the ground. Then Dr. Armstrong jumped up and went over to him, kneeling beside him. When he raised his head his eyes were bewildered. He said in a low, awestruck whisper, "My God! he's dead."

They didn't take it in. Not at once. Dead? *Dead?* That young Norse God in the prime of his health and strength. Struck down all in a moment. Healthy young men didn't die like that, choking over a whisky and soda. . . . No, they couldn't take it in.

Dr. Armstrong was peering into the dead man's face. He sniffed at the blue, twisted lips. Then he picked up the glass from which Anthony Marston had been drinking.

General Macarthur said, "Dead? D'you mean the fellow just choked and—and died?"

The physician said, "You can call it choking, if you like. He died of asphyxiation right enough."

He was sniffing now at the glass. He dipped a finger into the dregs and very cautiously just touched the finger with the tip of his tongue. His expression altered.

General Macarthur said, "Never knew a man could die like that—just of a choking fit!"

Emily Brent said in a clear voice, "In the midst of life we are in death."

Dr. Armstrong stood up. He said brusquely, "No, a man doesn't die of a mere choking fit. Marston's death wasn't what we call a natural death."

Vera said almost in a whisper, "Was there—something—in the whisky?"

Armstrong nodded. "Yes. Can't say exactly. Everything points to one of the cyanides. No distinctive smell of prussic acid, probably potassium cyanide. It acts pretty well instantaneously."

51

The judge said sharply, "It was in his glass?"

"Yes."

The doctor strode to the table where the drinks were. He removed the stopper from the whisky and smelt and tasted it. Then he tasted the soda water. He shook his head. "They're both all right."

Lombard said, "You mean—he must have put the stuff in his glass *himself?*"

Armstrong nodded with a curiously dissatisfied expression. He said, "Seems like it."

Blore said, "Suicide, eh? That's a queer go."

Vera said slowly, "You'd never think that *he* would kill himself. He was so alive. He was—oh—enjoying himself! When he came down the hill in his car this evening he looked—he looked—oh, I can't *explain!*"

But they knew what she meant. Anthony Marston, in the height of his youth and manhood, had seemed like a being who was immortal. And now, crumpled and broken, he lay on the floor. Dr. Armstrong said, "Is there any possibility other than suicide?"

Slowly everyone shook his head. There could be no other explanation. The drinks themselves were untampered with. They had all seen Anthony Marston go across and help himself. It followed therefore that any cyanide in the drink must have been put there by Anthony Marston himself. And yet—why should Anthony Marston commit suicide?

Blore said thoughtfully, "You know, doctor, it doesn't seem right to me. I shouldn't have said Mr. Marston was a suicidal type of gentleman."

Armstrong answered, "I agree."

ii.

They had left it like that. What else was there to say? Together Armstrong and Lombard had carried the inert body of Anthony Marston to his bedroom and had laid him there covered over with a sheet.

When they came downstairs again, the others were standing in a group, shivering a little, though the night was not cold. Emily Brent said, "We'd better go to bed. It's late."

It was past twelve o'clock. The suggestion was a wise one—yet everyone hesitated. It was as though they clung to each other's company for reassurance. The judge said, "Yes, we must get some sleep."

Rogers said, "I haven't cleared yet—in the dining room."

Lombard said curtly, "Do it in the morning."

Armstrong said to him, "Is your wife all right?"

"I'll go and see, sir."

He returned a minute or two later. "Sleeping beautiful, she is."

"Good," said the doctor. "Don't disturb her."

"No, sir. I'll just put things straight in the dining room and make sure everything's locked up right. and then I'll turn in." He went across the hall into the dining room.

The others went upstairs, a slow, unwilling procession.

If this had been an old house, with creaking wood, and dark shadows, and heavily paneled walls, there might have been an eerie feeling. But this house was the essence of modernity. There were no dark corners—no possible sliding panels—it was flooded with electric light—everything was new and bright and shining. There was nothing hidden in this house, nothing concealed. It had no atmosphere about it. Somehow, that was the most frightening thing of all. . . .

They exchanged good nights on the upper landing. Each of them went into his or her own room, and each of them automatically, almost without conscious thought, locked the door. . . .

iii.

In his pleasant, softly tinted room, Mr. Justice Wargrave removed his garments and prepared himself for bed. He was thinking about Edward Seton. He remembered Seton very well. His fair hair, his blue eyes, his habit of looking you straight in the face with a pleasant air of straightforwardness. That was what had made so good an impression on the jury.

Llewellyn, for the Crown, had bungled it a bit. He had been overvehement, had tried to prove too much. Matthews, on the other hand, for the Defense, had been good. His points had told. His cross-examinations had been deadly. His handling of his client in the witness box had been masterly.

And Seton had come through the ordeal of cross-examination well. He had not got excited or overvehement. The jury had been impressed. It had seemed to Matthews, perhaps, as though everything had been over bar the shouting.

The judge wound up his watch carefully and placed it by the bed. He remembered exactly how he had felt sitting there—listening, making notes, appreciating everything, tabulating every scrap of evidence that told against the prisoner. He'd enjoyed that case! Matthews' final speech had been first class. Llewellyn, coming after it, had failed to remove the good impression that the defending counsel had made. And then had come his own summing up . . .

Carefully, Mr. Justice Wargrave removed his false teeth and dropped them into a glass of water. The shrunken lips fell in. It was a cruel mouth now, cruel and predatory. Hooding his eyes, the judge smiled to himself. He'd cooked Seton's goose all right!

With a slightly rheumatic grunt, he climbed into bed and turned out the electric light.

iv.

Downstairs in the dining room, Rogers stood puzzled. He was staring at the china figures in the center of the table. He muttered to himself, "That's a rum go! I could have sworn there were ten of them."

v.

General Macarthur tossed from side to side. Sleep would not come to him. In the darkness he kept seeing

Arthur Richmond's face. He'd liked Arthur—he'd been damned fond of Arthur. He'd been pleased that Leslie liked him too.

Leslie was so capricious. Lots of good fellows that Leslie would turn up her nose at and pronounce dull. "Dull!" Just like that. But she hadn't found Arthur Richmond dull. They'd got on well together from the beginning. They'd talked of plays and music and pictures together. She'd teased him, made fun of him, ragged him. And he, Macarthur, had been delighted at the thought that Leslie took quite a motherly interest in the boy.

Motherly indeed! Damn fool not to remember that Richmond was twenty-eight to Leslie's twenty-nine. He'd loved Leslie. He could see her now. Her heart-shaped face, and her dancing, deep-gray eyes, and the brown curling mass of her hair. He'd loved Leslie and he'd believed in her absolutely.

Out there in France, in the middle of all the hell of it, he'd sat thinking of her, taken her picture out of the breast pocket of his tunic. And then—he'd found out!

It had come about exactly in the way things happened in books. The letter in the wrong envelope. She'd been writing to them both and she'd put her letter to Richmond in the envelope addressed to her husband. Even now, all these years after, he could feel the shock of it—the pain. . . . God, it had hurt!

And the business had been going on some time. The letter made that clear. Week ends! Richmond's last leave . . . Leslie—Leslie and Arthur!

God damn the fellow! Damn his smiling face, his brisk "Yes, sir." Liar and hypocrite! Stealer of another man's wife!

It had gathered slowly—that cold, murderous rage. He'd managed to carry on as usual—to show nothing. He'd tried to make his manner to Richmond just the same. Had he succeeded? He thought so. Richmond hadn't suspected. Inequalities of temper were easily accounted for out there, where men's nerves where continually snapping under the strain. Only young Armitage had looked at him curiously once or twice. Quite a young chap, but he'd had perceptions, that boy. Armitage, perhaps, had guessed—when the time came.

He'd sent Richmond deliberately to death. Only a miracle could have brought him through unhurt. That miracle didn't happen. Yes, he'd sent Richmond to his death and he wasn't sorry. It had been easy enough. Mistakes were being made all the time, officers being sent to death needlessly. All was confusion, panic. People might say afterwards, "Old Macarthur lost his nerve a bit, made some colossal blunders, sacrificed some of his best men." They couldn't say more.

But young Armitage was different. He'd looked at his commanding officer very oddly. He'd known, perhaps, that Richmond was being deliberately sent to death. (And after the war was over—had Armitage talked?)

Leslie hadn't known. Leslie had wept for her lover (he supposed) but her weeping was over by the time he'd come back to England. He'd never told her that he'd found her out. They'd gone on together—only, somehow, she hadn't seemed very real any more. And then, three or four years later, she'd got double pneumonia and died. That had been a long time ago. Fifteen years—sixteen years?

And he'd left the Army and come to live in Devon—bought the sort of little place he'd always meant to have. Nice neighbors—pleasant part of the world. There was a bit of shooting and fishing. He'd gone to church on Sundays. (But not the day that the lesson was read about David putting Uriah in the forefront of the battle. Somehow he couldn't face that. Gave him an uncomfortable feeling.)

Everybody had been very friendly. At first, that is. Later, he'd had an uneasy feeling that people were talking about him behind his back. They eyed him differently, somehow. As though they'd heard something—some lying rumor . . . (Armitage? Supposing Armitage had talked?)

He'd avoided people after that—withdrawn into himself. Unpleasant to feel that people were discussing you.

And all so long ago. So—so purposeless now. Leslie had faded into the distance and Arthur Richmond, too. Nothing of what had happened seemed to matter any more. It made life lonely, though. He'd taken to shunning his old Army friends. (If Armitage had talked, they'd know about it.)

And now—this evening—a hidden voice had blared out that old hidden story. Had he dealt with it all right? Kept a stiff upper lip? Betrayed the right amount of feeling—indignation, disgust—but no guilt, no discomfiture? Difficult to tell. Surely nobody could have taken the accusation seriously. There had been a pack of other nonsense, just as farfetched. That charming girl—the voice had accused her of drowning a child! Idiotic! Some madman throwing crazy accusations about! Emily Brent, too—actually a niece of old Tom Brent of the Regiment. It had accused her of murder! Anyone could see with half an eye that the woman was as pious as could be—the kind that was hand and glove with parsons.

Damned curious business, the whole thing! Crazy, nothing less. Ever since they had got here—when was that? Why, damn it, it was only this afternoon! Seemed a good bit longer than that. He thought: I wonder when we shall get away again. Tomorrow, of course, when the motorboat came from the mainland.

Funny, just this minute he didn't want much to get away from the island. . . . To go back to the mainland, back to his little house, back to all the troubles and worries. Through the open window he could hear the waves breaking on the rocks—a little louder now than earlier in the evening. Wind was getting up, too. He thought: Peaceful sound. Peaceful place. . . . He thought: Best of an island is once you get there—you can't go any further . . . you've come to the end of things. . . . *He knew, suddenly, that he didn't want to leave the island.*

vi.

Vera Claythorne lay in bed, wide awake, staring up at the ceiling. The light beside her was on. She was frightened of the dark. She was thinking: Hugo . . . Hugo . . . Why do I feel you're so near to me tonight? . . . Somewhere quite close . . . Where is he really? I don't know. I never shall know. He just went away—right away—out of my life.

It was no good trying not to think of Hugo. He was close to her. She *had* to think of him—to remember . . . Cornwall . . . The black rocks, the smooth yellow sand. Mrs. Hamilton, stout, good humored. Cyril, whining a little always, pulling at her hand. *"I want to swim out to the rock, Miss Claythorne. Why can't I swim out to the rock?"* Looking up—meeting Hugo's eyes watching her.

The evenings after Cyril was in bed . . . *"Come out for a stroll, Miss Claythorne."* *"I think perhaps I will."* . . . The decorous stroll down to the beach. The moonlight—the soft Atlantic air. And then, Hugo's arms round her.

"I love you. I love you. You know I love you, Vera?"

Yes, she knew. (Or thought she knew.)

"I can't ask you to marry me. I've not got a penny. It's all I can do to keep myself. Queer, you know, once, for three months, I had the chance of being a rich man to look forward to. Cyril wasn't born until three months, after Maurice died. If he'd been a girl . . ."

If the child had been a girl, Hugo would have come into everything. He'd been disappointed, he admitted, *"I hadn't built on it, of course. But it was a bit of a knock. Oh, well, luck's luck! Cyril's a nice kid. I'm awfully fond of him."* And he was fond of him, too. Always ready to play games or amuse his small nephew. No rancor in Hugo's nature.

Cyril wasn't really strong. A puny child—no stamina. The kind of child, perhaps, who wouldn't live to grow up . . .

And then—?

"Miss Claythorne, why can't I swim to the rock?" Irritating whiny repetition.

"It's too far, Cyril."

"But, Miss Claythorne . . ."

Vera got up. She went to the dressing table and swallowed three aspirins. She thought: I wish I had some proper sleeping stuff.

She thought: If *I* were doing away with myself I'd take an overdose of veronal—something like that—not cyanide! She shuddered as she remembered Anthony Marston's convulsed purple face.

As she passed the mantelpiece, she looked up at the framed doggerel.

Ten little Indian boys went out to dine;
One choked his little self and then there were nine.

She thought to herself: It's horrible—just like us this evening. . . .

Why had Anthony Marston wanted to die? *She* didn't want to die. She couldn't imagine wanting to die. . . . Death was for—the other people. . . .

6

DR. ARMSTRONG was dreaming. . . . It was very hot in the operating room. . . . Surely they'd got the temperature too high? The sweat was rolling down his face. His hands were clammy. Difficult to hold the scalpel firmly . . . How beautifully sharp it was. . . . Easy to do a murder with a knife like that. And of course he *was* doing a murder. . . .

The woman's body looked different. It had been a large, unwieldy body. This was a spare, meager body. And the face was hidden. Who was it that he had to kill? He couldn't remember. But he *must* know! Should he ask Sister? Sister was watching him. No, he couldn't ask her. She was suspicious, he could see that.

But who was it on the operating table? They shouldn't have covered up the face like that. . . . If he could only see the face . . . Ah! that was better. A young probationer was pulling off the handkerchief.

Emily Brent, of course. It was Emily Brent that he had to kill. How malicious her eyes were! Her lips were moving. What was she saying? *"In the midst of life we are in death. . . ."*

She was laughing now. No, nurse, don't put the handkerchief back. I've got to see. I've got to give the anesthetic. Where's the ether? I must have brought the ether with me. What have you done with the ether, Sister? Château Neuf du Pape? Yes, that will do quite as well. Take the handkerchief away, nurse.

Of course! I knew it all the time! *It's Anthony Marston!* His face is purple and convulsed. But he's not dead—he's laughing. I tell you he's laughing! He's shaking the operating table. Look out, man, look out. Nurse, steady it—steady—it—

With a start Dr. Armstrong woke up. It was morning. Sunlight was pouring into the room. And someone was leaning over him—shaking him. It was Rogers. Rogers, with a white face, saying, "Doctor—doctor!"

Dr. Armstrong woke up completely. He sat up in bed. He said sharply, "What is it?"

"It's the wife, doctor. *I can't get her to wake.* My God! I can't get her to wake. And—and she don't look right to me."

Dr. Armstrong was quick and efficient. He wrapped himself in his dressing gown and followed Rogers.

He bent over the bed where the woman was lying peacefully on her side. He lifted the cold hand, raised the eyelid. It was some few minutes before he straightened himself and turned from the bed.

Rogers whispered, "Is—she—is she—?" He passed a tongue over dry lips.

Armstrong nodded. "Yes, she's gone."

His eyes rested thoughtfully on the man before him. Then they went to the table by the bed, to the washstand, then back to the sleeping woman.

Rogers said, "Was it—was it—'er 'eart, doctor?"

Dr. Armstrong was a minute or two before replying. Then he said, "What was her health like normally?"

Rogers said, "She was a bit rheumaticky."

"Any doctor been attending her recently?"

"Doctor?" Rogers stared. "Not been to a doctor for years—neither of us."

"You'd no reason to believe she suffered from heart trouble?"

"No, doctor. I never knew of anything."

Armstrong said, "Did she sleep well?"

Now Rogers' eyes evaded his. The man's hands came together and turned and twisted uneasily. He muttered. "She didn't sleep extra well—no."

The doctor said sharply, "Did she take things to make her sleep?"

Rogers stared at him, surprised. "Take things? To make her sleep? Not that I knew of. I'm sure she didn't."

Armstrong went over to the washstand. There were a certain number of bottles on it. Hair lotion, lavender water, cascara, glycerin of cucumber for the hands, a mouthwash, tooth paste and some Elliman's. Rogers helped by pulling out the drawers of the dressing table. From there they moved on to the chest of drawers. But there was no sign of sleeping draughts or tablets. Rogers said, "She didn't have nothing last night, sir, except what you gave her. . . ."

ii.

When the gong sounded for breakfast at nine o'clock it found everyone up and awaiting the summons. General Macarthur and the judge had been pacing the terrace outside, exchanging desultory comments on the political situation. Vera Claythorne and Philip Lombard had been up to the summit of the island behind the house. There they had discovered William Henry Blore, standing staring at the mainland. He said, "No sign of that motorboat yet. I've been watching for it."

Vera said, smiling, "Devon's a sleepy county. Things are usually late."

Philip Lombard was looking the other way, out to sea. He said abruptly, "What d'you think of the weather?"

Glancing up at the sky, Blore remarked, "Looks all right to me."

Lombard pursed up his mouth into a whistle. He said, "It will come on to blow before the day's out."

Blore said, "Squally—eh?"

From below them came the boom of a gong. Philip Lombard said, "Breakfast? Well, I could do with some."

As they went down the steep slope Blore said to Lombard in a ruminating voice, "You know, it beats me—why that young fellow wanted to do himself in! I've been worrying about it all night."

Vera was a little ahead. Lombard hung back slightly. He said. "Got any alternative theory?"

"I'd want some proof. Motive, to begin with. Well off I should say he was."

Emily Brent came out of the drawing-room window to meet them. She said sharply, "Is the boat coming?"

"Not yet." said Vera.

They went in to breakfast. There was a vast dish of eggs and bacon on the sideboard and tea and coffee. Rogers held the door open for them to pass in, then shut it from the outside.

Emily Brent said, "That man looks ill this morning."

Dr. Armstrong, who was standing by the window, cleared his throat. He said, "You must excuse any—er—shortcomings this morning. Rogers has had to do the best he can for breakfast single-handed. Mrs. Rogers has—er—not been able to carry on this morning."

Emily Brent said sharply, "What's the matter with the woman?"

Dr. Armstrong said easily, "Let us start our breakfast. The eggs will be cold. Afterwards, there are several matters I want to discuss with you all."

They took the hint. Plates were filled, coffee and tea were poured. The meal began. Discussion of the island was, by mutual consent, tabooed. They spoke instead in a desultory fashion of current events. The news from abroad, events in the world of sport, the latest reappearance of the Loch Ness monster.

Then, when plates were cleared, Dr. Armstrong moved back his chair a little, cleared his throat importantly and spoke. He said, "I thought it better to wait until you had had your breakfast before telling you of a sad piece of news. Mrs. Rogers died in her sleep."

There were startled and shocked ejaculations. Vera exclaimed, "How awful! Two deaths on this island since we arrived!"

Mr. Justice Wargrave, his eyes narrowed, said in his small, precise, clear voice, "H'm—very remarkable—what was the cause of death?"

Armstrong shrugged his shoulders. "Impossible to say offhand."

"There must be an autopsy?"

"I certainly couldn't give a certificate. I have no knowledge whatsoever of the woman's state of health."

Vera said, "She was a very nervous-looking creature. And she had a shock last night. It might have been heart failure, I suppose?"

Dr. Armstrong said dryly, "Her heart certainly failed to beat—but what caused it to fail is the question."

One word fell from Emily Brent. It fell hard and clear into the listening group. "Conscience!" she said.

Armstrong turned to her. "What exactly do you mean by that, Miss Brent?"

Emily Brent, her lips tight and hard, said, "You all heard. She was accused, together with her husband, of having deliberately murdered her former employer—an old lady."

"And you think?"

Emily Brent said, "I think that that accusation was true. You all saw her last night. She broke down completely and fainted. The shock of having her wickedness brought home to her was too much for her. She literally died of fear."

Dr. Armstrong shook his head doubtfully. "It is a possible theory," he said. "One cannot adopt it without more exact knowledge of her state of health. If there was cardiac weakness—"

Emily Brent said quietly, "Call it, if you prefer, an Act of God."

Everyone looked shocked. Mr. Blore said uneasily, "That's carrying things a bit far, Miss Brent."

She looked at them with shining eyes. Her chin went up. She said, "You regard it as impossible that a sinner should be struck down by the wrath of God! I do not!"

The judge stroked his chin. He murmured in a slightly

ironic voice, "My dear lady, in my experience of ill-doing, Providence leaves the work of conviction and chastisement to us mortals—and the process is often fraught with difficulties. There are no short cuts."

Emily Brent shrugged her shoulders. Blore said sharply, "What did she have to eat and drink last night after she went up to bed?"

Armstrong said, "Nothing."

"She didn't take anything? A cup of tea? A drink of water? I'll bet you she had a cup of tea. That sort always does."

"Rogers assures me she had nothing whatsoever."

"Ah," said Blore. "But he *might* say so!" His tone was so significant that the doctor looked at him sharply.

Philip Lombard said, "So that's your idea?"

Blore said aggressively, "Well, why not? We all heard that accusation last night. May be sheer moonshine—just plain lunacy! On the other hand, it may not. Allow for the moment that it's true. Rogers and his missus polished off that old lady. Well, where does that get you? They've been feeling quite safe and happy about it—"

Vera interrupted. In a low voice she said, "No, I don't think Mrs. Rogers ever felt safe."

Blore looked slightly annoyed at the interruption. "Just like a woman," his glance said. He resumed, "That's as may be. Anyway there's no active danger to them as far as they know. Then, last night, some unknown lunatic spills the beans. What happens? The woman cracks—she goes to pieces. Notice how her husband hung over her as she was coming round. Not all husbandly solicitude! Not on your life! He was like a cat on hot bricks. Scared out of his life as to what she might say.

"And there's the position for you! They've done a murder and got away with it. But if the whole thing's going to be raked up, what's going to happen? Ten to one, the woman will give the show away. She hasn't got the nerve to stand up and brazen it out. She's a living danger to her husband, that's what she is. He's all right. *He*'ll lie with a straight face till kingdom comes—but he can't be sure of *her!* And if *she* goes to pieces, his neck's in danger!

So he slips something into a cup of tea and makes sure that her mouth is shut permanently."

Armstrong said slowly, "There was no empty cup by her bedside—there was nothing there at all. I looked."

Blore snorted. "Of course there wouldn't be! First thing he'd do when she'd drunk it would be to take that cup and saucer away and wash it up carefully."

There was a pause. Then General Macarthur said doubtfully, "It may be so. But I should hardly think it possible that a man would do that—to his wife."

Blore gave a short laugh. He said, "When a man's neck's in danger, he doesn't stop to think too much about sentiment."

There was a pause. Before anyone could speak, the door opened and Rogers came in. He said, looking from one to the other, "Is there anything more I can get you? I'm sorry there was so little toast, but we've run right out of bread. The new bread hasn't come over from the mainland yet."

Mr. Justice Wargrave stirred a little in his chair. He asked, "What time does the motorboat usually come over?"

"Between seven and eight, sir. Sometimes it's a bit after eight. Don't know what Fred Narracott can be doing this morning. If he's ill he'd send his brother."

Philip Lombard said, "What's the time now?"

"Ten minutes to ten, sir."

Lombard's eyebrows rose. He nodded slowly to himself. Rogers waited a minute or two. General Macarthur spoke suddenly and explosively. "Sorry to hear about your wife, Rogers. Doctor's just been telling us."

Rogers inclined his head. "Yes, sir. Thank you, sir." He took up the empty bacon dish and went out. Again there was a silence.

iii.

On the terrace outside Philip Lombard said, "About this motorboat—"

Blore looked at him. Blore nodded his head. He said, "I

know what you're thinking, Mr. Lombard. I've asked myself the same question. Motorboat ought to have been here nigh on two hours ago. It hasn't come. Why?"

"Found the answer?" asked Lombard.

It's not an accident—that's what I say. It's part and parcel of the whole business. It's all bound up together."

Philip Lombard said, "It won't come, you think?"

A voice spoke behind him—a testy, impatient voice. "The motorboat's not coming," he said.

Blore turned his square shoulder slightly and viewed the last speaker thoughtfully. "You think not too, General?"

General Macarthur said sharply, "Of course it won't come. We're counting on the motorboat to take us off the island. That's the meaning of the whole business. *We're not going to leave the island*. . . . None of us will ever leave. . . . It's the end, you see—the end of everything. . . ." He hesitated, then he said in a low, strange voice, "That's peace—real peace. To come to the end—not to have to go on. . . . Yes, peace. . . ."

He turned abruptly and walked away. Along the terrace, then down the slope towards the sea—obliquely—to the end of the island where loose rocks went out into the water. He walked a little unsteadily, like a man who was only half-awake.

Blore said, "There goes another one who's balmy! Looks as though it'll end with the whole lot going that way."

Philip Lombard said, "I don't fancy *you* will, Blore."

The ex-Inspector laughed. "It would take a lot to send me off my head." He added dryly, "And I don't think you'll be going that way either, Mr. Lombard."

Philip Lombard said, "I feel quite sane at the minute, thank you."

iv.

Dr. Armstrong came out onto the terrace. He stood there hesitating. To his left were Blore and Lombard. To his right was Wargrave, slowly pacing up and down, his head bent down. Armstrong, after a moment of indecision, turned towards the latter. But at that moment Rogers came quickly out of the house. "Could I have a word with you, sir, please?"

Armstrong turned. He was startled at what he saw.

Rogers' face was working. Its color was grayish green. His hands shook. It was such a contrast to his restraint of a few minutes ago that Armstrong was quite taken aback. "Please, sir, if I could have a word with you. Inside, sir."

The doctor turned back and re-entered the house with the frenzied butler. He said, "What's the matter, man? Pull yourself together."

"In here, sir, come in here." He opened the dining-room door. The doctor passed in. Rogers followed him and shut the door behind him.

"Well," said Armstrong, "what is it?"

The muscles of Rogers' throat were working. He was swallowing. He jerked out, "There's things going on, sir, that I don't understand."

Armstrong said sharply, "Things? What things?"

"You'll think I'm crazy, sir. You'll say it isn't anything. But it's got to be explained, sir. It's got to be explained. Because it doesn't make any sense."

"Well, man, tell me what it is. Don't go on talking in riddles."

Rogers swallowed again. He said, "It's those little fig-ures, sir. In the middle of the table. The little china figures. Ten of them, there were. I'll swear to that, ten of them."

Armstrong said, "Yes, ten. We counted them last night at dinner."

Rogers came nearer. "That's just it, sir. Last night, when I was clearing up, there wasn't but nine, sir. I noticed it and thought it queer. But that's all I thought. And now, sir, this morning. I didn't notice when I laid the breakfast. I was upset and all that. But now, sir, when I came to clear away. See for yourself if you don't believe me. *There's only eight, sir!* Only eight! It doesn't make sense, does it? *Only eight . . .*"

7

AFTER BREAKFAST, Emily Brent had suggested to Vera Claythorne that they should walk up to the summit again and watch for the boat. Vera had acquiesced.

The wind had freshened. Small white crests were appearing on the sea. There were no fishing boats out—and no sign of the motorboat. The actual village of Sticklehaven could not be seen, only the hill above it, a jutting-out cliff of red rock concealed the actual little bay.

Emily Brent said, "The man who brought us out yesterday seemed a dependable sort of person. It is really very odd that he should be so late this morning."

Vera did not answer. She was fighting down a rising feeling of panic. She said to herself angrily, "You must keep cool. This isn't like you. You've always had excellent nerves." Aloud she said after a minute or two, "I wish he would come. I—I want to get away."

Emily Brent said dryly, "I've no doubt we all do."

Vera said, "It's all so extraordinary. . . . There seems no—no meaning in it all."

The elderly woman beside her said briskly, "I'm very annoyed with myself for being to easily taken in. Really that letter is absurd when one comes to examine it. But I had no doubts at the time—none at all."

Vera murmured mechanically, "I suppose not."

"One takes things for granted too much," said Emily Brent.

Vera drew a deep shuddering breath. She said, "Do you really think—what you said at breakfast?"

"Be a little more precise, my dear. To what in particular are you referring?"

Vera said in a low voice, "Do you really think that Rogers and his wife did away with that old lady?"

Emily Brent gazed thoughtfully out to sea. Then she

said, "Personally, I am quite sure of it. What do you think?"

"I don't know what to think."

Emily Brent said, "Everything goes to support the idea. The way the woman fainted. And the man dropped the coffee tray, remember. Then the way he spoke about it —it didn't ring true. Oh, yes, I'm afraid they did it."

Vera said, "The way she looked—scared of her own shadow! I've never seen a woman look so frightened. . . . She must have been always haunted by it. . . ."

Miss Brent murmured, "I remember a text that hung in my nursery as a child. 'Be sure thy sin will find thee out.' It's very true, that. 'Be sure thy sin will find thee out.'"

Vera scrambled to her feet. She said, "But, Miss Brent—Miss Brent—in that case—"

"Yes, my dear?"

"The others? What about the others?"

"I don't quite understand you."

"All the other accusations—they—*they* weren't true? But if it's true about the Rogerses—" She stopped, unable to make her chaotic thought clear.

Emily Brent's brow, which had been frowning perplexedly, cleared. She said, "Ah, I understand you now. Well, there is that Mr. Lombard. He admits to having abandoned twenty men to their deaths."

Vera said, "They were only natives. . . ."

Emily Brent said sharply, "Black or white, they are our brothers."

Vera thought: Our black brothers—our black brothers. Oh, I'm going to laugh. I'm hysterical. I'm not myself. . . .

Emily Brent continued thoughtfully, "Of course, some of the other accusations were very farfetched and ridiculous. Against the judge, for instance, who was only doing his duty in his public capacity. And the ex-Scotland Yard man. My own case, too." She paused and then went on, "Naturally, considering the circumstances, I was not going to say anything last night. It was not a fit subject to discuss before gentlemen."

"No?"

Vera listened with interest. Miss Brent continued se-

69

renely, "Beatrice Taylor was in service with me. *Not a nice girl*—as I found out too late. I was very much deceived in her. She had nice manners and was very clean and willing. I was very pleased with her. Of course all that was the sheerest hypocrisy! She was a loose girl with no morals. Disgusting! It was some time before I found out that she was what they call 'in trouble.'" She paused, her delicate nose wrinkling itself in distaste. "It was a great shock to me. Her parents were decent folk, too, who had brought her up very strictly. I'm glad to say they did not condone her behavior."

Vera said, staring at Miss Brent, "What happened?"

"Naturally I did not keep her an hour under my roof. No one shall ever say that I condoned immorality."

Vera said in a lower voice, "What happened—to her?"

Miss Brent said, "The abandoned creature, not content with having one sin on her conscience, committed a still graver sin. She took her own life."

Vera whispered, horror struck, "She killed herself?"

"Yes, she threw herself into the river."

Vera shivered. She stared at the calm, delicate profile of Miss Brent. She said, "What did you feel like when you knew she'd done that? Weren't you sorry? Didn't you blame yourself?"

Emily Brent drew herself up. "I? I had nothing with which to reproach myself."

Vera said, "But if your—hardness—drove her to it."

Emily Brent said sharply, "Her own action—her own sin —that was what drove her to it. If she had behaved like a decent modest young woman none of this would have happened."

She turned her face to Vera. There was no self-reproach, no uneasiness in those eyes. They were hard and self-righteous. Emily Brent sat on the summit of Indian Island, encased in her own armor of virtue. The little elderly spinster was no longer slightly ridiculous to Vera. Suddenly—she was terrible.

Dr. Armstrong came out of the dining room and once more came out on the terrace. The judge was sitting in a chair now, gazing placidly out to sea. Lombard and Blore were over to the left, smoking but not talking. As before, the doctor hesitated for a moment. His eyes rested speculatively on Mr. Justice Wargrave. He wanted to consult with someone. He was conscious of the judge's acute, logical brain. But nevertheless he wavered. Mr. Justice Wargrave might have a good brain but he was an elderly man. At this juncture, Armstrong felt what was needed was a man of action. He made up his mind. "Lombard, can I speak to you for a minute?"

Philip started. "Of course."

The two men left the terrace. They strolled down the slope towards the water. When they were out of earshot, Armstrong said, "I want a consultation."

Lombard's eyebrows went up. He said, "My dear fellow, I've no medical knowledge."

"No, no, I mean as to the general situation."

"Oh, that's different."

Armstrong said, "Frankly, what do you think of the position?"

Lombard reflected a minute. Then he said, "It's rather suggestive, isn't it?"

"What are your ideas on the subject of that woman? Do you accept Blore's theory?"

Philip puffed smoke into the air. He said, "It's perfectly feasible—taken alone."

"Exactly."

Armstrong's tone sounded relieved. Philip Lombard was no fool. The latter went on, "That is, accepting the premise that Mr. and Mrs. Rogers have successfully got away with murder in their time. And I don't see why they shouldn't. What do you think they did exactly? Poisoned the old lady?"

Armstrong said slowly, "It might be simpler than that. I asked Rogers this morning what this Miss Brady had suffered from. His answer was enlightening. I don't need to go into medical details, but in a certain form of cardiac trouble, amyl nitrite is used. When an attack comes on an ampoule of amyl nitrite is broken and it is inhaled. If amyl nitrite were withheld—well, the consequences might easily be fatal."

Philip Lombard said thoughtfully, "As simple as that. It must have been—rather tempting."

The doctor nodded. "Yes, no positive action. No arsenic to obtain and administer—nothing definite—just —negation! And Rogers hurried through the night to fetch a doctor and they both felt confident that no one could ever know."

"And, even if anyone knew, nothing could ever be proved against them," added Philip Lombard. He frowned suddenly. "Of course—that explains a good deal."

Armstrong said, puzzled, "I beg your pardon."

Lombard said, "I mean—it explains Indian Island. There are crimes that cannot be brought home to their perpetrators. Instance, the Rogerses'. Another instance, old Wargrave, who committed his murder strictly within the law."

Armstrong said sharply, "You believe that story?"

Philip Lombard smiled. "Oh, yes, I believe it. Wargrave murdered Edward Seton all right, murdered him as surely as if he'd stuck a stiletto through him! But he was clever enough to do it from the judge's seat in wig and gown. So in the ordinary way you can't bring his little crime home to him."

A sudden flash passed like lightning through Armstrong's mind. *Murder in Hospital. Murder on the Operating Table. Safe—yes, safe as houses!* Philip Lombard was saying, "Hence—Mr. Owen—hence—Indian Island!"

Armstrong drew a deep breath. "Now we're getting down to it. What's the real purpose of getting us all here?"

Philip Lombard said, "What do *you* think?"

Armstrong said abruptly, "Let's go back a minute to this woman's death. What are the possible theories? Rogers killed her because he was afraid she would give the show away. Second possibility, she lost her nerve and took an easy way out herself."

Philip Lombard said, "Suicide, eh?"

"What do you say to that?"

Lombard said, "It could have been—yes—*if it hadn't been for Marston's death*. Two suicides within twelve hours is a little *too* much to swallow! And if you tell me that Anthony Marston, a young bull with no nerves and precious little brains, got the wind up over having mowed down a couple of kids and deliberately put himself out of the way—well, the idea's laughable! And anyway, how did he get hold of the stuff? From all I've ever heard, potassium cyanide isn't the kind of stuff you take about with you in your waistcoat pocket. But that's your line of country."

Armstrong said, "Nobody in their senses carries potassium cyanide. It might be done by someone who was going to take a wasps' nest."

"The ardent gardener or landowner, in fact? Again, not Anthony Marston. It strikes me that cyanide is going to need a bit of explaining. Either Anthony Marston meant to do away with himself before he came here, and therefore came prepared—or else—"

Armstrong prompted him. "Or else?"

Philip Lombard grinned. "Why make me say it? When it's on the tip of your own tongue. *Anthony Marston was murdered, of course.*"

iii.

Dr. Armstrong drew a deep breath. "And Mrs. Rogers?"

Lombard said slowly, "I could believe in Anthony's suicide (with difficulty) if it weren't for Mrs. Rogers. I could believe in Mrs. Rogers' suicide (easily) if it weren't for Anthony Marston. I can believe that Rogers put his wife out of the way—if it were not for the unexplained death of Anthony Marston. But what we need is a theory to explain two deaths following rapidly on each other."

Armstrong said, "I can perhaps give you some help towards that theory." And he repeated the facts that Rogers had given him about the disappearance of the two little china figures.

Lombard said, "Yes, little china Indian figures . . . There were certainly ten last night at dinner. And now there are eight, you say?"

Dr. Armstrong recited:

"Ten little Indian boys going out to dine;
One went and choked himself and then there were
*   nine.*

"Nine little Indian boys sat up very late;
One overslept himself and then there were eight."

The two men looked at each other. Philip Lombard grinned and flung away his cigarette. "Fits too damned well to be a coincidence! Anthony Marston dies of asphyxiation or choking last night after dinner, and Mother Rogers oversleeps herself with a vengeance."

"And therefore?" said Armstrong.

Lombard took him up. "And therefore another kind of puzzle. The nigger in the woodpile! X! Mr. Owen! U. N. Owen. One Unknown Lunatic at Large!"

"Ah!" Armstrong breathed a sigh of relief. "You agree. But you see what it involves? Rogers swore that there was no one but ourselves and him and his wife on the island."

"Rogers is wrong! Or possibly Rogers is lying!"

Armstrong shook his head. "I don't think he's lying. The man's scared. He's scared nearly out of his senses."

Philip Lombard nodded. He said, "No motorboat this morning. That fits in. Mr. Owen's little arrangements again to the fore. Indian Island is to be isolated until Mr. Owen has finished his job."

Armstrong had gone pale. He said, "You realize— the man must be a raving maniac!"

Philip Lombard said, and there was a new ring in his voice, "There's one thing Mr. Owen didn't realize."

"What's that?"

"This island's more or less a bare rock. We shall make short work of searching it. We'll soon ferret out U. N. Owen, Esq."

Dr. Armstrong said warningly, "He'll be dangerous."

Philip Lombard laughed. "Dangerous? Who's afraid of the big bad wolf? *I'll* be dangerous when I get hold of him!"

He paused and said, "We'd better rope in Blore to help us. He'll be a good man in a pinch. Better not tell the women. As for the others, the General's gaga, I think, and old Wargrave's forte is masterly inactivity. The three of us can attend to this job."

8

BLORE WAS easily roped in. He expressed immediate agreement with their arguments. "What you've said about those china figures, sir, makes all the difference. That's crazy, that is! There's only one thing. You don't think this Owen's idea might be to do the job by proxy, as it were?"

"Explain yourself, man."

"Well, I mean like this. After the racket last night this young Mr. Marston gets the wind up and poisons himself. And Rogers, *he* gets the wind up too and bumps off his wife! All according to U. N. O.'s plan."

Armstrong shook his head. He stressed the point about the cyanide. Blore agreed. "Yes, I'd forgotten that. Not a natural thing to be carrying about with you. But how did it get into his drink, sir?"

Lombard said, "I've been thinking about that. Marston had several drinks that night. Between the time he had his last one and the time he finished the one before it, there was quite a gap. During that time his glass was lying about on some table or other. I think, though I can't be sure, it was on the little table near the window. The window was open. Somebody could have slipped a dose of the cyanide into the glass."

Blore said unbelievingly, "Without our all seeing him, sir?"

Lombard said dryly, "We were all—rather concerned elsewhere."

Armstrong said slowly, "That's true. We'd all been attacked. We were walking about, moving about the room. Arguing, indignant, intent on our own business. I think it *could* have been done. . . ."

Blore shrugged his shoulders. "Fact is, it must have been done! Now then, gentlemen, let's make a start. Nobody's got a revolver, by any chance? I suppose that's too much to hope for."

Lombard said, "I've got one." He patted his pocket.

Blore's eyes opened very wide. He said in an overcasual tone: "Always carry that about with you, sir?"

Lombard said, "Usually. I've been in some tight places, you know."

"Oh," said Blore and added, "Well, you've probably never been in a tighter place than you are today! If there's a lunatic hiding on this island, he's probably got a young arsenal on him—to say nothing of a knife or dagger or two."

Armstrong coughed. "You may be wrong there, Blore. Many homicidal lunatics are very quiet, unassuming people. Delightful fellows."

Blore said, "I don't feel this one is going to be of that kind, Dr. Armstrong."

ii.

The three men started on their tour of the island. It proved unexpectedly simple. On the northwest side, towards the coast, the cliffs fell sheer to the sea below, their surface unbroken. On the rest of the island there were no trees and very little cover. The three men worked carefully and methodically, beating up and down from the highest point to the water's edge, narrowly scanning the least irregularity in the rock which might point to the entrance to a cave. But there were no caves.

They came at last, skirting the water's edge, to where General Macarthur sat looking out to sea. It was very peaceful here with the lap of the waves breaking over the rocks. The old man sat very upright, his eyes fixed on the horizon. He paid no attention to the approach of the searchers. His oblivion of them made one at least faintly uncomfortable.

Blore thought to himself, 'Tisn't natural—looks as though he'd gone into a trance or something. He cleared his throat and said in a would-be conversational tone, "Nice peaceful spot you've found for yourself, sir."

The General frowned. He cast a quick look over his shoulder. He said, "There is so little time—so little time. I really must insist that no one disturbs me."

Blore said genially, "We won't disturb you. We're just making a tour of the island, so to speak. Just wondered, you know, if someone might be hiding on it."

The General frowned and said, "You don't understand—you don't understand at all. Please go away."

Blore retreated. He said, as he joined the other two, "He's crazy. . . . It's no good talking to him."

Lombard asked with some curiosity, "What did he say?"

Blore shrugged his shoulders. "Something about there being no time and that he didn't want to be disturbed."

Dr. Armstrong frowned. He murmured, "I wonder now. . . ."

iii.

The search of the island was practically completed. The three men stood on the highest point looking over towards the mainland. There were no boats out. The wind was freshening. Lombard said, "No fishing boats out. There's a storm coming. Damned nuisance you can't see the village from here. We could signal or do something."

Blore said, "We might light a bonfire tonight."

Lombard said dryly, "It's easier of belief than the truth! all probably been provided for."

"In what way, sir?"

"How do I know? Practical joke, perhaps. We're to be marooned here, no attention is to be paid to signals, etc.

Possibly the village has been told there's a wager on. Some damn fool story anyway."

Blore said dubiously, "Think they'd swallow that?"

Lombard said drily, "It's easier of belief than the truth! If the village were told that the island was to be isolated until Mr. Unknown Owen had quietly murdered all his guests—do you think they'd believe that?"

Dr. Armstrong said, "There are moments when I can't believe it myself. And yet—"

Philip Lombard, his lips curling back from his teeth, said, *"And yet*—that's just it! You've said it, doctor!"

Blore was gazing down into the water. He said, "Nobody could have clambered down here, I suppose?"

Armstrong shook his head. "I doubt it. It's pretty sheer. And where could he hide?"

Blore said, "There might be a hole in the cliff. If we had a boat now, we could row round the island."

Lombard said, "If we had a boat, we'd all be halfway to the mainland by now!"

"True enough, sir."

Lombard said suddenly, "We can make sure of this cliff. There's only one place where there *could* be a recess —just a little to the right below here. If you fellows can get hold of a rope, you can let me down to make sure."

Blore said, "Might as well *be* sure. Though it seems absurd—on the face of it! I'll see if I can get hold of something." He started off briskly down to the house.

Lombard stared up at the sky. The clouds were beginning to mass themselves together. The wind was increasing. He shot a sideways look at Armstrong. He said, "You're very silent, doctor. What are you thinking?"

Armstrong said slowly, "I was wondering exactly how mad old Macarthur was. . . ."

iv.

Vera had been restless all the morning. She had avoided Emily Brent with a kind of shuddering aversion. Miss Brent herself had taken a chair just round the corner of the house so as to be out of the wind. She sat

78

there knitting. Every time Vera thought of her she seemed to see a pale drowned face with seaweed entangled in the hair. . . . A face that had once been pretty—impudently pretty perhaps—and which was now beyond the reach of pity or terror. And Emily Brent, placid and righteous, sat knitting.

On the main terrace, Mr. Justice Wargrave sat huddled in a porter's chair. His head was poked down well into his neck. When Vera looked at him, she saw a man standing in the dock—a young man with fair hair and blue eyes and a bewildered, frightened face. Edward Seton. And in imagination she saw the judge's old hands put the black cap on his head and begin to pronounce sentence. . . .

After a while Vera strolled slowly down to the sea. She walked along towards the extreme end of the island where an old man sat staring out to the horizon. General Macarthur stirred at her approach. His head turned—there was a queer mixture of questioning and apprehension in his look. It startled her. He stared intently at her for a minute or two. She thought to herself: How queer. It's almost as though he *knew*. . . .

He said, "Oh! it's you! You've come. . . ."

Vera sat down beside him. She said, "Do you like sitting here looking out to sea?"

He nodded his head gently. "Yes," he said. "It's pleasant. It's a good place, I think, to wait."

"To wait?" said Vera sharply. "What are you waiting for?"

He said gently, "The end. But I think you know that, don't you? It's true, isn't it? We're all waiting for the end."

She said unsteadily, "What do you mean?"

General Macarthur said gravely, *"None of us are going to leave the island.* That's the plan. You know it, of course, perfectly. What, perhaps, you can't understand is the relief!"

Vera said wonderingly, "The relief?"

He said, "Yes. Of course, you're very young . . . you haven't got to that yet. But it does come! The blessed relief when you know that you've done with it all—that you haven't got to carry the burden any longer. You'll feel that too some day. . . ."

Vera said hoarsely, "I don't understand you." Her fingers worked spasmodically. She felt suddenly afraid of this quiet old soldier.....

He said musingly, "You see, I loved Leslie. I loved her very much. . . ."

Vera said questioningly, "Was Leslie your wife?"

"Yes, my wife. . . . I loved her—and I was very proud of her. She was so pretty—and so gay." He was silent for a minute or two, then he said, "Yes, I loved Leslie. That's why I did it."

Vera said, "You mean—" and paused.

General Macarthur nodded his head gently. "It's not much good denying it now—not when we're all going to die. *I sent Richmond to his death.* I suppose, in a way, it was murder. Curious. *Murder*—and I've always been such a law-abiding man! But it didn't seem like that at the time. I had no regrets. 'Serves him damned well right!'— that's what I thought. But afterwards—"

In a hard voice, Vera said, "Well, afterwards?"

He shook his head vaguely. He looked puzzled and a little distressed. "I don't know. I—don't know. It was all different, you see. I don't know if Leslie ever guessed . . . I don't think so. But you see, I didn't know about her any more. She'd gone far away where I couldn't reach her. And then she died—and I was alone. . . ."

Vera said, "Alone—alone—" and the echo of her voice came back to her from the rocks.

General Macarthur said, "You'll be glad, too, when the end comes."

Vera got up. She said sharply, "I don't know what you mean!"

He said, "I *know,* my child, I *know.* . . ."

"You don't. You don't understand at all. . . ."

General Macarthur looked out to sea again. He seemed unconscious of her presence behind him. He said very gently and softly, "Leslie . . . ?"

When Blore returned from the house with a rope coiled over his arm, he found Armstrong where he had left him staring down into the depths. Blore said breathlessly, "Where's Mr. Lombard?"

Armstrong said carelessly, "Gone to test some theory or other. He'll be back in a minute. Look here, Blore, I'm worried."

"I should say we were all worried."

The doctor waved an impatient hand. "Of course—of course. I don't mean it that way. I'm thinking of old Macarthur."

"What about him, sir?"

Dr. Armstrong said grimly, "What we're looking for is a madman. *What price Macarthur?*"

Blore said incredulously, "You mean he's homicidal?"

Armstrong said doubtfully, "I shouldn't have said so. Not for a minute. But of course I'm not a specialist in mental diseases. I haven't really had any conversation with him—I haven't studied him from that point of view."

Blore said doubtfully, "Gaga, yes! But I wouldn't have said—"

Armstrong cut in with a slight effort as of a man who pulls himself together. "You're probably right! Damn it all, there *must* be someone hiding on the island! Ah! here comes Lombard."

They fastened the rope carefully. Lombard said, "I'll help myself all I can. Keep a lookout for a sudden strain on the rope."

After a minute or two, while they stood together watching Lombard's progress, Blore said, "Climbs like a cat, doesn't he?" There was something odd in his voice.

Dr. Armstrong said, "I should think he must have done some mountaineering in his time."

"Maybe."

There was a silence and the ex-Inspector said, "Funny sort of cove altogether. D'you know what I think?"

"What?"

"He's a wrong 'un!"

Armstrong said doubtfully, "In what way?"

Blore grunted. Then he said, "I don't know—exactly. But I wouldn't trust him a yard."

Dr. Armstrong said, "I suppose he's led an adventurous life."

Blore said, "I bet some of his adventures have had to be kept pretty dark." He paused and then went on, "Did you happen to bring a revolver along with you, doctor?"

Armstrong stared. "Me? Good Lord, no. Why should I?"

Blore said, *"Why did Mr. Lombard?"*

Armstrong said doubtfully, "I suppose—habit."

Blore snorted.

A sudden pull came on the rope. For some moments they had their hands full. Presently, when the strain relaxed, Blore said, "There are habits *and* habits! Mr. Lombard takes a revolver to out-of-the-way places, right enough, *and* a primus and a sleeping bag and a supply of bug powder, no doubt! But habit wouldn't make him bring the whole outfit down here! It's only in books people carry revolvers around as a matter of course."

Dr. Armstrong shook his head perplexedly. They leaned over and watched Lombard's progress. His search was thorough and they could see at once that it was futile. Presently he came up over the edge of the cliff. He wiped the perspiration from his forehead. "Well," he said. "We're up against it. It's the house or nowhere."

v i .

The house was easily searched. They went through the few outbuildings first and then turned their attention to the building itself. Mrs. Rogers' yard measure found in the kitchen dresser assisted them. But there were no hidden spaces left unaccounted for. Everything was plain and straightforward, a modern structure devoid of concealments. They went through the ground floor first. As they mounted to the bedroom floor, they saw through the landing window Rogers carrying out a tray of cocktails to the terrace. Philip Lombard said lightly, "Wonderful animal, the good servant. Carries on with an impassive countenance."

Armstrong said appreciatively, "Rogers is a first-class butler, I'll say that for him!"

Blore said, "His wife was a pretty good cook, too. That dinner—last night—"

They turned in to the first bedroom. Five minutes later they faced each other on the landing. No one hiding—no possible hiding place. Blore said, "There's a little stair here."

Dr. Armstrong said, "It leads up to the servants' room."

Blore said, "There must be a place under the roof—for cisterns, water tank, etc. It's the best chance—and the only one!"

And it was then, as they stood there, that they heard the sound from above. A soft, furtive footfall overhead.

They all heard it. Armstrong grasped Blore's arm. Lombard held up an admonitory finger. "Quiet—listen."

It came again—someone moving softly, furtively, overhead.

Armstrong whispered, "He's actually in the bedroom itself. The room where Mrs. Rogers' body is."

Blore whispered back, "Of course! Best hiding place he could have chosen! Nobody likely to go there. Now then—quiet as you can."

They crept stealthily upstairs. On the little landing outside the door of the bedroom they paused again. Yes, someone was in the room. There was a faint creak from within. Blore whispered, "Now."

He flung open the door and rushed in, the other two close behind him. Then all three stopped dead. Rogers was in the room, his hands full of garments.

vii.

Blore recovered himself first. He said, "Sorry—er—Rogers. Heard someone moving about in here, and thought—well—" He stopped.

Rogers said, "I'm sorry, gentlemen. I was just moving

my things. I take it there will be no objection if I take one of the vacant guest chambers on the floor below? The smallest room."

It was to Armstrong that he spoke, and Armstrong replied, "Of course. Of course. Get on with it." He avoided looking at the sheeted figure lying on the bed.

Rogers said, "Thank you, sir."

He went out of the room with his arm full of belongings and went down the stairs to the floor below. Armstrong moved over to the bed and, lifting the sheet, looked down on the peaceful face of the dead woman. There was no fear there now. Just emptiness. Armstrong said, "Wish I'd got my stuff here. I'd like to know what drug it was." Then he turned to the other two. "Let's get finished. I feel it in my bones we're not going to find anything."

Blore was wrestling with the bolts of a low manhole. He said, "That chap moves damned quietly. A minute or two ago we saw him in the garden. None of us heard him come upstairs."

Lombard said, "I suppose that's why we assumed it must be a stranger moving about up here."

Blore disappeared into a cavernous darkness. Lombard pulled a torch from his pocket and followed. Five minutes later three men stood on an upper landing and looked at each other. They were dirty and festooned with cobwebs and their faces were grim. There was no one on the island but their eight selves.

9

LOMBARD SAID slowly, "So we've been wrong—wrong all along! Built up a nightmare of superstition and fantasy all because of the coincidence of two deaths!"

Armstrong said gravely, "And yet, you know, the argument holds. Hang it all, I'm a doctor, I know something about suicides. Anthony Marston wasn't a suicidal type."

Lombard said doubtfully, "It couldn't, I suppose, have been an accident?"

Blore snorted, unconvinced. "Damned queer sort of accident," he grunted.

There was a pause, then Blore said, "About the woman——" and stopped.

"Mrs. Rogers?"

"Yes. It's possible, isn't it, that that might have been an accident?"

Philip Lombard said, "An accident? In what way?"

Blore looked slightly embarrassed. His red-brick face grew a little deeper in hue. He said, almost blurting out the words, "Look here, doctor, you did give her some dope, you know."

Armstrong stared at him. "Dope? What do you mean?"

"Last night. You said yourself you'd give her something to make her sleep."

"Oh, that, yes. A harmless sedative."

"What was it exactly?"

"I gave her a mild dose of trional. A perfectly harmless preparation."

Blore grew redder still. He said, "Look here—not to mince matters—you didn't give her an overdose, did you?"

Dr. Armstrong said angrily, "I don't know what you mean."

Blore said, "It's possible, isn't it, that you may have made a mistake? These things do happen once in a while."

Armstrong said sharply, "I did nothing of the sort. The suggestion is ridiculous." He stopped and added in a cold, biting tone, "Or do you suggest that I gave her an overdose on purpose?"

Philip Lombard said quickly, "Look here, you two, got to keep our heads. Don't let's start slinging accusations about."

Blore said sullenly, "I only suggested the doctor had made a mistake."

Dr. Armstrong smiled with an effort. He said, showing

his teeth in a somewhat mirthless smile, "Doctors can't afford to make mistakes of that kind, my friend."

Blore said deliberately. "It wouldn't be the first you've made—if that gramophone record is to be believed!"

Armstrong went white. Philip Lombard said quickly and angrily to Blore, "What's the sense of making yourself offensive? We're all in the same boat. We've got to pull together. What about your own pretty little spot of perjury?"

Blore took a step forward, his hands clenched. He said in a thick voice, "Perjury be damned! That's a foul lie! You may try and shut me up, Mr. Lombard, but there's things I want to know—and one of them is about *you!*"

Lombard's eyebrows rose. "About me?"

"Yes. I want to know why you brought a revolver down here on a pleasant social visit."

Lombard said, "You do. do you?"

"Yes, I do, Mr. Lombard."

Lombard said unexpectedly, "You know, Blore, you're not nearly such a fool as you look."

"That's as may be. What about that revolver?"

Lombard smiled. "I brought it because I expected to run into a spot of trouble."

Blore said suspiciously, "You didn't tell us that last night." Lombard shook his head.

"You were holding out on us?" Blore persisted.

"In a way, yes," said Lombard.

"Well, come on, out with it."

Lombard said slowly, "I allowed you all to think that I was asked here in the same way as most of the others. That's not quite true. As a matter of fact I was approached by a mysterious Johnny—Morris his name was. He offered me a hundred guineas to come down here and keep my eyes open—said I'd got a reputation for being a good man in a tight place."

"Well?" Blore prompted impatiently.

Lombard said with a grin, "That's all."

Dr. Armstrong said, "But surely he told you more than that?"

"Oh, no, he didn't. Just shut up like a clam. I could

take it or leave it—those were his words. I was hard up. I took it."

Blore looked unconvinced. He said, "Why didn't you tell us all this last night?"

"My dear man—" Lombard shrugged eloquent shoulders. "How was I to know that last night wasn't exactly the eventuality I was here to cope with? I lay low and told a noncommittal story."

Dr. Armstrong said shrewdly, "But now—you think differently?"

Lombard's face changed. It darkened and hardened. He said, "Yes. I believe now that I'm in the same boat as the rest of you. That hundred guineas was just Mr. Owen's little bit of cheese to get me into the trap along with the rest of you." He said slowly, *"For we are in a trap—* I'll take my oath on that! Mrs. Rogers' death! Tony Marston's! The disappearing Indian boys on the dinner table! Oh, yes, Mr. Owen's hand is plainly to be seen—*but where the devil is Mr. Owen himself?"*

Downstairs the gong pealed a solemn call to lunch.

ii.

Rogers was standing by the dining-room door. As the three men descended the stairs he moved a step or two forward. He said in a low, anxious voice, "I hope lunch will be satisfactory. There is cold ham and cold tongue, and I've boiled some potatoes. And there's cheese and biscuits and some tinned fruits."

Lombard said, "Sounds all right. Stores are holding out, then?"

"There is plenty of food, sir—of a tinned variety. The larder is very well stocked. A necessity, that, I should say, sir, on an island where one may be cut off from the mainland for a considerable period."

Lombard nodded. Rogers murmured as he followed the three men into the dining room: "It worries me that Fred Narracott hasn't been over today. It's peculiarly unfortunate, as you might say."

"Yes," said Lombard, "peculiarly unfortunate describes it very well."

Miss Brent came into the room. She had just dropped a ball of wool and was carefully rewinding the end of it. As she took her seat at table she remarked, "The weather is changing. The wind is quite strong and there are white horses on the sea."

Mr. Justice Wargrave came in. He walked with a slow measured tread. He darted quick looks from under his bushy eyebrows at the other occupants of the dining room. He said, "You have had an active morning." There was a faint malicious pleasure in his voice.

Vera Claythorne hurried in. She was a little out of breath. She said quickly, "I hope you didn't wait for me. Am I late?"

Emily Brent said, "You're not the last. The General isn't here yet."

They sat round the table. Rogers addressed Miss Brent, "Will you begin, madam, or will you wait?"

Vera said, "General Macarthur is sitting right down by the sea. I don't expect he would hear the gong there and anyway"—she hesitated—"he's a little vague today, I think."

Rogers said quickly, "I will go down and inform him luncheon is ready."

Dr. Armstrong jumped up. "I'll go," he said. "You others start lunch."

He left the room. Behind him he heard Rogers' voice. "Will you take cold tongue or cold ham, madam?"

iii.

The five people sitting round the table seemed to find conversation difficult. Outside sudden gusts of wind came up and died away. Vera shivered a little and said, "There is a storm coming."

Blore made a contribution to the discourse. He said conversationally, "There was an old fellow in the train from Plymouth yesterday. *He* kept saying a storm was coming. Wonderful how they know weather, these old salts."

Reader's Supplement

to

AND THEN THERE WERE NONE

AGATHA CHRISTIE (1891–1976)
(Reprinted with permission of Angus McBean, London)

BIOGRAPHICAL BACKGROUND

Suppose you met a solidly proportioned, blondish woman who looked and acted like a queen, and heard her say in a clipped British accent:

"I enjoy my food, hate the taste of any kind of alcohol, have tried and tried to like smoking but can't manage it. I adore flowers, am crazy about the sea, love the theater . . . loathe wireless and all loud noises."

Suppose you also learned that this queenly woman, at the age of sixteen, had studied voice and the piano in Paris, had practiced singing for six hours a day, but had abandoned a career in grand opera because she discovered she was too shy to appear in public. And suppose you were told that later in her life when she had achieved worldwide fame she absolutely refused to be interviewed, was rarely photographed, flatly declined luncheon invitations, and didn't permit her publisher to meet with her for twenty-five years!

Now, would you believe that this woman was once christened the "Queen of Crime," that she could write a story in which ten people are done in, that she could produce more than eighty novels and over a dozen plays in most of which someone (and often more than one) meets violent death? Yet this is a true picture of Agatha Christie, one of the great masters of mystery fiction, whose outward appearance and behavior completely belie her tremendous capacity for writing bloodcurdling tales of suspense and murder.

Agatha Mary Clarissa Miller was born in 1891 in Torquay, in the Devonshire district of England. She was the second daughter of Frederick Alvah Miller, a transplanted New York City resident, and an intelligent, charming English mother who had her own ideas about how to bring up children, ideas that changed from season to season. Agatha was but an infant when her father died. By the time she was ready for school, her mother had decided that public schools had almost destroyed the mind and spirit of her elder daughter. Accordingly, the future "Queen of Crime" received her entire early education at home, sheltered, as it were, from the evil influences of the outside world.

The obedient little girl was encouraged to write poems and stories. It is said that on one occasion her doting mother, who believed her children capable of any achievement, suggested that Agatha, confined to bed with a cold, write a short story. What is even more remarkable is that Agatha did write one! Perhaps a hint of things to come was present in these stories, which invariably were full of tragedy.

Agatha's interest in writing persisted. She became involved in detective fiction almost by chance. Her elder sister had stated that one didn't have to read long before knowing who had committed the crime in the average mystery. Accepting this complaint as a challenge, Agatha decided to write a story that would completely baffle even her sister. Out of this decision came *The Mysterious Affair at Styles*. This first effort was rejected by many publishers, but was finally accepted, and the "Queen" was on her way.

She served for a time as a volunteer worker in Red Cross hospitals during World War I and then married a Royal Flying Corps officer, Colonel Archibald Christie, in 1919. Her first marriage was not very successful. Her concern over it possibly led to a mysterious episode of her own in 1926. Agatha Christie, by then a renowned writer, suddenly disappeared. Her whereabouts baffled the police. When she did turn up, she was discovered singing and dancing in a Yorkshire inn as a member of a band! In 1928, Agatha divorced the colonel and two years later married Max Mallowan, an archeologist with whom she has led an interesting life ever since.

It is hard to say which of Agatha Christie's books is most popular. For a time, *The Murder of Roger Ackroyd* (1926) was considered the best, but that was before *And Then There Were None* (1939) appeared, first in serialized form in a magazine, then as a novel, and finally as a successful motion picture. In the latter story, also called *Ten Little Indians,* Agatha went to the furthest extremes to invent a trick ending, so much so that some critics objected to her "gimmick," but her readers loved it.

Many of her books contain standard detective characters who appear again and again. Hercule Poirot is perhaps the most famous—the little Belgian sleuth with his "little gray cells" that help him solve crimes almost as adroitly as does Sherlock Holmes. Miss Marple is another odd sort of detective, and so are a half dozen others.

Although Agatha Christie has written some romantic novels, under the pen name of Mary Westmacott, she has not enjoyed much success in this field. In 1954, her play *Witness for the Prosecution* was produced on Broadway and ran for years. She recently collected some of her short stories into editions for teen-agers, two of which are *Thirteen for Luck!* and *Double Sin.*

HISTORICAL BACKGROUND

In this book, as in many of her others, Agatha Christie establishes the setting of her story in the vicinity of Devon, a district very familiar to her. If you were to consult a map of England, you would find the area in the very southwesterly tip between Cornwall and Somerset, facing the English Channel on the south and the Bristol Channel on the northwest. The author was born in Torquay, which is about midpoint on the southern coast of Devon.

She tells us that Justice Wargrave is coming from Somerset (northeast of Devon), Macarthur from Dorset (east of Devon), Dr. Armstrong from Salisbury Plain (northeast of Somerset), and Mr. Blore from Plymouth (southwest of Torquay). You can almost picture Agatha sitting at her desk and running a line in a wide semicircle above her birthplace and deciding that this would be a good area from which to draw the central characters because she had a firsthand acquaintance with the land and climate. Indeed, when a storm plays an important part in the isolation of the guests, you can readily accept the possibility of such weather because the area is known for sudden violent outbursts of rain and fog.

Some other famous mystery story writers have used current events in their plots. For instance, Ian Fleming built situations around rockets or "moonrakers." In Agatha Christie's books, the land and its politics rarely figure prominently. Thus, even though the time of *And Then There Were None* is the late 1930's, we are not reminded that Europe is shaking under the threat of German agression.

Indian Island gets its character by being identified first as one of the places rich foreigners (Americans especially) were in the habit of purchasing to achieve status. Castles in Spain or villas in Italy were equally prized as romantic vacation retreats. Moreover, when one had a huge place on his hands, he had to fill it with people to escape loneliness. The weekend party, therefore, featuring hordes of friends, acquaintances, and interesting strangers, was quite the vogue—as it still is today on large estates here and abroad. This accounts for the willingness of the guests to come to Indian Island, despite the vagueness of the invitations. As Miss Brent puts it, a free vacation "was indeed something to take into consideration," even if one didn't know the host! (p. 14M)

Agatha Christie's list of guests is exactly what one would expect to find at a holiday gathering in a big house owned by a wealthy man. There would be some handsome, dashing devils like Marston, a few seemingly sweet young things like Vera, at least one tight-lipped spinster like Miss Brent, a mysterious adventurer or two like Lombard, a representative of the military like General Macarthur, several professional men like Dr. Armstrong and Justice Wargrave, often a hired detective to guard the owner's jewels and silver (Mr. Blore), and, of course, servants (Mr. and Mrs. Rogers). Throw in a dash of the world-renowned British crime detection bureau, Scotland Yard, and sinister-sounding episodes in the past of the central characters and you have all the ingredients of the proper background for a spine-tingling murder mystery!

Note: The page references on the following pages direct your attention to passages in the text (T for Top of page, M for Middle, and B for Bottom).

PICTORIAL BACKGROUND

Torquay, the birthplace of Agatha Christie, is in Devonshire. It is a fashionable watering place and has been advertised as the English Riviera. Named after the nearby Tor Abbey, founded in 1196, the town is built on a series of terraces rising up from the beaches. Much frequented as a winter resort, it has numerous villas and gardens, a beautiful promenade, libraries, and a museum.

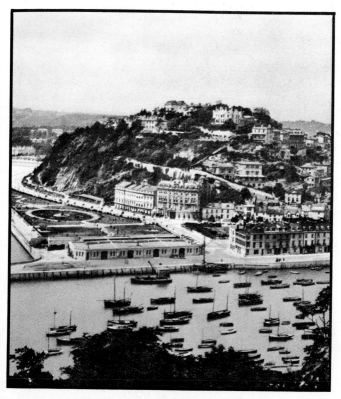

A VIEW OF THE TERRACES AT TORQUAY

Overlooking the lovely River Dart, Agatha Christie finds the peaceful atmosphere favorable for evolving the intricate plots that have made her books famous. From Dittisham, a nearby village, the Mayflower *set out for America hundreds of years ago when mystery plays were written in verse.*

AGATHA CHRISTIE WITH HER HUSBAND AT THEIR
DEVONSHIRE HOME

Vera Claythorne, in a third-class carriage with five other travelers in it, leaned her head back and shut her eyes. How hot it was traveling by train today! It would be nice to get to the sea! Really a great piece of luck getting this job. When you wanted a holiday post it nearly always meant looking after a swarm of children. . . . (p. 10M)

A THIRD-CLASS COACH ON AN ENGLISH TRAIN

Mr. Blore was in the slow train from Plymouth. There was only one other person in his carriage, an elderly seafaring gentleman with a bleary eye. At the present moment he had dropped off to sleep. Mr. Blore was writing carefully in a little notebook.

"That's the lot," he muttered to himself. . . . (p. 17B)

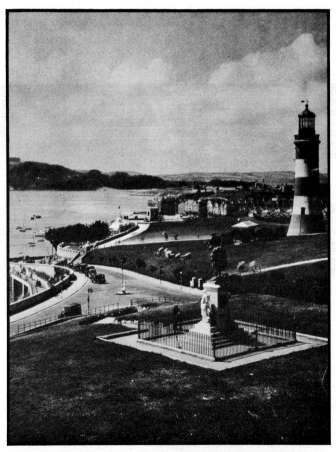

A STRIKING VIEW OF THE PLYMOUTH SHORELINE

Then they plunged into a maze of cross-country lanes. . . .

General Macarthur said, "Don't know this part of Devon at all. My little place is in East Devon—just on the borderline of Dorset."

Vera said, "It really is lovely here. The hills and the red earth and everything so green and luscious looking." (p. 22T)

THE DEVONSHIRE COUNTRYSIDE

They came up over a steep hill and down a zigzag track to Sticklehaven—a mere cluster of cottages with a fishing boat or two drawn up on the beach. Illuminated by the setting sun, they had their first glimpse of Indian Island jutting up out of the sea to the south.

Vera said, surprised, "It's a long way out." (p. 22M)

AN ENGLISH VILLAGE SIMILAR TO STICKLEHAVEN

Down the steep track into the village a car was coming. A car so fantastically powerful, so superlatively beautiful that it had all the nature of an apparition. At the wheel sat a young man, his hair blown back by the wind. In the blaze of the evening light he looked, not a man, but a young god, a Hero God out of some Northern Saga. (p. 23B)

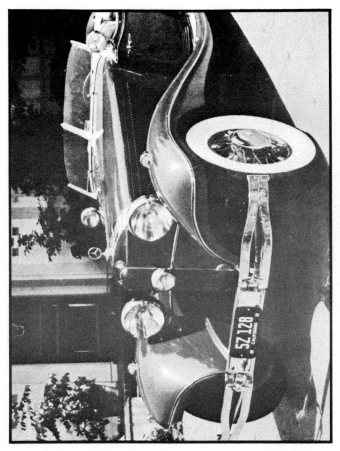

A FLASHY SPORTS CAR OF THE PERIOD

Fred Narracott sat by the engine thinking to himself that this was a queer lot. Not at all his idea of what Mr. Owen's guests were likely to be. He'd expected something altogether more classy. Togged-up women and gentlemen in yachting costume and all very rich and important looking.

Not at all like Mr. Elmer Robson's parties. (p. 24M)

THE OCCUPANTS OF THE MOTOR BOAT TO INDIAN ISLAND
(Reprinted with permission of 20th Century-Fox)

As the party ascended the steps, and came out on a terrace above, their spirits revived. In the open doorway of the house a correct butler was awaiting them, and something about his gravity reassured them. And then the house itself was really attractive, the view from the terrace magnificent. . . . (p. 25B)

A "CORRECT" ENGLISH BUTLER

Mr. Justice Wargrave thought to himself: Armstrong? Remember him in the witness box. Very correct and cautious. All doctors are damned fools. Harley Street ones are the worst of the lot. And his mind dwelt malevolently on a recent interview he had had with a suave personage in that very street. (p. 30T)

HARLEY STREET, LONDON, WHERE NUMEROUS
DOCTORS PRACTICE

Dinner was drawing to a close. . . . (p. 33T)

Actors in the motion picture: *(l. to r. around the table)
Vera (June Duprez), Philip (Louis Hayward), Tony
(Mischa Auer), General Macarthur (Sir C. Aubrey Smith),
Rogers (Richard Haydn), Judge Wargrave (Barry Fitz-
gerald), Dr. Armstrong (Walter Huston), Mr. Blore (Rol-
and Young), Emily (Judith Anderson)*

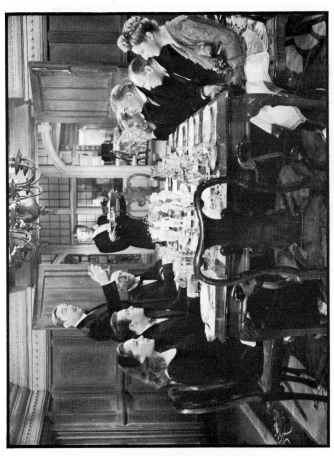

THE GUESTS ENJOY THEIR FIRST DINNER.
(Reprinted with permission of 20th Century-Fox)

Inside the second room a table had been brought up close to the wall which adjoined the drawing room. On the table was a gramophone—an old-fashioned type with a large trumpet attached. The mouth of the trumpet was against the wall, and Lombard, pushing it aside, indicated where two or three small holes had been unobtrusively bored through the wall. (p. 37M)

A GRAMOPHONE—1905

The judge wound up his watch carefully and placed it by the bed. He remembered exactly how he had felt sitting there—listening, making notes, appreciating everything, tabulating every scrap of evidence that told against the prisoner. He'd enjoyed that case. Matthews' final speech had been first class. (p. 54M)

A BRITISH COURTROOM SCENE

Dr. Armstrong came out onto the terrace. He stood there hesitating. To his left were Blore and Lombard. To his right was Wargrave, slowly pacing up and down, his head bent down. Armstrong, after a moment of indecision, turned towards the latter. But at that moment Rogers came quickly out of the house. (p. 66B)

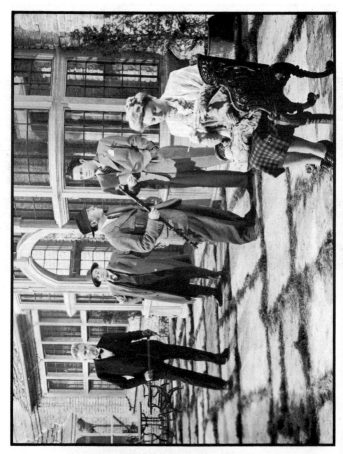

SOME OF THE GUESTS ON THE TERRACE
(Reprinted with permission of 20th Century-Fox)

The three men started on their tour of the island . . . the cliffs fell sheer to the sea below. . . . The three men worked carefully and methodically, beating up and down from the highest point to the water's edge, narrowly scanning the least irregularity in the rock which might point to the entrance to a cave. But there were no caves. (p. 76B)

A ROCKY COAST IN DEVONSHIRE

After a while Vera strolled slowly down to the sea. She walked along towards the extreme end of the island where an old man sat staring out to the horizon. General Macarthur stirred at her approach. His head turned—there was a queer mixture of questioning and apprehension in his look. It startled her. (p. 79M)

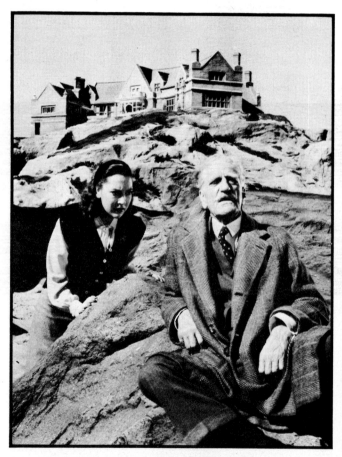

VERA AND GENERAL MACARTHUR AT THE SHORE
(Reprinted with permission of 20th Century-Fox)

The storm increased. The wind howled against the side of the house. Everyone was in the living room. They sat listlessly huddled together. And, surreptitiously, they watched each other. When Rogers brought in the tea tray, they all jumped. He said: "Shall I draw the curtains? It would make it more cheerful-like." (p. 105M)

A TEA TRAY AND SERVICE

They all moved inside the room, looking at the neatly set plates and cutlery. . . . It was Vera who saw it first. She caught the judge's arm and the grip of her athletic fingers made the old gentleman wince. She cried out, "The Indians! Look!"

There were only six china figures in the middle of the table. (p. 109B)

ANOTHER SHOCKING WARNING
(Reprinted with permission of 20th Century-Fox)

The terrace was peaceful and innocuous looking in the sunshine. They hesitated there a minute, then instead of entering by the front door, they made a cautious circuit of the house. They found Blore. He was spreadeagled on the stone terrace on the east side, his head crushed and mangled by a great block of white marble. (p. 148B)

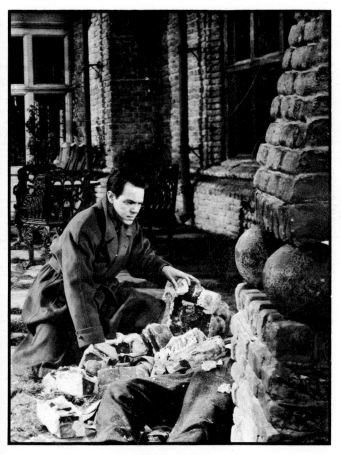

THE LATEST VICTIM. . . .
(Reprinted with permission of 20th Century-Fox)

Death was very near to Philip Lombard now. It had never, he knew, been nearer. Nevertheless he was not beaten yet. He said authoritatively, "Give that revolver to me."

    Vera laughed.

    Lombard said, "Come on, hand it over." (p. 153T)

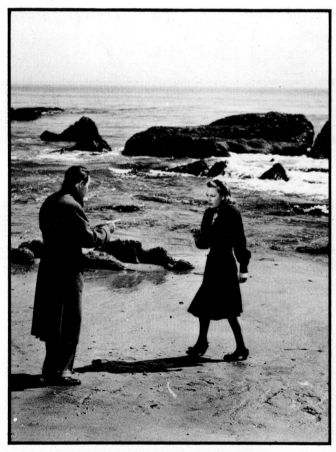

THE LAST TWO SURVIVORS IN A SHOWDOWN
(Reprinted with permission of 20th Century-Fox)

She opened the door. . . . She gave a gasp. . . . What was that—*hanging from the hook in the ceiling?* A rope with a noose all ready? And a chair to stand upon—a chair that could be kicked away. . . . That was what Hugo wanted. . . . *And of course that was the last line of the rhyme.* He went and hanged himself and then there were none. . . . *(p. 155M)*

. . . AND THEN THERE WERE NONE. . . .
(Reprinted with permission of 20th Century-Fox)

Sir Thomas Legge, Assistant Commissioner at Scotland Yard, said irritably, "But the whole thing's incredible."

Inspector Maine said respectfully, "I know, sir."

The A.C. went on, "Ten people dead on an island and not a living soul on it. It doesn't make sense!"

Inspector Maine said stolidly, "Nevertheless, it hap-pened, sir." (p. 156T)

SCOTLAND YARD, VIEWED FROM WESTMINSTER BRIDGE—1940's

VISUAL GLOSSARY

1—cosh (p. 92B)

2—truncheon (p. 92B)

3—stiletto (p. 72M)

4—torch (p. 84M)

5–grandfather chair (p. 90T) 7–gimlet (p. 115M)

6–siphon (p. 127T) 8–heliograph (p. 98M)

LITERARY ALLUSIONS AND NOTES

Even before this exciting murder mystery begins, the reader may encounter some problems with unfamiliar words and allusions. First, there is the title itself, a quotation from a nursery rhyme, "Ten Little Indians." Agatha Christie gives some explanation of why her setting is labeled Indian Island, but it is clear that the name is chosen to fit into the framework suggested by the nursery rhyme, just as the china figurines in the story carry out this theme. In fact, just to stick to the idea, the author piles up an unusual number of corpses. The title, *And Then There Were None,* is, of course, part of the last line of the familiar rhyme. Less familiar may be some details of the convenient Cast of Characters prefixed to the novel. For instance, American readers may not know British expressions such as *C.I.D.* (Criminal Investigation Department—a sort of British F.B.I.). Moreover, a classical reference such as "Charon ferrying the Styx" (referring to the mythological ferryman who was supposed to carry dead souls over the infernal river to their resting place in the afterlife) or a Latin legal phrase *corpora delicti* ("bodies of the crime," the victims) may baffle some. Explanations of additional references follow.

contadini **(p. 10T) (Italian):**
   Natives, peasants
games mistress (p. 11T):
   In a British school, the physical education instructress
sine qua non (p. 12B) (Latin):
   "Without which not," a prerequisite, an indispensable thing
Harley Street (p. 15M):
   A fashionable street in London known for its concentration of high-priced medical specialists—the mention gives Dr. Armstrong "class."
C.M.G., D.S.O. (p. 17B):
   These initials after General Macarthur's name are indicative of high military decorations (and an important

career as a soldier)—high-ranking officers are sometimes made "Commander of the Order of St. Michael and St. George" and bravery or other distinguished service is sometimes rewarded with the "Distinguished Service Order."

"Had one over the eight" (p. 18T):
Eight beers being considered permissible, one more than that, according to military slang of World War I, makes a man drunk.

War (p. 22M):
The capital letter makes us note that The Great War (World War I) is meant, the novel having just come out in its first printing the year World War II began (1939).

Saga (p. 24T):
Scandinavian literature gives us sagas (epic poems) in which brave and handsome heroes (to which young Anthony Marston is compared in appearance) are featured.

Ten little Indian boys (p. 28T):
Modern sensibilities have altered the original English children's poem that appears in Iona and Peter Opie's *Oxford Nursery Rhyme Book* (reprinted 1960). In general, Mrs. Christie's story rather closely follows the old rhyme, though her ingenuity is overtaxed by the "bumble-bee" and the "Zoo" aspects—for which she more than makes up with her brilliant "red herring." One can see that her setting (Devon) and her plot are dictated by the old rhyme. Of course no "bear" *hugs* one of the characters, but Mrs. Christie is close enough. Note that the familiarity of the original rhyme enables readers who know it from childhood to keep important details of the mystery in mind as the complicated plot unfolds.

gong (p. 32M):
It was the custom in large British country houses to call guests to dinner by beating on a gong, much as cooks in the Old West beat on a triangle or other convenient piece of iron to summon hungry cowboys to the chuckwagon.

cairngorm (p. 32B):
This is a yellowish quartz stone found in the mountains of Scotland. Set into a pin of Celtic design, cairngorms

are often worn by traditional little ladies or prim types who are prone to sweater and plaid skirt combinations. The brooch marks Emily as prim, proper, perhaps a bit dowdy or unfashionable.

"Swan Song" (p. 39T):
An old legend says that swans sing only just before their death. Thus a "swan song" is a farewell: in this case very appropriate and just ambiguous enough to pass as the title of a piece of music, thus not arousing Rogers' suspicions.

Caesar's wife (p. 46M):
Caesar's wife in ancient Rome was supposed to be not only virtuous but absolutely above suspicion.

pukka sahib (p. 46B) (Hindi):
This means "proper gentleman," an expression much used by retired colonels of the Indian Army and other Britons with a "colonial" background. The feminine is *mem sahib* (see p. 166B).

Sister (p. 49M):
A nurse in a hospital (not necessarily a nun)

"In the midst of life. . . ." (p. 51B):
It is a quotation from the Anglican *Book of Common Prayer,* the First Anthem for the Burial of the Dead.

David . . . Uriah (p. 56M):
"Set ye Uriah in the forefront of the hottest battle," ordered King David, according to *II Samuel,* 11:15, for the Hebrew King coveted the general's wife and wanted the husband killed. Of course the parallel is not exact, for here it is the husband who sends his wife's lover out to be killed, but one can see why General Macarthur might find a sermon on this text disturbing.

Château Neuf du Pape (p. 60T):
A red wine from France's vineyards

Elliman's (p. 61M):
A patent medicine

Loch Ness monster (p. 62B):
Speculation has raged for years over whether or not a prehistoric monster lives in the waters of Loch Ness in Scotland.

"Be sure . . ." (p. 69T):

A slight misquotation of "Be sure your sin will find you out," *Numbers,* 32:23. Presumably the error is Mrs. Christie's, for Miss Brent is supposed to be very knowledgeable about the Bible and would probably not make a mistake about a favorite quotation.

black cap (p. 79T):

British judges in high courts place a triangular black cap on their wigs when pronouncing sentences of death. The costume of such a judge, gray wig and scarlet robe, figures prominently later in the story.

trional (p. 85M):

A mild sleeping powder. Seconal would be better known to most laymen, but aficionados of detective fiction are traditionally well versed on such arcane drugs as curare, cyanide, and so on.

white horses (p. 88T):

White caps on the waves

cosh (p. 92B):

British underworld term for what Americans call a black-jack

heliographing (p. 98M):

This is a method of sending messages by Morse Code by reflecting the sun's rays off a mirror.

lav (p. 106T):

The butler betrays his class by first using the word *lav* (for "lavatory," strictly a place to wash one's hands) and then immediately correcting it to the more acceptable *bathroom* (itself a euphemism, generally speaking, but in this case really a place where a bath and shower are to be found).

echo answers where (p. 108B):

Lombard seems to know his Byron. He is quoting the poet's *Bride of Abydos:*

> Hark! To the hurried question of Despair:
> "Where is my child?"—an echo answers—
>   "where?"

a case in America (p. 112T):
The case is that of Lizzie Borden of Massachusetts who was acquitted of murdering her parents with an ax. The jingle of the time ran:

> Lizzie Borden took an ax
> And gave her father forty whacks.
> When she saw what she had done
> She gave her mother forty-one.

sang-froid (p. 114B) (French):
"Cold blood," imperturbability under strain, equanimity

"Thou shalt not be afraid. . . ." (p. 115M):
The comforting words of *Psalm* 91:3

flex (p. 138T):
British for electrical cord or cable

red herring (p. 144B):
From the practice of drawing a red herring—cured by salting and smoking—across the path to confuse hunting dogs, a red herring has come to mean a clue that puts one off the right track, makes one lose the scent of the quarry.

Broadmoor (p. 147B):
A prison in England

Priest's Hole (p. 149B):
In times when Catholicism was equivalent to sedition under English law, devout Roman Catholics hid the priests who came to their houses (to celebrate the Mass in secret) in concealed "priests' holes" in the floors whenever the Protestant police or other authorities threatened.

chloral (p. 156M):
A bitter, crystalline hydrate $CCl_3CH(OH)_2$ of the oily aldehyde chloral, it is called chloral hydrate and is used as a hypnotic.

Cain (p. 173T):
In *Genesis*. Adam and Eve's son Cain murdered his brother, Abel, in jealous rage and thereafter was banished to Nod, on the east of Eden, God putting a mark on his forehead so that all men would know him ("The Mark of Cain").

CRITICAL EXCERPTS

Now that you have read the novel, hailed as "Agatha Christie's masterpiece" by Rupert Hart-Davis, you may wish to reconsider it in light of critical pronouncements on detective fiction as a *genre,* and particularly on this mystery novel. Here are some critical excerpts from a variety of sources that provide insights that can enrich your understanding and appreciation of this famous work. We begin with a few apt quotations relevant to the murderer and the author who created him and move through general remarks of interest to book reviews that greeted *And Then There Were None* upon its initial appearance. We conclude with some observations that put the topic into perspective.

1. *Two quotations from Nietzsche, creator of the concept of a "Superman":*
"Everything absolute belongs to pathology."
"The idealist is incorrigible—if he is turned out of his heaven, he makes an ideal of his hell."

2. *The distinctive quality of a detective story, in which it differs from all other types of fiction, is that the satisfaction that it offers to the reader is primarily an intellectual satisfaction. This is not to say that it need be deficient in the other qualities appertaining to good fiction: in grace of diction, in humour, in interesting characterization, in picturesqueness of setting or in emotional presentation. On the contrary, it should possess all these qualities. It should be an interesting story, well and vivaciously told. But whereas in other fiction these are the primary, paramount qualities, in detective fiction they are secondary and subordinate to the intellectual interest, to which they must be, if necessary, sacrificed. The entertainment that the connoisseur looks for is an exhibition of mental gymnastics in which he is invited to take part; and the excellence of the entertainment must be judged by the completeness with which it satisfies the expectations of the*

type of reader to whom it is addressed . . . theologians, scholars, lawyers, and to a less extent, perhaps, doctors and men of science. Judging by the letters which I have received from time to time, the enthusiast par excellence is the clergyman of a studious and scholarly habit.

> R. Austin Freeman, "The Art of the Detective Story," *Nineteenth Century and After*, May 1924.

3. *In this connection ["a variation of this trick" of tracing the crime to the detective himself "is resorted to in one of Agatha Christie's Poirot books—The Murder of Roger Ackroyd"] it should be pointed out that a certain "gentleman's agreement" has grown up between the detective-story writer and the public—the outcome of a definite development in the relationship necessary for the projection of this type of fiction. And not only has the reader the right to expect and demand fair treatment from an author along the lines tacitly laid down and according to the principles involved, but an author who uses this trust for the purpose of tricking his co-solver of a criminal problem immediately forfeits all claim to the reading public's consideration.*

> Willard Huntington Wright, Introduction to *The Great Detective Stories*, Charles Scribner's Sons, 1927.

4. *In early mystery fiction, the problem tends to be, who did the crime? At first, while readers were still unsophisticated, the formula of the Most Unlikely Person had a good run. But the reader soon learned to see through this. If there was a single person in the story who appeared to have no motive for the crime and who was allowed to amble through to the penultimate chapter free from any shadow of suspicion, that character became a marked man or woman. "I knew he must be guilty because nothing was said about him," said the cunning reader. Thus we come to a new axiom laid down by Mr. G. K. Chesterton in a brilliant essay in the* New Statesman:

"the real criminal must be suspected at least once in the course of the story. Once he is suspected, and then (apparently) cleared, he is made safe from future suspicion. . . ." Probably the most baffling form of detective-story is still that in which suspicion is distributed equally among a number of candidates, one of whom turns out to be guilty.

> Dorothy L. Sayers, Introduction to *Great Short Stories of Detection, Mystery, and Horror*, Victor Gollancz, 1928; published in New York (1929) by Payson & Clarke as *Omnibus of Crime.*

5. *Revenge is an old, a primeval instinct: it came into action. The ethics of the tribe were not outraged, since it is improbable that it possessed much moral sense. It did not so much punish the murderer or thief in the spirit of superiority of the modern mouthpiece of Society, delivering the judicial homily to the occupant of the dock, as it set about "getting even" with him.*

Sometimes this revenge took the form of swift death; sometimes of death after due torture; at others of exile; and, again, of mutilation. It developed later, being unorganized, into the form of the vendetta, in which the blood relatives of the slain declared a feud against the family of the assassin. In this form revenge has persisted down to modern times in Latin countries, in the form of the Corsican vendetta, and, in the United States, in the blood-feud.

Indiscriminate revenge against the wrongdoer by the community or family, however, was inconvenient. At some time or other the community relegated the task to the judge and the gaoler. . . .

> George Godwin, *Cain, or The Future of Crime,* To-day and To-morrow Series, E. P. Dutton & Co., Inc., 1929.

6. . . . *For the mystery novel* Suspicion Handicap, *the field*

is limited. You know it wasn't the hero or the heroine who did the murder. You are practically sure it couldn't have been Reggie Banks, because he is a comic character, and any vestige of humor in any character in a mystery story automatically rules him out as a potential criminal. It can't have been Uncle Joe, because he is explicitly stated to be kind to dogs. So you assume it must have been some totally uninteresting minor character who hardly ever appears and who is disclosed on the last page as the son of the inventor whom the murdered man swindled forty years ago. At any rate, you know quite well it's one of them. . . .

If I were writing a mystery story I would go boldly out for the big sensation. I would not have the crime committed by anybody in the book at all. . . .

> P. G. Wodehouse, "About These Mystery Stories, *Saturday Evening Post,* 1929.

7. The criminal must be someone mentioned in the early part of the story, but must not be anyone whose thoughts the reader has been allowed to follow.

The mysterious stranger who turns up from nowhere in particular, from a ship as often as not, whose existence the reader had no means of suspecting from the outset, spoils the play altogether. The second half of the rule is more difficult to state precisely, especially in view of some remarkable performances by Mrs. Christie. It would be more exact to say that the author must not imply an attitude of mystification in the character who turns out to be the criminal.

> [Monsignor] Ronald A. Knox, Introduction to *The Best Detective Stories of 1928;* Faber & Faber, 1929; published in New York by Liveright as *The Best English Detective Stories of 1928.*

8. *I must say I have a special liking for those tales where one's field as a reader is to some extent determined and*

marked down. Supposing the circumstances make it necessary that the murder was committed by one staying in a certain house, one's attention is thus focused on a fixed number of people. This narrowing down of the possibles serves in a curious way to make the puzzle harder. You no longer try to reason on the assumption that anything is possible, but to choose out of a number of possibles the right solution.

> H. Douglas Thomson, *Masters of Mystery: A Study of the Detective Story*, Collins, 1931.

9. *In the first place—if you don't mind—don't kill the victim too soon. We like to get to know him a little first. I mean, don't start with his body. Don't have Inspector Higginbottom summoned hastily in paragraph 1 of page 1 to the Mansions Apartments because there's a dead body just found upstairs. The thrill is too short. We lost interest. Even when it turns out that there's been "foul play" it doesn't rouse us; we expected it. Not even when it turns out that the dead man is a leading member of the Stock Exchange; that's all right; we never heard of him anyway.*

Oh, no, give us a chance to learn to know the man a little, and like him, and then his death is like that of a friend; or let him be such a mean hound that we get to hate him; then when his body is found, who is happier than we are?

Now another little point. When you do find his body, don't have a string of people, a houseful of them, who have to be under suspicion one after the other, so that we can see it all coming—the butler, the private secretary, the French maid, the handy man (too handy, perhaps)—well, everybody knows the standing list. . . .

> Stephen Leacock, "Twenty Cents' Worth of Murder," *Too Much College*, Dodd, Mead & Company, Inc., 1939.

10. *If Mr. [E. R.] Punshon [in Murder Abroad] clings too tenaciously to his favourite detective [Bobby Owen], Mrs.*

Christie deserts her M. Poirot completely in her present novel . . . and replaces him by no one at all. If her latest story has scarcely any detection in it there is no scarcity of murders. Ten persons, ranging from a judge to a doctor, are induced by various pretexts to come for a visit to [Indian] Island, off the Devon coast, and are there cut off from the mainland. At a dinner on their first evening no host or hostess makes an appearance and instead a gramophone record accuses each and all of them of murders committed "outside the law." Then one by one they are struck down by the invisible avenger. On the dinner table are figures . . . and as each of the doomed party dies one of the figures vanishes. There is a certain feeling of monotony inescapable in the regularity of the deaths which is better suited to a serialized newspaper story than a full-length novel. Yet there is an ingenious problem to solve in naming the murderer. Who is the tenth little [Indian]? It will be an extremely astute reader who guesses correctly.

Anon., "Lone Investigator," *Times Literary Supplement,* November 11, 1939.

11. *For thirteen years Mrs. Christie's admirers have been waiting for her to reproduce the superlative form of* The Murder of Roger Ackroyd. *Once or twice their hopes have been raised:* The A.B.C. Murders *very nearly came up to scratch, but the common run of Poirot's adventures has produced little more than a half-light from the little grey cells. Now at last the expected* chef-d'oeuvre *has appeared.* Ten Little [Indians] *is as near a perfect crime puzzle as we are likely to see. It is short,* sans *Poirot, exciting, baffling, and scrupulously fair. To divulge any of the plot would be to take the edge off the reader's enjoyment. It should be enough to say that the book is Agatha Christie's masterpiece.*

Anon., "Murder with Padding," *The Spectator,* December 15, 1939.

12. *Apart from one little dubious proceeding there is no*

cheating; the reader is just bamboozled in a straightforward way from first to last. . . . If it were not for that iota of hanky-panky [And Then There Were None] *would be the most colossal achievement of a colossal career.*

Ralph Partridge, *New Statesman & Nation*, XVIII, 1939.

13. *We seek unsuccessfully among the guests for the invisible "host" of this house-to-morgue party. Scotland Yard is unsuccessful in a brief epilogue; a manuscript found in a bottle gives posthumous declaration from one of the ten. It is Agatha Christie run wild.*

M. L. Prevost, *Library Journal*, LXV, 1940.

14. *There is no doubt, probably, that this is a highly ingenious jigsaw by a master of puzzling, but don't try to believe it, or you'll be sunk at the half-way mark. Hercule Poirot* [*the egotistical and dapper Belgian detective featured in some of Mrs. Christie's novels*] *does not appear. Nor any other detective, for that matter.*

Will Cuppy, *Books*, 1940.

15. *For absolute horror and complete bafflement Agatha Christie's* And Then There Were None *takes all prizes.*

Marian Wiggin, *Boston Transcript*, 1940.

16. Crime, Place and Sleuth
Ten men and women, all with besmirched pasts, spend weekend on island off Devon coast. One by one they die.

Summing-Up
Hair-raising and completely inexplicable build-up not matched by rather fantastic explanation—but most readers won't mind that.

Verdict

Spectacular.

Anon., "The Criminal Record," *Saturday Review of Literature,* 1940.

17. *The whole thing is utterly impossible and utterly fascinating. It is the most baffling mystery that Agatha Christie has ever written, and if any other writer has ever surpassed it for sheer puzzlement the name escapes our memory. We are referring, of course, to mysteries that have logical explanations, as this one has. It is a tall story, to be sure, but it could have happened.*

Isaac Anderson, *The New York Times,* 1940.

18. *Slick, tricky idea which somehow doesn't quite come off, probably because of a forced emphasis on a group of manufactured people. Smart as anything, though, and you'll have to hand it to Miss Christie.*

Anon., *The New Yorker,* XVI, 1940.

19. *Detective fiction is distinguished from all other types of crime fiction by its insistence upon the normal. The abnormal event—theft, arson, murder—is explained in terms of the material, the natural, the logical. Crime is the stone thrown into a quiet pool. It is the oddly colored thread woven into a colorless pattern.*

The detective is the diagnostician. It is his business to study the ripples on the surface of the pool and to find the disturbing stone, his job to pick the elusive thread from the tapestry.

This insistence on the normal adds the illusion of reality. It is a piquant and subtle accompaniment to extraordinary behavior. Murder in a madhouse is a probability; therefore not so mysterious nor exciting, when it happens, as murder at the greengrocer's. One expects horrors from a monster created by Frankenstein. It is a more subtle titillation of the nerves to get them from an insignificant and respectable householder who is whimsically devoted to canaries.

> Alfred Hitchcock, Introduction to *The Pocket Book of Great Detectives*, Pocket Books, Inc., 1941.

20. *What it boils down to is this: that the fully evolved detective story is technically by far the trickiest form of fiction humanity has so far devised. For we have come to demand of it not only a mystery with a plausible solution, but over and above that, a mystery with a surprise solution which by rights we ought not to have been surprised at at all.*[1] *I am not, of course, to be understood as implying that because orthodox detective fiction is inordinately difficult to do well, it is therefore,* ipso facto, *inordinately well worth doing. Walking across Niagara Falls on a tight-rope is inordinately difficult to do; but we do not for that reason cherish Niagara Falls tight-rope walkers above all other men. No, the case for orthodox detective fiction depends on the fact that most of us get great satisfaction out of contemplating, now and again, a piece of virtuoso literary* contrivance. *Why this should be so I have no idea. None the less, it is so. And far from repining, we addicts ought to be grateful that the gods have given us minds eclectic enough to accommodate this specialised variety of literary pleasure along with all the others.*

> Edmund Crispin, Introduction to *Best Detective Stories*, Faber and Faber, 1961.

21. *Stories about murder, fictional or nonfictional, fascinate*

---

[1] *It is perhaps worth noting here that this business of fair play to the reader, of giving him throughout the narrative the evidence which ought to enable him to anticipate the solution, is not so much a matter of sportsmanship as of art. It avoids the feeling of arbitrariness which is evoked in us by a surprise ending not demonstrably conditioned by all that has gone before. For examples of the disappointing—because totally unprepared—type of surprise ending, see* Trent's Last Case, *or more recently Mr. Julian Symons'* The Colour of Murder. *[Mr. Crispin's note.—Ed.]*

us. Why? Many a publisher, many an educator, has asked himself that question. I think that fundamentally the answer is not very difficult to find. Murder is a clear-cut event. Whether or not we find the corpse or the murderer or the motive, we know that whenever a murder has occurred, two (at least two) human beings have clashed with an irrevocable result. So much in our life and literature is unclear and ambiguous; murder is certain. But if we want to understand it, it is always a challenge. My own studies indicate that its main characteristic is that it breaks through the routine of our life, and that it always has this breakthrough effect on two levels: the psychological and the social.

The principal characters in a murder—the person who commits it, the person who tries to find the murderer, and the people who have to decide what should be done with him—all present interesting psychological problems. Modern dynamic clinical psychiatry has taught us a great deal about motives, inhibitions, internal impulses, emotional crises. What we have learned from the psychopathology of minor emotional disorders has helped us to throw light on violent deeds, and conversely what we may glean from murder cases in their stark and exaggerated simplicity can help us to understand the more obscure details of harmless neurotic difficulties.

But however deep our depth psychology of the unconscious is, it remains superficial if it leaves out the objective social conditions under which people—all people—live. The pressures come not only from within but also from outside. Every murder case, especially if it comes to trial, throws a searchlight on the society in which it occurs, and we become aware of a fixed moment in social history.

> Fredric Wertham, M.D., Introduction to *Murder for Profit* by William Bolitho, 1926, reprinted by Time Incorporated, 1964.

22. *Mrs. Christie does much of the plotting for her books while munching apples in her bathtub. Because she finds the sight of flowers and trees a temptation to truancy, she prefers*

working indoors. She types her manuscripts on a portable machine using three fingers of each hand. The idea for a story gestates slowly with her, but once she has decided to put it on paper, she works ceaselessly for at least ten days so that it will become well advanced before it has a chance to become stale. Most of her novels are written in about six weeks.

Current Biography 1964. Charles Moritz, ed., H. W. Wilson Co., 1964.

23. *There seems to be little doubt that Agatha Christie, consciously or not, has patterned her style after that of Arthur Conan Doyle, creator of the master detective, Sherlock Holmes. There is a similar use of trick sequences to bring about mystery and violence: the poems in the guests' bedrooms (p. 28T), the Voice (p. 35T), the disappearing porcelain figures (p. 54B), the stolen shower curtain (p. 106T), and the missing wool. There is adherence to Doyle's tradition of ultimately resting the blame on the least likely suspect, although* And Then There Were None *goes even a step further! And there is the author's honesty of presentation of clues, albeit many are false leads. The reader is given all the facts available to anyone in the story, and the solution depends upon the interpretation of the facts, not upon unexpected turns of the plot.*

As has been mentioned before, Agatha Christie considers background relatively unimportant, and she uses it only to establish a setting where the crime itself will stand out. Although Indian Island sounds intriguing at first, it quickly becomes lost as a factor in the story, other than its isolation from the mainland. Were it not for this fact, the strange doings could have happened in a dozen other places where communication with the outside world was limited—a vacation retreat in the mountains, a beachside resort cut off by a flood, an inn where guests are trapped by a hurricane, etc.

Several other characteristics make Agatha Christie's style unique. Incredible as it may sound, she detests violence—if it is caused by blunt instruments, sharp-edged weapons, and earsplitting gun explosions. Of course, in this book, since she was dealing with an extraordinarily large number of murders, she had to concede to a few crude deaths. But, in general, she prefers refined, gentle means. As she has said, "I specialize in murders of quiet, domestic interest. Give me a nice deadly phial to play with and I am happy."

True to her word, she certainly starts off her wholesale slaughter of the Indian Island guests in a well-bred manner by using noiseless and unmessy poison!

Agatha Christie employs a variety of devices in her prose. She is fond, perhaps too fond, of the italicized word or expression for emphasis (p. 9B and throughout); loves to end a paragraph or a whole chapter with the three dots (. . .) signifying interrupted or on-going narration (p. 9B and elsewhere); and delights in rattling off a series of sentence fragments in an effort to duplicate conversational bursts, as in the paragraph beginning with "Indian Island! Why there . . ." (p. 11T) and Part IV of Chapter Two (p. 24B). Moreover, she likes the effect of contrast. Note how Dr. Armstrong and Tony Marston (p. 16B), as well as old men and boys (p. 17M), view swift-moving cars, and how both Wargrave and Lombard inquire about "this part of the world" (p. 20T & M). And, like other good mystery writers, she uses foreshadowing liberally, that is, a pointing ahead toward coming events to increase suspense (p. 19T).

Agatha Christie's dialogue is decidedly different from the vigorous, sometimes shocking, talk that appears so regularly in books by Mickey Spillane, James Cain, and Raymond Chandler. Agatha's characters talk like one another, and everybody is a lady or gentleman (p. 33M).

Critics like to say, "Style is the man." In this case, it most certainly is the lady. Agatha Christie writes as she thinks and lives. Her ladylike words and cultured murders reflect a comfortable mind dabbling in the gruesome.

Features of the Author's Style, Harry Shefter, RES edition of *And Then There Were None*, 1964.

24. *Most murders are crimes of passion of one sort or another: murders within the family: a jealous husband kills his wife; an overwrought wife kills her husband or child, and so on. A large percentage of such murderers never come to trial because they commit suicide. They have been faced with a crisis situation, have responded without self-control, and the result is disaster. There is a choice here, but it is merely the choice of running down a slope instead of trying to stop yourself from sliding down it. But the murder cases that make the headlines usually do so for a good reason: that the murders reveal a far more unusual kind of choice: that of the gambler, or adventurer, or leader. The murderer may be of a fairly high level of intelligence; he also feels a generalised resentment towards society. He pursues his train of thought—and emotion—logically, until it ends in murder. We may condemn the crime as ultimately stupid; but it would be blindness to apply* any *kind of blanket judgement: stupidity, wickedness, sickness, as if it was all of a piece. . . . A man without a vocation, or without the confidence to pursue it single-mindedly, takes the path of least resistance; of security and adjustment to social demands. . . . "Headline" murders may be the result of pressures that most people —fortunately—will never experience, and of choices that most people will never be called upon to make. Like the artist, this type of criminal possesses a certain independence of spirit that means when it comes to the real issue—his deepest obsession—he doesn't bother to consult other people, but simply goes ahead.*

Colin Wilson, Introduction to *A Casebook of Murder*, Mayflower Paperback, 1971, first published by Leslie Frewin, 1969.

Rogers went round the table collecting the meat plates. Suddenly, with the plates held in his hands, he stopped. He said in an odd, scared voice, "There's somebody running. . . ."

They could all hear it—running feet along the terrace. In that minute, they knew—knew without being told. . . . As by common accord, they all rose their feet. They stood looking towards the door. Dr. Armstrong appeared, his breath coming fast. He said, "General Macarthur—"

"Dead!" The word burst from Vera explosively.

Armstrong said, "Yes, he's dead. . . ." There was a pause—a long pause. Seven people looked at each other and could find no words to say.

iv.

The storm broke just as the old man's body was borne in through the door. The others were standing in the hall. There was a sudden hiss and roar as the rain came down.

As Blore and Armstrong passed up the stairs with their burden, Vera Claythorne turned suddenly and went into the deserted dining room. It was as they had left it. The sweet course stood ready on the sideboard untasted. Vera went up to the table. She was there a minute or two later when Rogers came softly into the room. He started when he saw her. Then his eyes asked a question. He said, "Oh, miss, I—I just came to see . . ."

In a loud, harsh voice that surprised herself Vera said, "You're quite right, Rogers. Look for yourself. *There are only seven.* . . ."

v.

General Macarthur had been laid on his bed. After making a last examination Armstrong left the room and came downstairs. He found the others assembled in the drawing room. Miss Brent was knitting. Vera Claythorne was standing by the window looking out at the hissing rain. Blore was sitting squarely in a chair, his hands on his knees. Lombard was walking restlessly up and down. At the far end of the room Mr. Justice Wargrave was sitting in a grandfather chair. His eyes were half-closed. They opened as the doctor came into the room. He said in a clear, penetrating voice, "Well, doctor?"

Armstrong was very pale. He said, "No question of heart failure or anything like that. Macarthur was hit with a life preserver or some such thing on the back of the head."

A little murmur went round, but the clear voice of the judge was raised once more. "Did you find the actual weapon used?"

"No."

"Nevertheless you are sure of your facts?"

"I am quite sure."

Mr. Justice Wargrave said quietly, "We know now exactly where we are."

There was no doubt now who was in charge of the situation. This morning Wargrave had sat huddled in his chair on the terrace refraining from any overt activity. Now he assumed command with the ease born of a long habit of authority. He definitely presided over the court. Clearing his throat, he once more spoke. "This morning, gentlemen, whilst I was sitting on the terrace, I was an observer of your activities. There could be little doubt of your purpose. You were searching the island for an unknown murderer?"

"Quite right, sir," said Philip Lombard.

The judge went on. "You had come, doubtless, to the same conclusion that I had—namely that the deaths of Anthony Marston and Mrs. Rogers were neither accidental nor were they suicides. No doubt you also reached a certain conclusion as to the purpose of Mr. Owen in enticing us to this island?"

Blore said hoarsely, "He's a madman! A loony."

The judge coughed. "That almost certainly. But it hardly affects the issue. Our main preoccupation is this —to save our lives."

Armstrong said in a trembling voice, "There's no one on the island, I tell you. *No one!*"

The judge stroked his jaw. He said gently, "In the

sense you mean, no. I came to that conclusion early this morning. I could have told you that your search would be fruitless. Nevertheless I am strongly of the opinion that 'Mr. Owen' (to give him the name he himself has adopted) *is* on the island. Very much so. Given the scheme in question which is neither more nor less than the execution of justice upon certain individuals for offenses which the law cannot touch, *there is only one way in which that scheme could be accomplished.* Mr. Owen could only come to the island in one way. It is perfectly clear. *Mr. Owen is one of us. . . ."*

vi.

"Oh, no, no, no . . ." It was Vera who burst out—almost in a moan.

The judge turned a keen eye on her. He said, "My dear young lady, this is no time for refusing to look facts in the face. We are all in grave danger. One of us is U. N. Owen. And we do not know which of us. Of the ten people who came to this island three are definitely cleared. Anthony Marston, Mrs. Rogers, and General Macarthur have gone beyond suspicion. There are seven of us left. Of those seven, one is, if I may so express myself, a bogus little Indian boy." He paused and looked round. "Do I take it that you all agree?"

Armstrong said, "It's fantastic—but I suppose you're right."

Blore said, "Not a doubt of it. And if you ask me, I've a very good idea—"

A quick gesture of Mr. Justice Wargrave's hand stopped him. The judge said quietly, "We will come to that presently. At the moment all I wish to establish is that we are in agreement on the facts."

Emily Brent, still knitting, said, "Your argument seems logical. I agree that one of us is possessed by a devil."

Vera murmured, "I can't believe it. . . . I can't. . . ."

Wargrave said, "Lombard?"

"I agree, sir, absolutely."

The judge nodded his head in a satisfied manner. He

said, "Now let us examine the evidence. To begin with, is there any reason for suspecting one particular person? Mr. Blore, you have, I think, something to say."

Blore was breathing hard. He said, "Lombard's got a revolver. He didn't tell the truth—last night. He admits it."

Philip Lombard smiled scornfully. He said, "I suppose I'd better explain again." He did so, telling the story briefly and succinctly.

Blore said sharply, "What's to prove it? There's nothing to corroborate your story."

The judge coughed. "Unfortunately," he said, "we are all in that position. There is only our own word to go upon." He leaned forward. "You have none of you yet grasped what a very peculiar situation this is. To my mind there is only one course of procedure to adopt. Is there anyone whom we can definitely eliminate from suspicion on the evidence which is in our possession?"

Dr. Armstrong said quickly, "I am a well-known professional man. The mere idea that I can be suspected of—"

Again a gesture of the judge's hand arrested a speaker before he finished his speech. Mr. Justice Wargrave said in his small, clear voice: "I, too, am a well-known person! But, my dear sir, that proves less than nothing! Doctors have gone mad before now. Judges have gone mad. So," he added, looking at Blore, "have policemen!"

Lombard said, "At any rate, I suppose you'll leave the women out of it."

The judge's eyebrows rose. He said in the famous "acid" tone that Counsel knew so well, "Do I understand you to assert that women are not subject to homicidal mania?"

Lombard said irritably, "Of course not. But all the same, it hardly seems possible—"

He stopped. Mr. Justice Wargrave, still in the same thin, sour voice, addressed Armstrong. "I take it, Dr. Armstrong, that a woman would have been physically capable of striking the blow that killed poor Macarthur?"

The doctor said calmly, "Perfectly capable—given a suitable instrument, such as a rubber truncheon or cosh."

"It would require no undue exertion of force?"

"Not at all."

Mr. Justice Wargrave wriggled his tortoiselike neck. He said, "The other two deaths have resulted from the administration of drugs. That, no one will dispute, is easily compassed by a person of the smallest physical strength."

Vera cried angrily, "I think you're mad!"

His eyes turned slowly till they rested on her. It was the dispassionate stare of a man well used to weighing humanity in the balance. She thought: He's just seeing me as a—as a specimen. And—the thought came to her with real surprise—he doesn't like me much!

In measured tones the judge was saying, "My dear young lady, do try and restrain your feelings. I am not accusing you." He bowed to Miss Brent. "I hope, Miss Brent, that you are not offended by my insistence that *all* of us are equally under suspicion?"

Emily Brent was knitting. She did not look up. In a cold voice she said, "The idea that I should be accused of taking a fellow creature's life—not to speak of the lives of *three* fellow creatures—is, of course, quite absurd to anyone who knows anything of my character. But I quite appreciate the fact that we are all strangers to one another and that in those circumstances nobody can be exonerated without the fullest proof. There is, as I have said, a devil amongst us."

The judge said, "Then we are agreed. There can be no elimination on the ground of character or position alone."

Lombard said, "What about Rogers?"

The judge looked at him unblinkingly. "What about him?"

Lombard said, "Well, to my mind, Rogers seems pretty well ruled out."

Mr. Justice Wargrave said, "Indeed, and on what grounds?"

Lombard said, "He hasn't got the brains, for one thing. And for another, his wife was one of the victims."

The judge's heavy eyebrows rose once more. He said, "In my time, young man, several people have come before me accused of the murders of their wives—*and* have been found guilty."

"Oh! I agree. Wife murder is perfectly possible—almost natural, let's say! But not this particular kind! I can believe in Rogers killing his wife because he was scared of her breaking down and giving him away, or because he'd taken a dislike to her, or because he wanted to link up with some nice little bit rather less long in the tooth. But I can't see him as the lunatic Mr. Owen dealing out crazy justice and starting on his own wife for a crime they both committed."

Mr. Justice Wargrave said, "You are assuming hearsay to be evidence. We do not know that Rogers and his wife conspired to murder their employer. That may have been a false statement, made so that Rogers should appear to be in the same position as ourselves. Mrs. Rogers' terror last night may have been due to the fact that she realized her husband was mentally unhinged."

Lombard said, "Well, have it your own way. U. N. Owen is one of us. No exceptions allowed. We all qualify."

Mr. Justice Wargrave said, "My point is that there can be no exceptions allowed on the score of *character, position,* or *probability.* What we must now examine is the possibility of eliminating one or more persons on the *facts.* To put it simply, is there among us one or more persons who could not possibly have administered either cyanide to Anthony Marston, or an overdose of sleeping draught to Mrs. Rogers, and who had no opportunity of striking the blow that killed General Macarthur?"

Blore's rather heavy face lit up. He leant forward. "Now you're talking, sir!" he said. "That's the stuff! Let's go into it. As regards young Marston I don't think there's anything to be done. It's already been suggested that someone from outside slipped something into the dregs of his glass before he refilled it for the last time. A person actually in the room could have done that even more easily. I can't remember if Rogers was in the room, but any of the rest of us could certainly have done it."

He paused, then went on. "Now take the woman Rogers. The people who stand out there are her husband and the doctor. Either of them could have done it as easy as winking—"

Armstrong sprang to his feet. He was trembling. "I protest— This is absolutely uncalled for! I swear that the dose I gave the woman was perfectly—"

"Dr. Armstrong." The small, sour voice was compelling. The doctor stopped with a jerk in the middle of his sentence. The small, cold voice went on. "Your indignation is very natural. Nevertheless you must admit that the facts have got to be faced. Either you or Rogers *could* have administered a fatal dose with the greatest ease. Let us now consider the position of the other people present. What chance had I, had Inspector Blore, had Miss Brent, had Miss Claythorne, had Mr. Lombard of administering poison? Can any one of us be completely and entirely eliminated?" He paused. "I think not."

Vera said angrily, "I was nowhere near the woman! All of you can swear to that."

Mr. Justice Wargrave waited a minute, then he said, "As far as my memory serves me the facts were these— will anyone please correct me if I make a misstatement? Mrs. Rogers was lifted onto the sofa by Anthony Marston and Mr. Lombard and Dr. Armstrong went to her. He sent Rogers for brandy. There was then a question raised as to where the voice we had just heard had come from. We all went into the next room with the exception of Miss Brent, who remained in this room—alone with the unconscious woman."

A spot of color came into Emily Brent's cheeks. She stopped knitting. She said, "This is outrageous!"

The remorseless small voice went on. "When we returned to this room, you, Miss Brent, were bending over the woman on the sofa."

Emily Brent said, "Is common humanity a criminal offense?"

Mr. Justice Wargrave said, "I am only establishing facts. Rogers then entered the room with the brandy which, of course, he could quite well have doctored before entering the room. The brandy was administered to the woman and shortly afterwards her husband and Dr. Armstrong assisted her up to bed where Dr. Armstrong gave her a sedative."

Blore said, "That's what happened. Absolutely. And

that lets out the judge, Mr. Lombard, myself and Miss Claythorne."

His voice was loud and jubilant. Mr. Justice Wargrave, bringing a cold eye to bear upon him, murmured, "Ah, but does it? We must take into account *every possible eventuality*."

Blore stared. He said, "I don't get you."

Mr. Justice Wargrave said, "Upstairs in her room, Mrs. Rogers is lying in bed. The sedative that the doctor has given her begins to take effect. She is vaguely sleepy and acquiescent. Supposing that at that moment there is a tap on the door and someone enters bringing her, shall we say, a tablet, or a draught, with the message that 'the doctor says you're to take this.' Do you imagine for one minute that she would not have swallowed it obediently without thinking twice about it?"

There was a silence. Blore shifted his feet and frowned, Philip Lombard said, "I don't believe in that story for a minute. Besides, none of us left this room for hours afterwards. There was Marston's death and all the rest of it."

The judge said, "Someone could have left his or her bedroom—later."

Lombard objected, "But then Rogers would have been up there."

Dr. Armstrong stirred. "No," he said. "Rogers went downstairs to clear up in the dining room and pantry. Anyone could have gone up to the woman's bedroom then without being seen."

Emily Brent said, "Surely, doctor, the woman would have been fast asleep by then under the influence of the drug you had administered?"

"In all likelihood, yes. But it is not a certainty. Until you have prescribed for a patient more than once you cannot tell their reaction to different drugs. There is, sometimes, a considerable period before a sedative takes effect. It depends on the personal idiosyncrasy of the patient towards that particular drug."

Lombard said, "Of course you *would* say that, doctor. Suits your book—eh?"

Again Armstrong's face darkened with anger. But again that passionless, cold little voice stopped the words on his lips. "No good result can come from recrimination. Facts are what we have to deal with. It is established, I think, that there is a possibility of such a thing as I have outlined occurring. I agree that its probability value is not high; though there again, it depends on who that person might have been. The appearance of Miss Brent or of Miss Claythorne on such an errand would have occasioned no surprise in the patient's mind. I agree that the appearance of myself, or of Mr. Blore, or of Mr. Lombard could have been, to say the least of it, unusual, but I still think the visit would have been received without the awakening of any real suspicion."

Blore said, "And that gets us—*where?*"

v i i .

Mr. Justice Wargrave, stroking his lip and looking quite passionless and inhuman, said, "We have now dealt with the second killing, and have established the fact that no one of us can be completely exonerated from suspicion." He paused and went on. "We come now to the death of General Macarthur. That took place this morning. I will ask anyone who considers that he or she has an alibi to state it in so many words. I myself will state at once that I have no valid alibi. I spent the morning sitting on the terrace and meditating on the singular position in which we all find ourselves. I sat on that chair on the terrace for the whole morning until the gong went, but there were, I should imagine, several periods during the morning when I was quite unobserved and during which it would have been possible for me to walk down to the sea, kill the General, and return to my chair. There is only my word for the fact that I never left the terrace. In the circumstances that is not enough. There must be *proof.*"

Blore said, "I was with Mr. Lombard and Dr. Armstrong all the morning. They'll bear me out."

Dr. Armstrong said, "You went to the house for a rope."

Blore said, "Of course I did. Went straight there and straight back. You know I did."

Armstrong said, "You were a long time. . . ."

Blore turned crimson. He said, "What the hell do you mean by that, Dr. Armstrong?"

Armstrong repeated, "I only said you were a long time."

"Had to find it, didn't I? Can't lay your hands on a coil of rope all in a minute."

Mr. Justice Wargrave said, "During Inspector Blore's absence, were you two gentlemen together?"

Armstrong said hotly, "Certainly. That is, Lombard went off for a few minutes. I remained where I was."

Lombard said with a smile, "I wanted to test the possibilities of heliographing to the mainland. Wanted to find the best spot. I was only absent a minute or two."

Armstrong nodded. He said, "That's right. Not long enough to do a murder, I assure you."

The judge said, "Did either of you two glance at your watches?"

"Well, no."

Philip Lombard said, "I wasn't wearing one."

The judge said evenly, "A minute or two is a vague expression." He turned his head to the upright figure with the knitting lying on her lap. "Miss Brent?"

Emily Brent said, "I took a walk with Miss Claythorne up to the top of the island. Afterwards I sat on the terrace in the sun."

The judge said, "I don't think I noticed you there."

"No, I was round the corner of the house to the east. It was out of the wind there."

"And you sat there till lunch time?"

"Yes."

"Miss Claythorne?"

Vera answered readily and clearly. "I was with Miss Brent early this morning. After that I wandered about a bit. Then I went down and talked to General Macarthur."

Mr. Justice Wargrave interrupted. He said, "What time was that?"

Vera for the first time was vague. She said, "I don't know. About an hour before lunch, I think—or it might have been less."

Blore asked, "Was it after we'd spoken to him or before?"

Vera said, "I don't know. He—he was very queer." She shivered.

"In what way was he queer?" the judge wanted to know.

Vera said in a low voice, "He said we were all going to die—he said he was waiting for the end. He—he frightened me. . . ."

The judge nodded. He said, "What did you do next?"

"I went back to the house. Then, just before lunch, I went out again and up behind the house. I've been terribly restless all day."

Mr. Justice Wargrave stroked his chin. He said, "There remains Rogers. Though I doubt if his evidence will add anything to our sum of knowledge."

Rogers, summoned before the court, had very little to tell. He had been busy all the morning about household duties and with the preparation of lunch. He had taken cocktails onto the terrace before lunch and had then gone up to remove his things from the attic to another room. He had not looked out of the window during the morning and had seen nothing that could have any bearing upon the death of General Macarthur. He would swear definitely that there had been eight china figures upon the dining table when he laid the table for lunch.

At the conclusion of Rogers' evidence there was a pause. Mr. Justice Wargrave cleared his throat. Lombard murmured to Vera Claythorne, "The summing up will now take place!"

The judge said, "We have inquired into the circumstances of these three deaths to the best of our ability. Whilst probability in some cases is against certain people being implicated, yet we cannot say definitely that any one person can be considered as cleared of all complicity. I reiterate my positive belief that of the seven persons assembled in this room one is a dangerous and probably insane criminal. There is no evidence before us as to who that person is. All we can do at the present juncture is to consider what measures we can take for communicating with the mainland for help, and in the event of help being delayed (as is only too possible given the state of the weather) what measures we must adopt to ensure our safety.

"I would ask you all to consider this carefully and to give me any suggestions that may occur to you. In the meantime I warn everybody to be upon his or her guard. So far the murderer has had an easy task, since his victims have been unsuspicious. From now on, it is our task to suspect each and every one amongst us. Forewarned is forearmed. Take no risks and be alert to danger. That is all."

Philip Lombard murmured beneath his breath, "The court will now adjourn. . . ."

10

"Do you believe it?" Vera asked. She and Philip Lombard sat on the window sill of the living room. Outside the rain poured down and the wind howled in great shuddering gusts against the window panes. Philip Lombard cocked his head slightly on one side before answering. Then he said, "You mean, do I believe that old Wargrave is right when he says it's one of us?"

"Yes."

Philip Lombard said slowly, "It's difficult to say. Logically, you know, he's right, and yet—"

Vera took the words out of his mouth. "And yet it seems so incredible!"

Philip Lombard made a grimace. "The whole thing's incredible! But after Macarthur's death there's no more doubt as to one thing. There's no question now of accidents or suicides. It's definitely murder. Three murders up to date."

Vera shivered. She said, "It's like some awful dream. I keep feeling that things like this *can't* happen!"

He said with understanding, "I know. Presently a tap

will come on the door, and early-morning tea will be brought in."

Vera said, "Oh, how I wish that could happen!"

Philip Lombard said gravely, "Yes, but it won't! We're all in the dream! And we've got to be pretty much upon our guard from now on."

Vera said, lowering her voice, "If—if it *is* one of them—which do you think it is?"

Philip Lombard grinned suddenly. He said, "I take it you are excepting our two selves? Well, that's all right. I know very well that I'm not the murderer, and I don't fancy that there's anything insane about you, Vera. You strike me as being one of the sanest and most level-headed girls I've come across. I'd stake my reputation on your sanity."

With a slightly wry smile, Vera said, "Thank you."

He said, "Come now, Miss Vera Claythorne, aren't you going to return the compliment?"

Vera hesitated a minute, then she said, "You've admitted, you know, that you don't hold human life particularly sacred, but all the same I can't see you as—as the man who dictated that gramophone record."

Lombard said, "Quite right. If I were to commit one or more murders it would be solely for what I could get out of them. This mass clearance isn't my line of country. Good, then we'll eliminate ourselves and concentrate on our five fellow prisoners. Which of them is U. N. Owen? Well, at a guess, and with absolutely nothing to go upon, I'd plump for Wargrave!"

"Oh!" Vera sounded surprised. She thought a minute or two and then said, "Why?"

"Hard to say exactly. But to begin with, he's an old man and he's been presiding over courts of law for years. That is to say, he's played God Almighty for a good many months every year. That must go to a man's head eventually. He gets to see himself as all-powerful, as holding the power of life and death—and it's possible that his brain might snap and he might want to go one step farther and be Executioner and Judge Extraordinary."

Vera said slowly, "Yes, I suppose that's *possible.* . . ."

Lombard said, "Who do you plump for?"

Without any hesitation Vera answered, "Dr. Armstrong."

Lombard gave a low whistle. "The doctor, eh? You know, I should have put him last of all."

Vera shook her head. "Oh, no! Two of the deaths have been poison. That rather points to a doctor. And then you can't get over the fact that the only thing we are certain Mrs. Rogers had was the sleeping draught that *he* gave her."

Lombard admitted, "Yes, that's true."

Vera persisted, "If a doctor went mad, it would be a long time before anyone suspected. And doctors overwork and have a lot of strain."

Philip Lombard said, "Yes, but I doubt if he could have killed Macarthur. He wouldn't have had time during that brief interval when I left him—not, that is, unless he fairly hared down there and back again, and I doubt if he's in good enough training to do that and show no signs of it."

Vera said, "He didn't do it then. He had an opportunity later."

"When?"

"When he went down to call the General to lunch."

Philip whistled again very softly. He said, "So you think he did it then? Pretty cool thing to do."

Vera said impatiently, "What risk was there? He's the only person here with medical knowledge. He can swear the body's been dead at least an hour and who's to contradict him?"

Philip looked at her thoughtfully. "You know," he said, "that's a clever idea of yours. I wonder—"

ii.

"Who is it, Mr. Blore? That's what I want to know. Who is it?" Rogers' face was working. His hands were clenched tightly round the polishing leather that he had just then been using.

Ex-Inspector Blore said, "Eh, my lad, that's the question!"

"One of us, 'is lordship said. Which one? That's what I want to know. Who's the fiend in 'uman form?"

"That," said Blore, "is what we all would like to know."

Rogers said shrewdly, "But you've got an idea, Mr. Blore. You've got an idea, 'aven't you?"

"I may have an idea," said Blore slowly. "But that's a long way from being sure. I may be wrong. All I can say is that if I'm right the person in question is a very cool customer—a very cool customer indeed."

Rogers wiped the perspiration from his forehead. He said hoarsely, "It's like a bad dream, that's what it is."

Blore said, looking at him curiously, "Got any ideas yourself, Rogers?"

The butler shook his head. He said hoarsely, "I don't know. I don't know at all. And that's what's frightening the life out of me. To have no idea . . ."

iii.

Dr. Armstrong said violently, "We must get out of here—we must—we must! At all costs!"

Mr. Justice Wargrave looked thoughtfully out of the smoking-room window. He played with the cord of his eyeglasses. He said, "I do not, of course, profess to be a weather prophet. But I should say that it is very unlikely that a boat could reach us—even if they knew of our plight—under twenty-four hours—and even then only if the wind drops."

Dr. Armstrong dropped his head in his hands and groaned. He said, "And in the meantime we may all be murdered in our beds?"

"I hope not," said Mr. Justice Wargrave. "I intend to take every possible precaution against such a thing happening."

It flashed across Dr. Armstrong's mind that an old man like the judge was far more tenacious of life than a younger man would be. He had often marveled at that fact in his professional career. Here was he, junior to the judge by perhaps twenty years, and yet with a vastly inferior sense of self-preservation.

Mr. Justice Wargrave was thinking: Murdered in our beds! These doctors are all the same—they think in clichés. A thoroughly commonplace mind.

The doctor said, "There have been three victims already, remember."

"Certainly. But you must remember that they were unprepared for the attack. We are forewarned."

Dr. Armstrong said bitterly, "What can we do? Sooner or later—"

"I think," said Mr. Justice Wargrave, "that there are several things we can do."

Armstrong said, "We've no idea, even, who it can be—"

The judge stroked his chin and murmured, "Oh, you know, I wouldn't quite say that."

Armstrong stared at him. "Do you mean you *know?*"

Mr. Justice Wargrave said cautiously, "As regards actual evidence, such as is necessary in court, I admit that I have none. But it appears to me, reviewing the whole business, that one particular person is sufficiently clearly indicated. Yes, I think so."

Armstrong stared at him. He said, "I don't understand."

iv.

Miss Brent was upstairs in her bedroom. She took up her Bible and went to sit by the window. She opened it. Then, after a minute's hesitation, she set it aside and went over to the dressing table. From a drawer in it she took out a small black-covered notebook. She opened it and began writing.

A terrible thing has happened. General Macarthur is dead. (His cousin married Elsie MacPherson.) There is no doubt but that he was murdered. After luncheon the judge made us a most interesting speech. He is convinced that the murderer is one of us. That means that one of us is possessed by a devil. I had already suspected that. Which of us is it?

They are all asking themselves that. I alone know. . . .

She sat for some time without moving. Her eyes grew vague and filmy. The pencil straggled drunkenly in her fingers. In shaking loose capitals she wrote: THE MURDERER'S NAME IS BEATRICE TAYLOR. . . . Her eyes closed. Suddenly, with a start, she awoke. She looked down at the notebook. With an angry exclamation she scored through the vague, unevenly scrawled characters of the last sentence. She said in a low voice: "Did *I* write that? Did I? *I must be going mad. . . .*"

v.

The storm increased. The wind howled against the side of the house. Everyone was in the living room. They sat listlessly huddled together. And, surreptitiously, they watched each other. When Rogers brought in the tea tray, they all jumped. He said: "Shall I draw the curtains? It would make it more cheerful-like."

Receiving an assent to this, the curtains were drawn and the lamps turned on. The room grew more cheerful. A little of the shadow lifted. Surely, by tomorrow, the storm would be over and someone would come—a boat would arrive. . . .

Vera Claythorne said, "Will you pour out tea, Miss Brent?"

The elder woman replied, "No, you do it, dear. That teapot is so heavy. And I have lost two skeins of my gray knitting wool. So annoying." Vera moved to the tea table. There was a cheerful rattle and clink of china. Normality returned.

Tea! Blessed ordinary everyday afternoon tea! Philip Lombard made a cheery remark. Blore responded. Dr. Armstrong told a humorous story. Mr. Justice Wargrave, who ordinarily hated tea, sipped approvingly.

Into this relaxed atmosphere came Rogers. And Rogers was upset. He said nervously and at random, "Excuse me, sir, but does anyone know what's become of the bath-room curtain?"

Lombard's head went up with a jerk. "The bathroom curtain? What the devil do you mean, Rogers?"

"It's gone, sir, clean vanished. I was going round draw-ing all the curtains and the one in the lav—bathroom wasn't there any longer."

Mr. Justice Wargrave asked, "Was it there this morn-ing?"

"Oh, yes, sir."

Blore said, "What kind of a curtain was it?"

"Scarlet oilsilk, sir. It went with the scarlet tiles."

Lombard said, "And it's gone?"

"Gone, sir."

They stared at each other. Blore said heavily, "Well—after all—what of it? It's mad—but so's everything else. Anyway, it doesn't matter. You can't kill anybody with an oilsilk curtain. Forget about it."

Rogers said, "Yes, sir, thank you, sir." He went out, shutting the door behind him.

Inside the room, the pall of fear had fallen anew. Again, surreptitiously, they watched each other.

vi.

Dinner came, was eaten, and cleared away. A simple meal, mostly out of tins. Afterwards, in the living room, the strain was almost too great to be borne. At nine o'clock, Emily Brent rose to her feet. She said, "I'm going to bed."

Vera said, "I'll go to bed too."

The two women went up the stairs and Lombard and Blore came with them. Standing at the top of the stairs, the two men watched the women go into their respective rooms and shut the doors. They heard the sound of two bolts being shot and the turning of two keys. Blore said with a grin, "No need to tell 'em to lock their doors!"

Lombard said, "Well, *they*'re all right for the night, at any rate!"

He went down again and the other followed him.

vii.

The four men went to bed an hour later. They went up together. Rogers, from the dining room where he was setting the table for breakfast, saw them go up. He heard them pause on the landing above. Then the judge's voice spoke. "I need hardly advise you, gentlemen, to lock your doors."

Blore said, "And, what's more, put a chair under the handle. There are ways of turning locks from the outside."

Lombard murmured, "My dear Blore, the trouble with you is you know too much!"

The judge said gravely, "Good night, gentlemen. May we all meet safely in the morning!"

Rogers came out of the dining room and slipped halfway up the stairs. He saw four figures pass through four doors and heard the turning of four locks and the shooting of four bolts. He nodded his head. "That's all right," he muttered.

He went back into the dining room. Yes, everything was ready for the morning. His eye lingered on the center plaque of looking glass and the seven little china figures. A sudden grin transformed his face. He murmured, "I'll see no one plays tricks tonight, at any rate."

Crossing the room he locked the door to the pantry. Then, going through the other door to the hall he pulled the door to, locked it and slipped the key into his pocket. Then, extinguishing the lights, he hurried up the stairs and into his new bedroom.

There was only one possible hiding place in it, the tall wardrobe, and he looked into that immediately. Then, locking and bolting the door, he prepared for bed. He said to himself, "No more Indian tricks tonight. I've seen to that. . . ."

11

PHILIP LOMBARD had the habit of waking at daybreak. He did so on this particular morning. He raised himself on an elbow and listened. The wind had somewhat abated but was still blowing. He could hear no sound of rain. . . . At eight o'clock the wind was blowing more strongly, but Lombard did not hear it. He was asleep again.

At nine-thirty he was sitting on the edge of his bed looking at his watch. He put it to his ear. Then his lips drew back from his teeth in that curious wolflike smile characteristic of the man. He said very softly, "I think the time has come to do something about this."

At twenty-five minutes to ten he was tapping on the closed door of Blore's room. The latter opened it cautiously. His hair was tousled and his eyes were still dim with sleep. Philip Lombard said affably, "Sleeping the clock round? Well, shows you've got an easy conscience."

Blore said shortly, "What's the matter?"

Lombard answered, "Anybody called you—or brought you any tea? Do you know what time it is?"

Blore looked over his shoulder at a small traveling clock by his bedside. He said, "Twenty-five to ten. Wouldn't have believed I could have slept like that. Where's Rogers?"

Philip Lombard said, "It's a case of echo answers where."

"What d'you mean?" asked the other sharply.

Lombard said, "I mean that Rogers is missing. He isn't in his room or anywhere else. And there's no kettle on and the kitchen fire isn't even lit."

Blore swore under his breath. He said, "Where the devil can he be? Out on the island somewhere? Wait till I get some clothes on. See if the others know anything."

Philip Lombard nodded. He moved along the line of

closed doors. He found Armstrong up and nearly dressed. Mr. Justice Wargrave, like Blore, had to be roused from sleep. Vera Claythorne was dressed. Emily Brent's room was empty.

The little party moved through the house. Rogers' room, as Philip Lombard had already ascertained, was untenanted. The bed had been slept in, and his razor and sponge and soap were wet. Lombard said, "He got up, all right."

Vera said in a low voice which she tried to make firm and assured, "You don't think he's—hiding somewhere —waiting for us?"

Lombard said, "My dear girl, I'm prepared to think anything of anyone! My advice is that we keep together until we find him."

Armstrong said, "He must be out on the island somewhere."

Blore, who had joined them, dressed but still unshaved, said, "Where's Miss Brent got to—that's another mystery?"

But as they arrived in the hall, Emily Brent came in through the front door. She had on a mackintosh. She said, "The sea is as high as ever. I shouldn't think any boat could put out today."

Blore said, "Have you been wandering about the island alone, Miss Brent? Don't you realize that that's an exceedingly foolish thing to do?"

Emily Brent said, "I assure you, Mr. Blore, that I kept an extremely sharp lookout."

Blore grunted. He said, "Seen anything of Rogers?"

Miss Brent's eyebrows rose. "Rogers? No, I haven't seen him this morning. Why?"

Mr. Justice Wargrave, shaved, dressed and with his false teeth in position, came down the stairs. He moved to the open dining-room door. He said, "Ha, laid the table for breakfast, I see."

Lombard said, "He might have done that last night."

They all moved inside the room, looking at the neatly set plates and cutlery. At the row of cups on the sideboard. At the felt mats placed ready for the coffee urn. It was Vera who saw it first. She caught the judge's arm and the grip of her athletic fingers made the old gentleman wince. She cried out, "The Indians! Look!"

There were only six china figures in the middle of the table.

ii.

They found him shortly afterwards. He was in the little wash house across the yard. He had been chopping sticks in preparation for lighting the kitchen fire. The small chopper was still in his hand. A bigger chopper, a heavy affair, was leaning against the door—the metal of it stained a dull brown. It corresponded only too well with the deep wound in the back of Rogers' head. . . .

iii.

"Perfectly clear," said Armstrong. "The murderer must have crept up behind him, swung the chopper once and brought it down on his head as he was bending over."

Blore was busy on the handle of the chopper and the flour sifter from the kitchen. Mr. Justice Wargrave asked, "Would it have needed great force, doctor?"

Armstrong said gravely, "A woman could have done it if that's what you mean." He gave a quick glance round. Vera Claythorne and Emily Brent had retired to the kitchen. "The girl could have done it easily—she's an athletic type. In appearance Miss Brent is fragile looking, but that type of woman has often a' lot of wiry strength. And you must remember that anyone who's mentally unhinged has a good deal of unsuspected strength."

The judge nodded thoughtfully. Blore rose from his knees with a sigh. He said, "No fingerprints. Handle was wiped afterwards."

A sound of laughter was heard—they turned sharply. Vera Claythorne was standing in the yard. She cried out in a high, shrill voice, shaken with wild bursts of laughter, "Do they keep bees on this island? Tell me that. Where do we go for honey? Ha! ha!"

They stared at her uncomprehendingly. It was as though the sane, well-balanced girl had gone mad before their eyes. She went on in that high, unnatural voice. "Don't stare like that! As though you thought I was mad. It's sane enough what I'm asking. Bees, hives, bees! Oh, don't you understand? Haven't you read that idiotic rhyme? It's up in all your bedrooms—put there for you to study! We might have come here straightaway if we'd had sense. *Seven little Indian boys chopping up sticks.* And the next verse. I know the whole thing by heart, I tell you! *Six little Indian boys playing with a hive.* And that's why I'm asking—do they keep bees on this island? —isn't it funny?—isn't it damned funny . . . ?"

She began laughing wildly again. Dr. Armstrong strode forward. He raised his hand and struck her a flat blow on the cheek. She gasped, hiccuped—and swallowed. She stood motionless a minute, then she said, "Thank you . . . I'm all right now." Her voice was once more calm and controlled—the voice of the efficient games mistress.

She turned and went across the yard into the kitchen saying, "Miss Brent and I are getting you breakfast. Can you—bring some sticks to light the fire?" The marks of the doctor's hand stood out red on her cheek.

As she went into the kitchen Blore said, "Well, you dealt with that all right, doctor."

Armstrong said apologetically, "Had to! We can't cope with hysteria on the top of everything else."

Philip Lombard said, "She's not a hysterical type."

Armstrong agreed. "Oh, no. Good healthy sensible girl. Just the sudden shock. It might happen to anybody."

Rogers had chopped a certain amount of firewood before he had been killed. They gathered it up and took it into the kitchen. Vera and Emily Brent were busy. Miss Brent was raking out the stove. Vera was cutting the rind off the bacon. Emily Brent said, "Thank you. We'll be as quick as we can—say half an hour to three-quarters. The kettle's got to boil."

Ex-Inspector Blore said in a low, hoarse voice to Philip Lombard, "Know what I'm thinking?"

Philip Lombard said, "As you're just about to tell me, it's not worth the trouble of guessing."

Ex-Inspector Blore was an earnest man. A light touch was incomprehensible to him. He went on heavily, "There was a case in America. Old gentleman and his wife—both killed with an ax. Middle of the morning. Nobody in the house but the daughter and the maid. Maid, it was proved, couldn't have done it. Daughter was a respectable middle-aged spinster. Seemed incredible. So incredible that they acquitted her. But they never found any other explanation." He paused. "I thought of that when I saw the ax—and then when I went into the kitchen and saw her there so neat and calm. Hadn't turned a hair! That girl, coming all over hysterical—well, that's natural—the sort of thing you'd expect—don't you think so?"

Philip Lombard said laconically, "It might be."

Blore went on. "But the other! So neat and prim—wrapped up in that apron—Mrs. Rogers' apron, I suppose—saying, 'Breakfast will be ready in half an hour or so.' If you ask me, that woman's as mad as a hatter! Lots of elderly spinsters go that way—I don't mean go in for homicide on the grand scale, but go queer in their heads. Unfortunately it's taken her this way. Religious mania—thinks she's God's instrument, something of that kind! She sits in her room, you know, reading her Bible."

Philip Lombard sighed and said, "That's hardly proof positive of an unbalanced mentality, Blore."

But Blore went on, ploddingly, perseveringly: "And then she was out—in her mackintosh, said she'd been down to look at the sea."

The other shook his head. He said, "Rogers was killed as he was chopping firewood—that is to say first thing when he got up. The Brent wouldn't have needed to wander about outside for hours afterwards. If you ask me, the murderer of Rogers would take jolly good care to be rolled up in bed snoring."

Blore said, "You're missing the point, Mr. Lombard. If the woman was innocent she'd be too dead scared to go wandering about by herself. She'd only do that *if she knew that she had nothing to fear*. That's to say *if she herself is the criminal*."

Philip Lombard said, "That's a good point. . . . Yes, I hadn't thought of that." He added with a faint grin, "Glad you don't still suspect me."

Blore said rather shamefacedly, "I did start by thinking of you—that revolver—and the queer story you told—or didn't tell. But I've realized now that that was really a bit too obvious." He paused and said, "Hope you feel the same about me."

Philip said thoughtfully, "I may be wrong, of course, but I can't feel that you've got enough imagination for this job. All I can say is, if you're the criminal, you're a damned fine actor and I take my hat off to you." He lowered his voice. "Just between ourselves, Blore, and taking into account that we'll probably both be a couple of stiffs before another day is out, you did indulge in that spot of perjury, I suppose?"

Blore shifted uneasily from one foot to the other. He said at last, "Doesn't seem to make much odds now. Oh, well, here goes. Landor was innocent right enough. The gang had got me squared and between us we got him put away for a stretch. Mind you, I wouldn't admit this—"

"If there were any witnesses," finished Lombard with a grin. "It's just between you and me. Well, I hope you made a tidy bit out of it."

"Didn't make what I should have done. Mean crowd, the Purcell gang. I got my promotion, though."

"And Landor got penal servitude and died in prison."

"I couldn't know he was going to die, could I?" demanded Blore.

"No, that was your bad luck."

"Mine? His, you mean."

"Yours, too. Because, as a result of it, it looks as though your own life is going to be cut unpleasantly short."

"Me?" Blore stared at him. "Do you think I'm going to

go the way of Rogers and the rest of them? Not me! I'm watching out for myself pretty carefully, I can tell you."

Lombard said, "Oh, well—I'm not a betting man. And anyway if you were dead I wouldn't get paid."

"Look here, Mr. Lombard, what do you mean?"

Philip Lombard showed his teeth. He said, "I mean, my dear Blore, that in my opinion you haven't got a chance!"

"What?"

"Your lack of imagination is going to make you absolutely a sitting target. A criminal of the imagination of U. N. Owen can make rings round you any time he—or she—wants to."

Blore's face went crimson. He demanded angrily, "And what about you?"

Philip Lombard's face went hard and dangerous. He said, "I've a pretty good imagination of my own. I've been in tight places before now and got out of them! I think—I won't say more than that but I *think* I'll get out of this one."

v.

The eggs were in the frying pan. Vera, at the stove, thought to herself: Why did I make a hysterical fool of myself? That was a mistake. Keep calm, my girl, keep calm. After all, she'd always prided herself on her level-headedness!

"Miss Claythorne was wonderful—kept her head—started off swimming after Cyril at once."

Why think of that now? All that was over—over. . . . Cyril had disappeared long before she got near the rock. She had felt the current take her, sweeping her out to sea. She had let herself go with it—swimming quietly, floating—till the boat arrived at last. . . . They had praised her courage and her *sang-froid*. . . . But not Hugo. Hugo had just—looked at her. . . . God, how it hurt, even now, to think of Hugo. . . . *Where was he? What was he doing? Was he engaged—married?*

Emily Brent said sharply, "Vera, that bacon is burning."

"Oh, sorry, Miss Brent, so it is. How stupid of me."

Emily Brent lifted out the last egg from the sizzling fat. Vera, putting fresh pieces of bacon in the frying pan, said curiously, "You're wonderfully calm, Miss Brent."

Emily Brent said, pressing her lips together, "I was brought up to keep my head and never to make a fuss."

Vera thought mechanically: Repressed as a child . . . That accounts for a lot. . . . She said, "Aren't you afraid?" She paused and then added, "Or don't you mind dying?"

Dying! It was as though a sharp little gimlet had run into the solid congealed mass of Emily Brent's brain. Dying? But *she* wasn't going to die! The others would die—yes—but not she, Emily Brent. This girl didn't understand! Emily wasn't afraid, naturally—none of the Brents were afraid. All her people were Service people. They faced death unflinchingly. They led upright lives just as she, Emily Brent, had led an upright life. . . . She had never done anything to be ashamed of. . . . And so, naturally, *she* wasn't going to die. . . .

"The Lord is mindful of His own." *"Thou shalt not be afraid for the terror by night; nor for the arrow that flieth by day. . . ."* It was daylight now—there was no terror. *"We shall none of us leave this island."* Who had said that? General Macarthur, of course, whose cousin had married Elsie MacPherson. He hadn't seemed to *care*. He had seemed—actually—to *welcome* the idea! Wicked! Almost impious to feel that way. Some people thought so little of death that they actually took their own lives. *Beatrice Taylor.* . . . Last night she had dreamed of Beatrice—dreamt that she was outside pressing her face against the window and moaning, asking to be let in. But Emily Brent hadn't wanted to let her in. Because, if she did, something terrible would happen. . . .

Emily came to herself with a start. That girl was looking at her very strangely. She said in a brisk voice, "Everything's ready, isn't it? We'll take the breakfast in."

Breakfast was a curious meal. Everyone was very polite. . . . "May I get you some more coffee, Miss Brent?" . . . "Miss Claythorne, a slice of ham?" . . . "Another piece of bacon?" . . . Six people, all outwardly self-possessed and normal.

And within? Thoughts that ran round in a circle like squirrels in a cage. . . . *"What next? What next? Who? Which?"* . . . *"Would it work? I wonder. It's worth trying. If there's time. My God, if there's time. . . ."* *"Religious mania, that's the ticket. . . . Looking at her, though, you can hardly believe it. . . . Suppose I'm wrong. . . ."* *"It's crazy—everything's crazy. I'm going crazy. Wool disappearing—red silk curtains—it doesn't make sense. I can't get the hang of it. . . ."* *"The damned fool, he believed every word I said to him. It was easy. . . . I must be careful, though, very careful."* *"Six of those little china figures . . . only six—how many will there be by tonight? . . ."*

"Who'll have the last egg?"

"Marmalade?"

"Thanks, can I give you some ham?"

Six people, behaving normally at breakfast. . . .

12

■

THE MEAL was over. Mr. Justice Wargrave cleared his throat. He said in a small, authoritative voice, "It would be advisable, I think, if we met to discuss the situation. Shall we say in half an hour's time in the drawing room?"

Everyone made a sound suggestive of agreement. Vera began to pile plates together. She said, "I'll clear away and wash up."

Philip Lombard said, "We'll bring the stuff out to the pantry for you."

"Thanks."

Emily Brent, rising to her feet, sat down again. She said, "Oh, dear."

The judge said, "Anything the matter, Miss Brent?"

Emily said apologetically, "I'm sorry. I'd like to help Miss Claythorne, but I don't know how it is. I feel just a little giddy."

"Giddy, eh?" Dr. Armstrong came towards her. "Quite natural. Delayed shock. I can give you something to—"

"No!" The word burst from her lips like an exploding shell. It took everyone aback. Dr. Armstrong flushed a deep red.

There was no mistaking the fear and suspicion in her face. He said stiffly, "Just as you please, Miss Brent."

She said, "I don't wish to take anything—anything at all. I will just sit here quietly till the giddiness passes off."

They finished clearing away the breakfast things. Blore said, "I'm a domestic sort of man. I'll give you a hand, Miss Claythorne."

Vera said, "Thank you."

Emily Brent was left alone sitting in the dining room. For a while she heard a faint murmur of voices from the pantry. The giddiness was passing. She felt drowsy now, as though she could easily go to sleep. There was a buzzing in her ears—or was it a real buzzing in the room? She thought: It's like a bee—a bumblebee.

Presently she saw the bee. It was crawling up the window pane. Vera Claythorne had talked about bees this morning.

Bees and honey . . . She liked honey. Honey in the comb, and strain it yourself through a muslin bag. Drip, drip, drip . . .

There was somebody in the room . . . somebody all wet and dripping. . . . *Beatrice Taylor came from the river.* . . . She had only to turn her head and she would see her.

But she couldn't turn her head. . . .

If she were to call out . . . But she couldn't call out. . . . There was no one else in the house. She was all alone. . . . She heard footsteps—soft, dragging footsteps coming up behind her. The stumbling footsteps of the drowned girl. . . . There was a wet, dank smell in her nostrils. . . . On the window pane the bee was buzzing—buzzing. . . . And then she felt the prick. The bee sting on the side of her neck. . . .

ii.

In the drawing room they were waiting for Emily Brent. Vera Claythorne said, "Shall I go and fetch her?"

Blore said quickly, "Just a minute."

Vera sat down again. Everyone looked inquiringly at Blore. He said, "Look here, everybody, my opinion's this: we needn't look farther for the author of these deaths than the dining room at this minute. I'd take my oath that woman's the one we're after!"

Armstrong said, "And the motive?"

"Religious mania. What do you say, doctor?"

Armstrong said, "It's perfectly possible. I've nothing to say against it. But of course we've no proof."

Vera said, "She was very odd in the kitchen when we were getting breakfast. Her eyes——" She shivered.

Lombard said, "You can't judge her by that. We're all a bit off our heads by now!"

Blore said, "There's another thing. She's the only one who wouldn't give an explanation after that gramophone record. Why? Because she hadn't any to give."

Vera stirred in her chair. She said, "That's not quite true. She told me—afterwards."

Wargrave said, "What did she tell you, Miss Claythorne?"

Vera repeated the story of Beatrice Taylor. Mr. Justice Wargrave observed, "A perfectly straightforward story. I personally should have no difficulty in accepting it. Tell me, Miss Claythorne, did she appear to be troubled by a sense of guilt or a feeling of remorse for her attitude in the matter?"

"None whatever," said Vera. "She was completely unmoved."

Blore said, "Hearts as hard as flints, these righteous spinsters! Envy, mostly!"

Mr. Justice Wargrave said, "It is now five minutes to eleven. I think we should summon Miss Brent to join our conclave."

Blore said, "Aren't you going to take any action?"

The judge said, "I fail to see what action we can take. Our suspicions are, at the moment, only suspicions. I will, however, ask Dr. Armstrong to observe Miss Brent's demeanor very carefully. Let us now go into the dining room."

They found Emily Brent sitting in the chair in which they had left her. From behind they saw nothing amiss, except that she did not seem to hear their entrance into the room.

And then they saw her face—suffused with blood, with blue lips and starting eyes. Blore said, "My God, she's dead!"

iii.

The small, quiet voice of Mr. Justice Wargrave said, "One more of us acquitted—too late!"

Armstrong was bent over the dead woman. He sniffed the lips, shook his head, peered into the eyelids. Lombard said impatiently, "How did she die, doctor? She was all right when we left her here!"

Armstrong's attention was riveted on a mark on the right side of the neck. He said, "That's the mark of a hypodermic syringe."

There was a buzzing sound from the window. Vera cried, "Look—a bee—*a bumblebee*. Remember what I said this morning!"

Armstrong said grimly, "It wasn't that bee that stung her! A human hand held the syringe."

The judge asked, "What poison was injected?"

Armstrong answered, "At a guess, one of the cyanides. Probably potassium cyanide, same as Anthony Marston. She must have died almost immediately by asphyxiation."

Vera cried, "But that *bee?* It can't be *coincidence!*"

Lombard said grimly, "Oh, no, it isn't coincidence! It's our murderer's touch of local color! He's a playful beast. Likes to stick to his damnable nursery jingle as closely as possible!" For the first time his voice was uneven, almost shrill. It was as though even his nerves, seasoned by a long career of hazards and dangerous undertakings, had given out at last. He said violently, "It's mad!—absolutely mad—we're all mad!"

The judge said calmly, "We have still, I hope, our reasoning powers. *Did anyone bring a hypodermic syringe to this house?*"

Dr. Armstrong, straightening himself, said in a voice that was not too well assured, "Yes, I did."

Four pairs of eyes fastened on him. He braced himself against the deep, hostile suspicion of those eyes. He said, "Always travel with one. Most doctors do."

Mr. Justice Wargrave said calmly, "Quite so. Will you tell us, doctor, where that syringe is now?"

"In the suitcase in my room."

Wargrave said, "We might, perhaps, verify that fact."

The five of them went upstairs, a silent procession. The contents of the suitcase were turned out on the floor. The hypodermic syringe was not there.

iv.

Armstrong said violently, "Somebody must have taken it!"

There was silence in the room. Armstrong stood with his back to the window. Four pairs of eyes were on him, black with suspicion and accusation. He looked from Wargrave to Vera and repeated helplessly—weakly, "I tell you someone must have taken it."

Blore was looking at Lombard, who returned his gaze. The judge said, "There are five of us here in this room. *One of us is a murderer.* The position is fraught with grave danger. Everything must be done in order to safeguard the four of us who are innocent. I will now ask you, Dr. Armstrong, what drugs you have in your possession?"

Armstrong replied, "I have a small medicine case here. You can examine it. You will find some sleeping stuff—trional and sulphonal tablets—a packet of bromide, bicarbonate of soda, aspirin. Nothing else. I have no cyanide in my possession."

The judge said, "I have myself, some sleeping tablets—sulphonal, I think they are. I presume they would be lethal if a sufficiently large dose were given. You, Mr. Lombard, have in your possession a revolver."

Philip Lombard said sharply, "What if I have?"

"Only this. I propose that the doctor's supply of drugs, my own sulphonal tablets, your revolver and anything else of the nature of drugs or firearms should be collected together and placed in a safe place. That after this is done, we should each of us submit to a search—both of our persons and of our effects."

Lombard said, "I'm damned if I'll give up my revolver!"

Wargrave said sharply, "Mr. Lombard, you are a very strongly built and powerful young man, but ex-Inspector Blore is also a man of powerful physique. I do not know what the outcome of a struggle between you would be but I can tell you this. On Blore's side, assisting him to the best of our ability, will be myself, Dr. Armstrong and Miss Claythorne. You will appreciate, therefore, that the odds against you if you choose to resist will be somewhat heavy."

Lombard threw his head back. His teeth showed in what was almost a snarl. "Oh, very well, then. Since you've got it all taped out."

Mr. Justice Wargrave nodded his head. "You are a sensible young man. Where is this revolver of yours?"

"In the drawer of the table by my bed."

"Good."

"I'll fetch it."

"I think it would be desirable if we went with you."

Philip said with a smile that was still nearer a snarl, "Suspicious devil, aren't you?"

They went along the corridor to Lombard's room. Philip strode across to the bed table and jerked open the drawer. Then he recoiled with an oath. The drawer of the bed table was empty.

v.

"Satisfied?" asked Lombard. He had stripped to the skin and he and his room had been meticulously searched by the other three men. Vera Claythorne was outside in the corridor. The search proceeded methodically. In turn, Armstrong, the judge and Blore submitted to the same test.

The four men emerged from Blore's room and approached Vera. It was the judge who spoke. "I hope you will understand, Miss Claythorne, that we can make no exceptions. That revolver must be found. You have, I presume, a bathing dress with you?"

Vera nodded.

"Then I will ask you to go into your room and put it on and then come out to us here."

Vera went into her room and shut the door. She reappeared in under a minute dressed in a tight-fitting silk rucked bathing dress.

Wargrave nodded approval. "Thank you, Miss Claythorne. Now if you will remain here, we will search your room."

Vera waited patiently in the corridor until they emerged. Then she went in, dressed, and came out to where they were waiting. The judge said, "We are now assured of one thing. There are no lethal weapons or drugs in the possession of any of us five. That is one point to the good. We will now place the drugs in a safe place. There is, I think, a silver chest, is there not, in the pantry?"

Blore said, "That's all very well, but who's to have the key? You, I suppose."

Mr. Justice Wargrave made no reply. He went down to the pantry and the others followed him. There was a small case there designed for the purpose of holding silver and plate. By the judge's directions, the various drugs were placed in this and it was locked. Then, still on War-

122

grave's instructions, the chest was lifted into the plate cupboard and this in turn was locked. The judge then gave the key of the chest to Philip Lombard and the key of the cupboard to Blore. He said, "You two are the strongest physically. It would be difficult for either of you to get the key from the other. It would be impossible for any of us three to do so. To break open the cupboard—or the plate chest—would be a noisy and cumbrous proceeding and one which could hardly be carried out without attention being attracted to what was going on."

He paused, then went on, "We are still faced by one very grave problem. *What has become of Mr. Lombard's revolver?*"

Blore said, "Seems to me its owner is the most likely person to know that."

A white dint showed in Philip Lombard's nostrils. He said, "You damned pig-headed fool! I tell you it's been stolen from me!"

Wargrave asked, "When did you see it last?"

"Last night. It was in the drawer when I went to bed—ready in case anything happened."

The judge nodded. He said, "It must have been taken this morning during the confusion of searching for Rogers or after his dead body was discovered."

Vera said, "It must be hidden somewhere about the house. We must look for it."

Mr. Justice Wargrave's finger was stroking his chin. He said, "I doubt if our search will result in anything. Our murderer has had plenty of time to devise a hiding place. I do not fancy we shall find that revolver easily."

Blore said forcefully, "I don't know where the revolver is, but I'll bet I know where something else is—that hypodermic syringe. Follow me."

He opened the front door and led the way round the house. A little distance away from the dining-room window he found the syringe. Beside it was a smashed china figure—a sixth broken Indian boy. Blore said in a satisfied voice, "Only place it could be. After he'd killed her, he opened the window and threw out the syringe and picked up the china figure from the table and followed on with that."

There were no prints on the syringe. It had been carefully wiped. Vera said in a determined voice, "Now let us look for the revolver."

Mr. Justice Wargrave said: "By all means. But in doing so let us be careful to keep together. Remember, if we separate, the murderer gets his chance."

They searched the house carefully from attic to cellar, but without result. The revolver was still missing.

13

"ONE OF *us* . . . *One of us* . . . *One of us* . . ."* Three words, endlessly repeated, dinning themselves hour after hour into receptive brains. Five people—five frightened people. Five people who watched each other, who now hardly troubled to hide their state of nervous tension. There was little pretense now—no formal veneer of conversation. They were five enemies linked together by a mutual instinct of self-preservation.

And all of them, suddenly, looked less like human beings. They were reverting to more bestial types. Like a wary old tortoise, Mr. Justice Wargrave sat hunched up, his body motionless, his eyes keen and alert. Ex-Inspector Blore looked coarser and clumsier in build. His walk was that of a slow, padding animal. His eyes were bloodshot. There was a look of mingled ferocity and stupidity about him. He was like a beast at bay ready to charge its pursuers. Philip Lombard's senses seemed heightened, rather than diminished. His ears reacted to the slightest sound. His step was lighter and quicker, his body was lithe and graceful. And he smiled often, his lips curling back from his long, white teeth.

Vera Claythorne was very quiet. She sat most of the time huddled in a chair. Her eyes stared ahead of her into space. She looked dazed. She was like a bird that has dashed its head against glass and that has been picked up by a human hand. It crouches there, terrified, unable to move, hoping to save itself by its immobility.

Armstrong was in a pitiable condition of nerves. He twitched and his hands shook. He lighted cigarette after cigarette and stubbed them out almost immediately. The forced inaction of their position seemed to gall him more than the others. Every now and then he broke out into a torrent of nervous speech. "We—we shouldn't just sit here doing nothing! There must be *something*—surely, surely, there is *something* that we can do? If we lit a bonfire—"

Blore said heavily, "In this weather?"

The rain was pouring down again. The wind came in fitful gusts. The depressing sound of the pattering rain nearly drove them mad. By tacit consent, they had adopted a plan of campaign. They all sat in the big drawing room. Only one person left the room at a time. The other four waited till the fifth returned.

Lombard said, "It's only a question of time. The weather will clear. Then we can do something—signal—light fires—make a raft—something!"

Armstrong said with a sudden cackle of laughter, "A question of time—*time?* We can't afford time! We shall all be dead. . . ."

Mr. Justice Wargrave said, and his small, clear voice was heavy with passionate determination, "Not if we are careful. *We must be very careful. . . .*"

The midday meal had been duly eaten—but there had been no conventional formality about it. All five of them had gone to the kitchen. In the larder they had found a great store of tinned foods. They had opened a tin of tongue and two tins of fruit. They had eaten standing round the kitchen table. Then, herding close together, they had returned to the drawing room—to sit there—sit —watching each other. . . .

And by now the thoughts that ran through their brains were abnormal, feverish, diseased. . . . "It's Armstrong. . . . I saw him looking at me sideways just then . . . his eyes are mad . . . quite mad. . . . Perhaps he isn't a doctor at all. . . . That's it, of course! . . . He's a lunatic, escaped from some doctor's house—pretending to be a doctor. . . . It's true . . . shall I tell them? . . . Shall I scream out? . . . No, it won't do to put him on his guard. . . . Besides, he can seem so sane. . . . What time is it? . . . Only a quarter past three! . . . Oh, God, I shall go mad myself. . . . *Yes, it's Armstrong.* . . . He's watching me now. . . ."

"They won't get *me!* I can take care of myself. . . . I've been in tight places before. . . . Where the hell is that revolver? . . . Who took it? . . . Who's got it? . . . Nobody's got it—we know that. We were all searched. . . . Nobody *can* have it. . . . *But someone knows where it is.* . . ."

"They're going mad . . . they'll all go mad. . . . Afraid of death . . . we're all afraid of death. . . . *I'm* afraid of death. . . . Yes, but that doesn't stop death coming. . . . *'The hearse is at the door, sir.'* Where did I read that? The girl . . . I'll watch the girl. Yes, I'll watch the girl. . . ."

"Twenty to four . . . only twenty to four . . . perhaps the clock has stopped. . . . I don't understand—no, I don't understand. . . . This sort of thing can't happen . . . *it is happening.* . . . Why don't we wake up? Wake up—Judgment Day—no, not that! If I could only think. . . . My head—something's happening in my head—it's going to burst—it's going to split. . . . This sort of thing can't happen. . . . What's the time? Oh, God! it's only a quarter to four."

"I must keep my head. . . . I must keep my head. . . . If only I keep my head . . . It's all perfectly clear—all worked out. But nobody must suspect. It may do the trick. It must! Which one? That's the question—which one? I think—yes, I rather think—yes—*him.*"

When the clock struck five they all jumped. Vera said, "Does anyone—want tea?"

There was a moment's silence. Blore said, "I'd like a cup."

Vera rose. She said, "I'll go and make it. You can all stay here."

Mr. Justice Wargrave said gently, "I think, my dear young lady, we would all prefer to come and watch you make it."

Vera stared, then gave a short, rather hysterical laugh. She said, "Of course! You would!"

Five people went into the kitchen. Tea was made and

drunk by Vera and Blore. The other three had whisky— opening a fresh bottle and using a siphon from a nailed-up case. The judge murmured with a reptilian smile, "We must be very careful. . . ."

They went back again to the drawing room. Although it was summer the room was dark. Lombard switched on the lights but they did not come on. He said, "Of course! The engine's not been run today since Rogers hasn't been there to see to it." He hesitated and said, "We could go out and get it going, I suppose."

Mr. Justice Wargrave said, "There are packets of candles in the larder, I saw them, better use those."

Lombard went out. The other four sat watching each other. He came back with a box of candles and a pile of saucers. Five candles were lit and placed about the room. The time was a quarter to six.

ii.

At twenty past six, Vera felt that to sit there longer was unbearable. She would go to her room and bathe her aching head and temples in cold water. She got up and went towards the door. Then she remembered and came back and got a candle out of the box. She lighted it, let a little wax pour into a saucer and stuck the candle firmly to it. Then she went out of the room, shutting the door behind her and leaving the four men inside. She went up the stairs and along the passage to her room. As she opened her door, she suddenly halted and stood stock still. Her nostrils quivered. The sea . . . The smell of the sea at St. Tredennick . . .

That was it. She could not be mistaken. Of course one smelt the sea on an island anyway, but this was different. It was the smell there had been on the beach that day— with the tide out and the rocks covered with seaweed drying in the sun . . . *"Can I swim out to the island, Miss Claythorne?" "Why can't I swim out to the island? . . ."* Horrid whiny spoilt little brat! If it weren't for him, Hugo would be rich . . . able to marry the girl he loved. . . .

Hugo . . . Surely—surely—Hugo was beside her? No, waiting for her in the room . . .

She took a step forward. The draught from the window caught the flame of the candle. It flickered and went out. . . . In the dark she was suddenly afraid. . . . "Don't be a fool," Vera Claythorne urged herself. "It's all right. The others are downstairs. All four of them. There's no one in the room. There can't be. You're imagining things, my girl."

But that smell—that smell of the beach at St. Tredennick . . . That wasn't imagined. *It was true.* . . .

And there *was* someone in the room. . . . She had heard something—surely she had heard something. . . . And then, as she stood there, listening—a cold, clammy hand touched her throat—a wet hand, smelling of the sea. . . .

iii.

Vera screamed. She screamed and screamed—screams of the utmost terror—wild, desperate cries for help. She did not hear the sounds from below, of a chair being overturned, of a door opening, of men's feet running up the stairs. She was conscious only of supreme terror. Then, restoring her sanity, lights flickered in the doorway —candles—men hurrying into the room.

"What the devil?" "What's happened?" "Good God, what is it?"

She shuddered, took a step forward, collapsed on the floor. She was only half-aware of someone bending over her, of someone forcing her head down between her knees.

Then at a sudden exclamation, a quick "My God, look at that!" her senses returned. She opened her eyes and raised her head. She saw what it was the men with the candles were looking at. A broad ribbon of wet seaweed was hanging down from the ceiling. It was that which in the darkness had swayed against her throat. It was that which she had taken for a clammy hand, a drowned hand come back from the dead to squeeze the life out of her!

She began to laugh hysterically. She said, "It was sea-weed—only seaweed—and that's what the smell was. . . ."

And then the faintness came over her once more—waves upon waves of sickness. Again someone took her head and forced it between her knees.

Eons of time seemed to pass. They were offering her something to drink—pressing the glass against her lips. She smelt brandy. She was just about to gulp the spirit gratefully down when, suddenly, a warning note—like an alarm bell—sounded in her brain. She sat up, pushing the glass away. She said sharply, "Where did this come from?"

Blore's voice answered. He stared a minute before speaking. He said, "I got it from downstairs."

Vera cried, "I won't drink it. . . ."

There was a moment's silence, then Lombard laughed. He said with appreciation, "Good for you, Vera! You've got your wits about you—even if you have been scared half out of your life. I'll get a fresh bottle that hasn't been opened." He went swiftly out.

Vera said uncertainly, "I'm all right now. I'll have some water."

Armstrong supported her as she struggled to her feet. She went over to the basin, swaying and clutching at him for support. She let the cold tap run and then filled the glass.

Blore said resentfully, "That brandy's all right."

Armstrong said, "How do you know?"

Blore said angrily, "I didn't put anything in it. That's what you're getting at, I suppose."

Armstrong said, "I'm not saying you did. You might have done it, or someone might have tampered with the bottle for just this emergency."

Lombard came swiftly back into the room. He had a new bottle of brandy in his hands and a corkscrew. He thrust the sealed bottle under Vera's nose. "There you are, my girl. Absolutely no deception." He peeled off the tin foil and drew the cork. "Lucky there's a good supply of spirits in the house. Thoughtful of U. N. Owen."

Vera shuddered violently. Armstrong held the glass while Philip poured the brandy into it. He said, "You'd better drink this, Miss Claythorne. You've had a nasty shock."

Vera drank a little of the spirit. The color came back to her face. Philip Lombard said with a laugh, "Well, here's one murder that hasn't gone according to plan!"

Vera said almost in a whisper, "You think—that was what was meant?"

Lombard nodded. "Expected you to pass out through fright! Some people would have, wouldn't they, doctor?"

Armstrong did not commit himself. He said doubtfully, "H'm, impossible to say. Young, healthy subject—no cardiac weakness. Unlikely. On the other hand—" He picked up the glass of brandy that Blore had brought. He dipped a finger in it, tasted it gingerly. His expression did not alter. He said dubiously, "H'm, tastes all right."

Blore stepped forward angrily. He said, "If you're saying that I tampered with that, I'll knock your ruddy block off."

Vera, her wits revived by the brandy, made a diversion by saying, "Where's the judge?"

The three men looked at each other. *That's odd. . . .* Thought he came up with us." Blore said, *"So did I. . . .* What about it, doctor? You came up the stairs behind me."

Armstrong said, "I thought he was following me. . . . Of course, he'd be bound to go slower than we did. He's an old man."

They looked at each other again. Lombard said, "It's damned odd. . . ."

Blore cried, "We must look for him."

He started for the door. The others followed him, Vera last. As they went down the stairs Armstrong said over his shoulder: "Of course he *may* have stayed in the living room. . . ."

They crossed the hall. Armstrong called out loudly, "Wargrave, Wargrave, where are you?"

There was no answer. A deadly silence filled the house apart from the gentle patter of the rain. Then, in the entrance to the drawing-room door, Armstrong stopped dead. The others crowded up and looked over his shoulder. Somebody cried out.

130

Mr. Justice Wargrave was sitting in his high-backed chair at the end of the room. Two candles burnt on either side of him. But what shocked and startled the onlookers was the fact that he sat there robed in scarlet with a judge's wig upon his head. . . .

Dr. Armstrong motioned to the others to keep back. He himself walked across to the silent, staring figure, reeling a little as he walked like a drunken man. He bent forward, peering into the still face. Then, with a swift movement, he raised the wig. It fell to the floor, revealing the high bald forehead with in the very middle a round stained mark from which something had trickled. . . .

Dr. Armstrong raised the limp hand and felt for the pulse. Then he turned to the others. He said—and his voice was expressionless, dead, far away, *"He's been shot. . . ."*

Blore said, "God—*the revolver!"*

The doctor said, still in the same lifeless voice, "Got him through the head. Instantaneous."

Vera stooped to the wig. She said, and her voice shook with horror, *"Miss Brent's missing gray wool. . . ."*

Blore said, "And the scarlet curtain that was missing from the bathroom. . . ."

Vera whispered, "So this is what they wanted them for. . . ."

Suddenly Philip Lombard laughed—a high, unnatural laugh. *"Five little Indian boys going in for law; one got in Chancery and then there were four.* That's the end of Mr. Bloody Justice Wargrave. No more pronouncing sentence for him! No more putting on the black cap! Here's the last time *he'll* ever sit in court! No more summing up and sending innocent men to death. How Edward Seton would laugh if he were here! God, how he'd laugh!"

His outburst shocked and startled the others. Vera cried, "Only this morning you said *he* was the one!"

Philip Lombard's face changed—sobered. He said in a low voice, "I know I did. . . . Well, I was wrong. Here's one more of us who's been proved innocent—*too late!"*

14

■

THEY HAD carried Mr. Justice Wargrave up to his room and laid him on the bed. Then they had come down again and had stood in the hall looking at each other. Blore said heavily, "What do we do now?"

Lombard said briskly, "Have something to eat. We've got to eat, you know."

Once again they went into the kitchen. Again they opened a tin of tongue. They ate mechanically, almost without tasting. Vera said, "I shall never eat tongue again."

They finished the meal. They sat round the kitchen table staring at each other. Blore said, "Only four of us now. . . . *Who'll be the next?*"

Armstrong stared. He said, almost mechanically, "We must be very careful——" and stopped.

Blore nodded. "That's what *he* said. . . . And now he's dead!"

Armstrong said, "How did it happen, I wonder?"

Lombard swore. He said, "A damned clever double cross! That stuff was planted in Miss Claythorne's room and it worked just as it was intended to. Everyone dashes up there thinking *she's* being murdered. And so——in the confusion——someone——caught the old boy off his guard."

Blore said, "Why didn't anyone hear the shot?"

Lombard shook his head. "Miss Claythorne was screaming, the wind was howling, we were running about and calling out. No, it wouldn't be heard." He paused. "But that trick's not going to work again. He'll have to try something else next time."

Blore said, "He probably will." There was an unpleasant tone in his voice. The two men eyed each other.

Armstrong said, "Four of us, and we don't know which . . ."

Blore said, "I know. . . ."

Vera said, "I haven't the least doubt. . . ."

Armstrong said slowly, "I suppose I do know really. . . ."

Philip Lombard said, "I think I've got a pretty good idea now. . . ." Again they all looked at each other.

Vera staggered to her feet. She said, "I feel awful. I must go to bed. . . . I'm dead beat."

Lombard said, "Might as well. No good sitting watching each other."

Blore said, "I've no objection. . . ."

The doctor murmured, "The best thing to do—although I doubt if any of us will sleep."

They moved to the door. Blore said, "I wonder where that revolver is now? . . ."

ii.

They went up the stairs.

The next move was a little like a scene in a farce. Each one of the four stood with a hand on his or her bedroom door handle. Then, as though at a signal, each one stepped into the room and pulled the door shut. There were sounds of bolts and locks, of the moving of furniture. Four frightened people were barricaded in until morning.

iii.

Philip Lombard drew a breath of relief as he turned from adjusting a chair under the door handle. He strolled across to the dressing table. By the light of the flickering candle he studied his face curiously. He said softly to himself, "Yes, this business has got you rattled all right."

His sudden wolflike smile flashed out. He undressed quickly. He went over to the bed, placing his wristwatch on the table by the bed. Then he opened the drawer of the table. He stood there, staring down at the revolver that was inside it. . . .

Vera Claythorne lay in bed. The candle still burned beside her. As yet she could not summon the courage to put it out. She was afraid of the dark. . . .

She told herself again and again: *You're all right until morning. Nothing happened last night. Nothing will happen tonight. Nothing can happen. You're locked and bolted in. No one can come near you. . . .* And she thought suddenly: Of course! I can stay here! Stay here locked in! Food doesn't really matter! I can stay here—safely till help comes! Even if it's a day—or two days. . . .

Stay here. Yes, but could she stay here? Hour after hour—with no one to speak to, with nothing to do but *think . . .*

She'd begin to think of Cornwall—of Hugo—of—of what she'd said to Cyril. Horrid whiny little boy, always pestering her. . . . *"Miss Claythorne, why can't I swim out to the rock? I can. I know I can."*

Was it her voice that had answered? *"Of course you can, Cyril, really. I know that."*

"Can I go then, Miss Claythorne?"

"Well, you see, Cyril, your mother gets so nervous about you. I'll tell you what. Tomorrow you can swim out to the rock. I'll talk to your mother on the beach and distract her attention. And then, when she looks for you, there you'll be standing on the rock waving to her! It *will* be a surprise!"

"Oh, good egg, Miss Claythorne! That will be a lark!"

She'd said it now. Tomorrow! Hugo was going to Newquay. When he came back—it would be all over. . . .

Yes, but supposing it wasn't? Supposing it went wrong? Cyril might be rescued in time. And then—then he'd say, *"Miss Claythorne said I could."* Well, what of it? One must take *some* risk! If the worst happened she'd brazen it out. *"How can you tell such a wicked lie, Cyril? Of course I never said any such thing!"* They'd believe her all right. Cyril often told stories. He was an untruthful

134

child. Cyril would know, of course. But that didn't matter. . . . And anyway nothing *would* go wrong. She'd pretend to swim out after him. But she'd arrive too late. . . . Nobody would ever suspect. . . .

Had Hugo suspected? Was that why he had looked at her in that queer far-off way . . . ? Had Hugo *known?* Was that why he had gone off after the inquest so hurriedly?

He hadn't answered the one letter she had written to him. . . .

Hugo . . .

Vera turned restlessly in bed. No, no, she mustn't think of Hugo. It hurt too much! That was all over, over and done with. . . . Hugo must be forgotten. . . . Why, this evening, had she suddenly felt that Hugo was in the room with her?

She stared up at the ceiling, stared at the big black hook in the middle of the room. She'd never noticed that hook before. The seaweed had hung from that. . . .

She shivered as she remembered that cold, clammy touch on her neck. . . . She didn't like that hook on the ceiling. It drew your eyes, fascinated you . . . a big black hook. . . .

v .

Ex-Inspector Blore sat on the side of his bed. His small eyes, red-rimmed and bloodshot, were alert in the solid mass of his face. He was like a wild boar waiting to charge. He felt no inclination to sleep. The menace was coming very near now. . . . Six out of ten! For all his sagacity, for all his caution and astuteness, the old judge had gone the way of the rest.

Blore snorted with a kind of savage satisfaction. What was it the old geezer had said? "We must be very careful. . . ."

Self-righteous smug old hypocrite. Sitting up in court feeling like God Almighty. He'd got his all right. . . . No more being careful for him.

And now there were four of them. The girl, Lombard,

Armstrong and himself. Very soon another of them would go. . . . But it wouldn't be William Henry Blore. He'd see to that all right.

(But the revolver . . . What about the revolver? That was the disturbing factor—the revolver!)

Blore sat on his bed, his brow furrowed, his little eyes creased and puckered while he pondered the problem of the revolver. . . . In the silence he could hear the clocks strike downstairs. Midnight. He relaxed a little now—even went so far as to lie down on his bed. But he did not undress.

He lay there, thinking. Going over the whole business from the beginning, methodically. painstakingly, as he had been wont to do in his police officer days. It was thoroughness that paid in the end.

The candle was burning down. Looking to see if the matches were within easy reach of his hand, he blew it out. Strangely enough, he found the darkness disquieting. It was as though a thousand age-old fears awoke and struggled for supremacy in his brain. Faces floated in the air—the judge's face crowned with that mockery of gray wool—the cold dead face of Mrs. Rogers—the convulsed purple face of Anthony Marston. . . . Another face—pale, spectacled, with a small, straw-colored mustache . . . a face he had seen sometime or other—but when? Not on the island. No, much longer ago than that. Funny, that he couldn't put a name to it. . . . Silly sort of face really—fellow looked a bit of a mug.

Of course! It came to him with a real shock. Landor!

Odd to think he'd completely forgotten what Landor looked like. Only yesterday he'd been trying to recall the fellow's face, and hadn't been able to. And now here it was, every feature clear and distinct, as though he had seen it only yesterday. . . .

Landor had had a wife—a thin slip of a woman with a worried face. There'd been a kid too, a girl about fourteen. For the first time, he wondered what had become of them. . . .

(The revolver. What had become of the revolver? That was much more important. . . .) The more he thought about it the more puzzled he was. . . . He didn't understand this revolver business. . . . Somebody in the house had got that revolver. . . .

Downstairs a clock struck one. Blore's thoughts were cut short. He sat up on the bed, suddenly alert. For he had heard a sound—a very faint sound—somewhere outside his bedroom door. *There was someone moving about in the darkened house.* The perspiration broke out on his forehead. Who was it, moving secretly and silently along the corridors? Someone who was up to no good, he'd bet that!

Noiselessly, in spite of his heavy build, he dropped off the bed and with two strides was standing by the door listening. But the sound did not come again. Nevertheless Blore was convinced that he was not mistaken. He had heard a footfall just outside his door. The hair rose slightly on his scalp. He knew fear again. . . .

Someone creeping about stealthily in the night. . . . He listened—but the sound was not repeated.

And now a new temptation assailed him. He wanted, desperately, to go out and investigate. If he could only see who it was prowling about in the darkness. But to open his door would be the action of a fool. Very likely that was exactly what the other was waiting for. He might even have meant Blore to hear what he had heard, counting on him coming out to investigate.

Blore stood rigid—listening. He could hear sounds everywhere now, cracks, rustles, mysterious whispers—but his dogged, realistic brain knew them for what they were—the creations of his own heated imagination. And then suddenly he heard something that was *not* imagination. Footsteps, very soft, very cautious, but plainly audible to a man listening with all his ears as Blore was listening. They came softly along the corridor (both Lombard's and Armstrong's rooms were further from the stair head than his). They passed his door without hesitating or faltering.

And as they did so, Blore made up his mind. He meant to see who it was! The footsteps had definitely passed his door going to the stairs. Where was the man going? When Blore acted, he acted quickly, surprisingly so for a man who looked so heavy and slow. He tiptoed back to the bed, slipped matches into his pocket, detached the plug of the electric lamp by his bed, and picked it up winding the flex round it. It was a chromium affair with a heavy ebonite base—a useful weapon.

He sprinted noiselessly across the room, removed the chair from under the door handle and with precaution unlocked and unbolted the door. He stepped out into the corridor. There was a faint sound in the hall below. Blore ran noiselessly in his stockinged feet to the head of the stairs. At that moment he realized why it was he had heard all these sounds so clearly. The wind had died down completely and the sky must have cleared. There was faint moonlight coming in through the landing window and it illuminated the hall below. Blore had an instantaneous glimpse of a figure just passing out through the front door.

In the act of running down the stairs in pursuit, he paused. Once again, he had nearly made a fool of himself! This was a trap, perhaps, to lure him out of the house!

But what the other man didn't realize was that he had made a mistake, had delivered himself neatly into Blore's hands. For, of the three tenanted rooms upstairs, *one must now be empty*. All that had to be done was to ascertain *which!* Blore went swiftly back along the corridor. He paused first at Dr. Armstrong's door and tapped. There was no answer. He waited a minute, then went on to Philip Lombard's room. Here the answer came at once. "Who's there?"

"It's Blore. I don't think Armstrong is in his room. Wait a minute." He went on to the door at the end of the corridor. Here he tapped again. "Miss Claythorne. Miss Claythorne."

Vera's voice, startled, answered him. "Who is it? What's the matter?"

"It's all right, Miss Claythorne. Wait a minute. I'll come back."

He raced back to Lombard's room. The door opened as he did so. Lombard stood there. He held a candle in his left hand. He had pulled on his trousers over his pajamas. His right hand rested in the pocket of his pajama jacket. He said sharply, "What the hell's all this?"

Blore explained rapidly. Lombard's eyes lit up. *"Armstrong—eh? So he's our pigeon!"* He moved along to Armstrong's door. "Sorry, Blore, but I don't take anything on trust."

He rapped sharply on the panel. "Armstrong—Armstrong."

There was no answer. Lombard dropped to his knees and peered through the keyhole. He inserted his little finger gingerly into the lock. He said, "Key's not in the door on the inside."

Blore said, "That means he locked it on the outside and took it with him."

Philip nodded, "Ordinary precaution to take. *We'll get him, Blore. . . .* This time, *we'll get him!* Half a second."

He raced along to Vera's room. "Vera."

"Yes."

"We're hunting Armstrong. He's out of his room. Whatever you do, *don't open your door.* Understand?"

"Yes, I understand."

"If Armstrong comes along and says that I've been killed, or Blore's been killed, *pay no attention.* See? Only open your door if *both Blore and I* speak to you. Got that?"

Vera said, "Yes. I'm not a complete fool."

Lombard said, "Good."

He joined Blore. He said, "And now—after him! The hunt's up!"

Blore said, "We'd better be careful. He's got a revolver, remember."

Philip Lombard, racing down the stairs, chuckled. He said, "That's where you're wrong." He undid the front door, remarking, "Latch pushed back—so that he could get in again easily." He went on, "I've got that revolver!" He took it half out of his pocket as he spoke. "Found it put back in my drawer tonight."

Blore stopped dead on the doorstep. His face changed. Philip Lombard saw it. He said impatiently, "Don't be a damned fool, Blore! I'm not going to shoot you! Go back and barricade yourself in if you like! I'm off after Armstrong."

He started off into the moonlight. Blore, after a minute's hesitation, followed him. He thought to himself: I suppose I'm asking for it. But after all— After all he had tackled criminals armed with revolvers before now. Whatever else he lacked, Blore did not lack courage. Show him the danger and he would tackle it pluckily. He was not afraid of danger in the open, only of danger undefined and tinged with the supernatural.

vi.

Vera, left to wait results, got up and dressed. She glanced over once or twice at the door. It was a good solid door. It was both bolted and locked and had an oak chair wedged under the handle. It could not be broken open by force. Certainly not by Dr. Armstrong. He was not a physically powerful man. If she were Armstrong intent on murder, it was cunning that she would employ, not force.

She amused herself by reflecting on the means he might employ. He might, as Philip had suggested, announce that one of the other two men was dead. Or he might possibly pretend to be mortally wounded himself, might drag himself groaning to her door.

There were other possibilities. He might inform her that the house was on fire. More, he might actually set the house on fire. . . . Yes, that would be a possibility. Lure the other two men out of the house, then, having previously laid a trail of petrol, he might set light to it. And she, like an idiot, would remain barricaded in her room until it was too late.

She crossed over to the window. Not too bad. At a pinch one could escape that way. It would mean a drop— but there was a handy flowerbed.

She sat down and, picking up her diary, began to write in it in a clear, flowing hand. One must pass the time.

Suddenly she stiffened to attention. She had heard a sound. It was, she thought, a sound like breaking glass.

And it came from somewhere downstairs. She listened hard, but the sound was not repeated.

She heard, or thought she heard, stealthy sounds of footsteps, the creak of stairs, the rustle of garments—but there was nothing definite, and she concluded, as Blore had done earlier, that such sounds had their origin in her own imagination.

But presently she heard sounds of a more concrete nature. People moving about downstairs—the murmur of voices. Then the very decided sound of someone mounting the stairs—doors opening and shutting—feet going up to the attic overhead. More noises from there. Finally the steps came along the passage. Lombard's voice said, "Vera? You all right?"

"Yes. What's happened?"

Blore's voice said, "Will you let us in?"

Vera went to the door. She removed the chair, unlocked the door and slid back the bolt. She opened the door. The two men were breathing hard; their feet and the bottom of their trousers were soaking wet.

She said again, "What's happened?"

Lombard said, *"Armstrong's disappeared. . . ."*

vii.

Vera cried, "What?"

Lombard said, "Vanished clean off the island."

Blore concurred, "Vanished—that's the word! Like some damned conjuring trick."

Vera said impatiently, "Nonsense! He's hiding somewhere!"

Blore said, "No, he isn't! I tell you, there's nowhere to hide on this island. It's as bare as your hand! There's moonlight outside. As clear as day it is. *And he's not to be found."*

Vera said, "He doubled back into the house."

Blore said, "We thought of that. We've searched the house too. You must have heard us. *He's not here,* I tell you. He's gone—clean vanished, vamoosed. . . ."

Vera said incredulously, "I don't believe it."

Lombard said, "It's true, my dear." He paused and then said, "There's one other little fact. A pane in the dining-room window has been smashed—*and there are only three little Indian boys on the table.*"

15

■

THREE PEOPLE sat eating breakfast in the kitchen. Outside, the sun shone. It was a lovely day. The storm was a thing of the past. And with the change in the weather, a change had come in the mood of the prisoners on the island. They felt now like people just awakening from a nightmare. There was danger, yes, but it was danger in daylight. That paralyzing atmosphere of fear that had wrapped them round like a blanket yesterday while the wind howled outside was gone.

Lombard said, "We'll try heliographing today with a mirror from the highest point of the island. Some bright lad wandering on the cliff will recognize SOS when he sees it, I hope. In the evening we could try a bonfire—only there isn't much wood—and anyway they might just think it was song and dance and merriment."

Vera said, "Surely someone can read Morse. And then they'll come to take us off. Long before this evening."

Lombard said, "The weather's cleared all right, but the sea hasn't gone down yet. Terrific swell on! They won't be able to get a boat near the island before tomorrow."

Vera cried, "Another night in his place!"

Lombard shrugged his shoulders. "May as well face it! Twenty-four hours will do it, I think. If we can last out that, we'll be all right."

Blore cleared his throat. He said, "We'd better come to a clear understanding. *What's happened to Armstrong?*"

Lombard said, "Well, we've got one piece of evidence. Only three little Indian boys left on the dinner table. It looks as though Armstrong had got his quietus."

Vera said, "Then why haven't you found his dead body?"

Blore said, "Exactly."

Lombard shook his head. He said, "It's damned odd—no getting over it."

Blore said doubtfully, "It might have been thrown into the sea."

Lombard said sharply, "By whom? You? Me? You saw him go out of the front door. You come along and find me in my room. We go out and search together. When the devil had I time to kill him and carry his body round the island?"

Blore said, "I don't know. But I do know one thing."

Lombard said, "What's that?"

Blore said, "The revolver. It was your revolver. It's in your possession now. There's nothing to show that it hasn't been in your possession all along."

"Come now, Blore, we were all searched."

"Yes, you'd hidden it away before that happened. Afterwards you just took it back again."

"My good blockhead, I swear to you that it was put back in my drawer. Greatest surprise I ever had in my life when I found it there."

Blore said, "You ask us to believe a thing like that! Why the devil should Armstrong, or anyone else for that matter, put it back?"

Lombard raised his shoulders hopelessly. "I haven't the least idea. It's just crazy. The last thing one would expect. There seems no point in it."

Blore agreed. "No, there isn't. You might have thought of a better story."

"Rather proof that I'm telling the truth, isn't it?"

"I don't look at it that way."

Philip said, "You wouldn't."

Blore said, "Look here, Mr. Lombard, if you're an honest man, as you pretend—"

Philip murmured, "When did I lay claims to being an honest man? No, indeed, I never said that."

Blore went on stolidly, "If you're speaking the truth—there's only one thing to be done. As long as you have that revolver, Miss Claythorne and I are at your mercy.

The only fair thing is to put that revolver with the other things that are locked up—and you and I will hold the two keys still."

Philip Lombard lit a cigarette. As he puffed smoke, he said, "Don't be an ass."

"You won't agree to that?"

"No, I won't. That revolver's mine. I need it to defend myself—and I'm going to keep it."

Blore said, "In that case we're bound to come to one conclusion."

"That I'm U. N. Owen? Think what you damned well please. But I'll ask you, if that's so, why I didn't pot you with the revolver last night? I could have, about twenty times over."

Blore shook his head. He said, "I don't know—and that's a fact. You must have had some reason."

Vera had taken no part in the discussion. She stirred now and said, "I think you're both behaving like a pair of idiots."

Lombard looked at her. "What's this?"

Vera said, "You've forgotten the nursery rhyme. Don't you see there's a clue there?"

She recited in a meaning voice:

Four little Indian boys going out to sea;
A red herring swallowed one and then there were three.

She went on: "*A red herring*—that's the vital clue. *Armstrong's not dead.* . . . He took away the china Indian to make you think he was. You may say what you like—Armstrong's on the island still. His disappearance is just a red herring across the track. . . ."

Lombard sat down again. He said, "You know, you may be right."

Blore said, "Yes, but if so, where is he? We've searched the place. Outside and inside."

Vera said scornfully, "We all searched for the revolver, didn't we, and couldn't find it? But it was somewhere all the time!"

Lombard murmured, "There's a slight difference in size, my dear, between a man and a revolver."

Vera said, "I don't care—I'm sure I'm right."

Blore murmured, "Rather giving himself away, wasn't it? Actually mentioning a red herring in the verse. He could have written it up a bit different."

Vera cried, "But don't you *see*, he's *mad*? It's all mad! The whole thing of going by the rhyme is mad! Dressing up the judge, killing Rogers when he was chopping sticks—drugging Mrs. Rogers so that she overslept herself—arranging for a bumblebee when Miss Brent died! It's like some horrible child playing a game. It's all got to fit in."

Blore said, "Yes, you're right." He thought a minute. "At any rate there's no Zoo on the island. He'll have a bit of trouble getting over that."

Vera cried, "Don't you see? *We're the Zoo.* . . . Last night, we were hardly human any more. *We're the Zoo.* . . ."

ii.

They spent the morning on the cliffs, taking it in turns to flash a mirror at the mainland. There were no signs that anyone saw them. No answering signals. The day was fine, with a slight haze. Below the sea heaved in a gigantic swell. There were no boats out. They had made another abortive search of the island. There was no trace of the missing physician.

Vera looked up at the house from where they were standing. She said, her breath coming with a slight catch in it, "One feels safer here, out in the open. . . . Don't let's go back into the house again."

Lombard said, "Not a bad idea. We're pretty safe here; no one can get at us without our seeing him a long time beforehand."

Vera said, "We'll stay here."

Blore said, "Have to pass the night somewhere. We'll have to go back to the house then."

Vera shuddered. "I can't bear it. I *can't* go through another night!"

Philip said, "You'll be safe enough—locked in your room."

Vera murmured, "I suppose so." She stretched out her hands, murmuring, "It's lovely—to feel the sun again. . . ." She thought, "How odd . . . I'm almost happy. And yet I suppose I'm actually in danger. . . . Somehow —now—nothing seems to matter . . . not in daylight. . . . I feel full of power—I feel that I can't die. . . ."

Blore was looking at his wristwatch. He said, "It's two o'clock. What about lunch?"

Vera said obstinately, "I'm not going back to the house. I'm going to say here—in the open."

"Oh, come now, Miss Claythorne. Got to keep your strength up, you know."

Vera said, "If I even see a tinned tongue, I shall be sick! I don't want any food. People go days on end with nothing sometimes when they're on a diet."

Blore said, "Well, I need my meals regular. What about you, Mr. Lombard?"

Philip said, "You know, I don't relish the idea of tinned tongue particularly. I'll stay here with Miss Claythorne."

Blore hesitated. Vera said, "I shall be quite all right. I don't think he'll shoot me as soon as your back is turned if that's what you're afraid of."

Blore said, "It's all right if you say so. But we agreed we ought not to separate."

Philip said, "You're the one who wants to go into the lion's den. I'll come with you if you like."

"No, you won't," said Blore. "You'll stay here."

Philip laughed. "So you're still afraid of me? Why, I could shoot you both this minute if I liked."

Blore said, "Yes, but that wouldn't be according to plan. It's one at a time, and it's got to be done in a certain way."

"Well," said Philip, "you seem to know all about it."

"Of course," said Blore, "it's a bit jumpy going up to the house alone—"

Philip said softly, "And therefore, *will I lend you my*

revolver? Answer, no, I will *not!* Not quite so simple as that, thank you."

Blore shrugged his shoulders and began to make his way up the steep slope to the house. Lombard said softly, "Feeding time at the Zoo! The animals are very regular in their habits!"

Vera said anxiously, "Isn't it very risky, what he's doing?"

"In the sense you mean—no, I don't think it is! Armstrong's not armed, you know, and anyway Blore is twice a match for him in physique and he's very much on his guard. And anyway it's a sheer impossibility that Armstrong can be in the house. I *know* he's not there."

"But—what other solution is there?"

Philip said softly, "There's Blore."

"Oh—do you really think—?"

"Listen, my girl. You heard Blore's story. You've got to admit that if it's true, *I can't possibly have had anything to do with Armstrong's disappearance.* His story clears me. *But it doesn't clear him.* We've only *his* word for it that he heard footsteps and saw a man going downstairs and out at the front door. The whole thing may be a lie. He may have got rid of Armstrong a couple of hours before that."

"How?"

Lombard shrugged his shoulders. "That we don't know. But if you ask me, we've only one danger to fear—and that danger is Blore! What do we know about the man? Less than nothing! All this ex-policeman story may be bunkum! He may be anybody—a mad millionaire—a crazy businessman—an escaped inmate of Broadmoor. One thing's certain. He *could* have done every one of these crimes."

Vera had gone rather white. She said in a slightly breathless voice, "And supposing he gets—us?"

Lombard said softly, patting the revolver in his pocket, "I'm going to take very good care he doesn't." Then he looked at her curiously. "Touching faith in me, haven't you, Vera? Quite sure I wouldn't shoot you?"

Vera said, "One has got to trust someone. . . . As a matter of fact I think you're wrong about Blore. I still think it's Armstrong." She turned to him suddenly. "Don't you feel—all the time—that there's *someone*. Someone watching and waiting?"

Lombard said slowly, "That's just nerves."

Vera said eagerly, "Then you *have* felt it?" She shivered. She bent a little closer. "Tell me—you don't think—" She broke off, went on, "I read a story once—about two judges that came to a small American town—from the Supreme Court. They administered justice—Absolute Justice. *Because—they didn't come from this world at all....*"

Lombard raised his eyebrows. He said, "Heavenly visitants, eh? No, I don't believe in the supernatural. This business is human enough."

Vera said, in a low voice, "Sometimes—I'm not sure...."

Lombard looked at her. He said, "That's conscience...." After a moment's silence he said very quietly, "So you *did* drown that kid after all?"

"I didn't! I didn't! You've no right to say that!"

He laughed easily. "Oh, yes, you did, my good girl! I don't know why. Can't imagine. There was a man in it probably. Was that it?"

A sudden feeling of lassitude, of intense weariness, spread over Vera's limbs. She said in a dull voice, "Yes—there was a man in it...."

Lombard said softly, "Thanks. That's what I wanted to know...."

Vera sat up suddenly. She exclaimed, "What was that? It wasn't an earthquake?"

Lombard said, "No, no. Queer, though—a thud shook the ground. And I thought—did you hear a sort of cry? I did."

They stared up at the house. Lombard said, "It came from there. We'd better go up and see."

"No, no, I'm not going."

"Please yourself. I am."

Vera said desperately, "All right. I'll come with you."

They walked up the slope to the house. The terrace was peaceful and innocuous looking in the sunshine. They hesitated there a minute; then instead of entering by the front door, they made a cautious circuit of the house. They found Blore. He was spreadeagled on the stone terrace on the east side, his head crushed and mangled by a great block of white marble.

Philip looked up. He said, "Whose is that window just above?"

Vera said in a low, shuddering voice, "It's mine— and *that's the clock from my mantelpiece*. . . . I remember now. It was—shaped like a bear. . . ." She repeated and her voice shook and quavered, "It was shaped like a bear. . . ."

iii.

Philip grasped her shoulder. He said, and his voice was urgent and grim, "This settles it. Armstrong is in hiding somewhere in that house. I'm going to get him."

But Vera clung to him. She cried, "Don't be a fool. It's *us* now! We're next! He *wants* us to look for him! He's *counting* on it!"

Philip stopped. He said thoughtfully, "There's something in that."

Vera cried, "At any rate, you do admit now I was right."

He nodded. "Yes—you win! It's Armstrong all right. But where the devil did he hide himself? We went over the place with a fine-tooth comb."

Vera said urgently, "If you didn't find him last night, you *won't find him now*. . . . That's common sense."

Lombard said reluctantly, "Yes, but—"

"He must have prepared a secret place beforehand— naturally—of course it's just what he would do. You know, like a Priest's Hole in old manor houses."

"This isn't an old house of that kind."

"He could have had one made."

Philip Lombard shook his head. He said, "We measured the place—that first morning. I'll swear there's no space unaccounted for."

Vera said, "There must be. . . ."

Lombard said, "I'd like to see—"

Vera cried, "Yes, you'd like to see! And he knows that! He's in there—waiting for you."

Lombard said, half bringing out the revolver from his pocket, "I've got this, you know."

"You said Blore was all right—that he was more than a match for Armstrong. So he was physically, and he was on the lookout too. But what you don't seem to realize is that Armstrong is *mad!* And a madman has all the advantages on his side. He's twice as cunning as anyone sane can be."

Lombard put back the revolver in his pocket. He said, "Come on, then."

iv.

Lombard said at last, "What are we going to do when night comes?"

Vera didn't answer. He went on accusingly, "You haven't thought of that?"

She said helplessly, "What *can* we do? Oh, my God, I'm *frightened.* . . ."

Philip Lombard said thoughtfully, "It's fine weather. There will be a moon. We must find a place—up by the top cliffs perhaps. We can sit there and wait for the morning. *We mustn't go to sleep.* . . . We must watch the whole time. And if anyone comes up towards us, I shall shoot!" He paused, "You'll be cold, perhaps, in that thin dress?"

Vera said with a raucous laugh, "Cold? I should be colder if I were dead!"

Philip Lombard said quietly, "Yes, that's true. . . ."

Vera moved restlessly. She said, "I shall go mad if I sit here any longer. Let's move about."

"All right."

They paced slowly up and down, along the line of the rocks overlooking the sea. The sun was dropping towards the west. The light was golden and mellow. It enveloped them in a golden glow. Vera said, with a sudden nervous little giggle, "Pity we can't have a bathe. . . ."

Philip was looking down towards the sea. He said

abruptly, "What's that, there? You see—by that big rock? No—a little further to the right."

Vera stared. She said, "It looks like somebody's clothes!"

"A bather, eh?" Lombard laughed. "Queer. I suppose it's only seaweed."

Vera said, "Let's go and look."

"It is clothes," said Lombard as they drew nearer. "A bundle of them. That's a boot. Come on, let's scramble along here."

They scrambled over the rocks. Vera stopped suddenly. She said, *"It's not clothes—it's a man. . . ."*

The man was wedged between two rocks, flung there by the tide earlier in the day. Lombard and Vera reached it in a last scramble. They bent down. *A purple discolored face—a hideous, drowned face. . . .* Lombard said, "My God! It's *Armstrong. . . ."*

16

■

EONS PASSED . . . worlds spun and whirled. . . . Time was motionless. . . . It stood still—it passed through a thousand ages. . . . No, it was only a minute or so. . . . Two people were standing looking down on a dead man. . . . Slowly, very slowly, Vera Claythorne and Philip Lombard lifted their heads and looked into each other's eyes. . . .

ii.

Lombard laughed. He said, "So that's it, is it, Vera?"

Vera said, "There's no one on the island—no one at all—*except us two. . . ."* Her voice was a whisper—nothing more.

Lombard said, "Precisely. So we know where we are, don't we?"

Vera said, "How was it worked—that trick with the marble bear?"

He shrugged his shoulders. "A conjuring trick, my dear —a very good one. . . ."

Their eyes met again. Vera thought, *Why did I never see his face properly before. A wolf—that's what it is —a wolf's face. . . . Those horrible teeth. . . .*

Lombard said, and his voice was a snarl—dangerous— menacing, "This is the end, you understand. We've come to the truth now. *And it's the end. . . ."*

Vera said quietly, "I understand. . . ." She stared out to sea. General Macarthur had stared out to sea—when— only yesterday? Or was it the day before? He too had said, *"This is the end. . . ."* He had said it with acceptance —almost with welcome. But to Vera the words—the thought—brought rebellion. No, it should not be the end. She looked down at the dead man. She said, "Poor Dr. Armstrong. . . ."

Lombard sneered. "What's this? Womanly pity?"

Vera said, "Why not? Haven't *you* any pity?"

He said, "I've no pity for you. Don't expect it!"

Vera looked down again at the body. She said, "We must move him. Carry him up to the house."

"To join the other victims, I suppose? All neat and tidy. As far as I'm concerned he can stay where he is."

Vera said, "At any rate, let's get him out of reach of the sea."

Lombard laughed. He said, "If you like."

He bent—tugging at the body. Vera leaned against him, helping him. She pulled and tugged with all her might. Lombard panted. "Not such an easy job."

They managed it, however, drawing the body clear of high-water mark. Lombard said as he straightened up, "Satisfied?"

Vera said, "Quite."

Her tone warned him. He spun round. Even as he clapped his hand to his pocket he knew that he would find it empty. She had moved a yard or two away and was facing him, revolver in hand.

Lombard said, "So that's the reason for your womanly solicitude! You wanted to pick my pocket."

She nodded. She held it steadily and unwaveringly.

Death was very near to Philip Lombard now. It had never, he knew, been nearer. Nevertheless he was not beaten yet. He said authoritatively, "Give that revolver to me."

Vera laughed.

Lombard said, "Come on, hand it over."

His quick brain was working. Which way—which method—talk her over—lull her into security—or a swift dash— All his life Lombard had taken the risky way. He took it now. He spoke slowly, argumentatively. "Now look here, my dear girl, you just listen—"

And then he sprang. Quick as a panther—as any other feline creature. . . . Automatically Vera pressed the trigger. . . . Lombard's leaping body stayed poised in midspring, then crashed heavily to the ground.

Vera came warily forward, the revolver ready in her hand. But there was no need of caution. Philip Lombard was dead—shot through the heart. . . .

iii.

Relief possessed Vera—enormous, exquisite relief. At last it was over. There was no more fear—no more steeling of her nerves. . . . She was alone on the island. . . . Alone with nine dead bodies. . . . But what did that matter? *She* was alive. . . . She sat there—exquisitely happy —exquisitely at peace. . . . No more fear. . . .

iv.

The sun was setting when Vera moved at last. Sheer reaction had kept her immobile. There had been no room in her for anything but the glorious sense of safety.

She realized now that she was hungry and sleepy. Principally sleepy. She wanted to throw herself on her bed and sleep and sleep and sleep. . . . Tomorrow, perhaps, they would come and rescue her—but she didn't really mind. She didn't mind staying here. Not now that she was alone. . . . Oh! blessed, blessed peace. . . .

She got to her feet and glanced up at the house. Nothing to be afraid of any longer! No terrors waiting for her! Just an ordinary well-built modern house. And yet, a little earlier in the day, she had not been able to look at it without shivering. . . .

Fear—what a strange thing fear was. . . . Well, it was over now. She had conquered—had triumphed over the most deadly peril. By her own quick-wittedness and adroitness she had turned the tables on her would-be destroyer.

She began to walk up towards the house. The sun was setting, the sky to the west was streaked with red and orange. It was beautiful and peaceful. . . . Vera thought: The whole thing might be a dream. . . .

How tired she was—terribly tired. Her limbs ached, her eyelids were drooping. Not to be afraid any more. . . . To sleep. Sleep . . . sleep . . . sleep . . . To sleep safely since she was alone on the island. One little Indian boy left all alone. She smiled to herself.

She went in at the front door. The house, too, felt strangely peaceful. Vera thought: ordinarily one wouldn't care to sleep where there's a dead body in practically every bedroom!

Should she go to the kitchen and get herself something to eat? She hesitated a moment, then decided against it. She was really too tired. . . . She paused by the dining-room door. There were still three little china figures in the middle of the table. Vera laughed. She said, "You're behind the times, my dears."

She picked up two of them and tossed them out through the window. She heard them crash on the stone of the terrace. The third little figure she picked up and held in her hand. She said, "You can come with me. We've won, my dear! We've won!"

The hall was dim in the dying light. Vera, the little Indian clasped in her hand, began to mount the stairs. Slowly, because her legs were suddenly very tired. *One little Indian boy left all alone.* How did it end? Oh, yes! *He got married and then there were none.*

Married . . . Funny, how she suddenly got the feeling again that Hugo was in the house . . . Very strong. Yes, Hugo was upstairs waiting for her. Vera said to herself: Don't be a fool. You're so tired that you're imagining the most fantastic things. . . .

Slowly up the stairs. . . . At the top of them something fell from her hand, making hardly any noise on the soft-pile carpet. She did not notice that she had dropped the revolver. She was only conscious of clasping a little china figure. How very quiet the house was. And yet—it didn't seem like an empty house. . . . Hugo, upstairs, waiting for her. . . .

One little Indian boy left all alone. What was the last line again? Something about being married—or was it something else? She had come now to the door of her room. Hugo was waiting for her inside—she was quite sure of it.

She opened the door. . . . She gave a gasp. . . . *What was that*—hanging from the hook in the ceiling? *A rope with a noose all ready? And a chair to stand upon—a chair that could be kicked away. . . . That was what Hugo wanted. . . .* And of course that was the last line of the rhyme. *He went and hanged himself and then there were none. . . .*

The little china figure fell from her hand. It rolled unheeded and broke against the fender. Like an automaton Vera moved forward. This was the end—here where the cold wet hand (Cyril's hand, of course) had touched her throat. . . .

"You can go to the rock, Cyril. . . ."

That was what murder was—as easy as that! But afterwards you went on remembering. . . .

She climbed up on the chair, her eyes staring in front of her like a sleepwalker's. . . . She adjusted the noose round her neck. Hugo was there to see she did what she had to do.

She kicked away the chair. . . .

EPILOGUE

SIR THOMAS LEGGE, Assistant Commissioner at Scotland Yard, said irritably, "But the whole thing's incredible!"

Inspector Maine said respectfully, "I know, sir."

The A.C. went on, "Ten people dead on an island and not a living soul on it. It doesn't make sense!"

Inspector Maine said stolidly, "Nevertheless, it *happened*, sir."

Sir Thomas Legge said, "Damn it all, Maine, somebody must have killed 'em."

"That's just our problem, sir."

"Nothing helpful in the doctor's report?"

"No, sir. Wargrave and Lombard were shot, the first through the head, the second through the heart. Miss Brent and Marston died of cyanide poisoning. Mrs. Rogers died of an overdose of chloral. Rogers' head was split open. Blore's head was crushed in. Armstrong died of drowning. Macarthur's skull was fractured by a blow on the back of the head and Vera Claythorne was hanged."

The A.C. winced. He said, "Nasty business—all of it." He considered for a minute or two. He said irritably, "Do you mean to say that you haven't been able to get anything helpful out of the Sticklehaven people? Dash it, they must know something."

Inspector Maine shrugged his shoulders. "They're ordinary decent seafaring folk. They know that the island was bought by a man called Owen—and that's about all the do know."

"Who provisioned the island and made all the necessary arrangements?"

"Man called Morris. Isaac Morris."

"And what does he say about it all?"

"He can't say anything, sir, he's dead."

The A.C. frowned. "Do we know anything about this Morris?"

"Oh, yes, sir, we know about him. He wasn't a very savory gentleman, Mr. Morris. He was implicated in that share-pushing fraud of Bennito's three years ago—we're sure of that though we can't prove it. And he was mixed up in the dope business. And again we can't prove it. He was a very careful man, Morris."

"And he was behind this island business?"

"Yes, sir, he put through the sale—though he made it clear that he was buying Indian Island for a third party, unnamed."

"Surely there's something to be found out on the financial angle, there?"

Inspector Maine smiled. "Not if you knew Morris! He can wangle figures until the best chartered accountant in the country wouldn't know if he was on his head or his heels! We've had a taste of that in the Bennito business. No, he covered his employer's tracks all right."

The other man sighed. Inspector Maine went on, "It was Morris who made all the arrangements down at Sticklehaven. Represented himself as acting for 'Mr. Owen.' And it was he who explained to the people down there that there was some experiment on—some bet about living on a 'desert island' for a week—and that no notice was to be taken of any appeal for help from out there."

Sir Thomas Legge stirred uneasily. He said, "And you're telling me that those people didn't smell a rat? Not even then?"

Maine shrugged his shoulders. He said, "You're forgetting, sir, that Indian Island previous belonged to young Elmer Robson, the American. He had the most extraordinary parties down there. I've no doubt the local people's eyes fairly popped out over them. But they got used to it and they'd begun to feel that anything to do with Indian Island would necessarily be incredible. It's natural, that, sir, when you come to think of it."

The Assistant Commissioner admitted gloomily that he supposed it was.

Maine said, "Fred Narracott—that's the man who took the party out there—did say one thing that was illuminating. He said he was surprised to see what sort of people these were. 'Not at all like Mr. Robson's parties.' I think it was the fact that they were all so normal and so quiet that made him override Morris' orders and take out a boat to the island after he'd heard about the SOS signals."

"When did he and the other men go?"

"The signals were seen by a party of boy scouts on the morning of the 11th. There was no possibility of getting out there that day. The men got there on the afternoon of the 12th at the first moment possible to run a boat ashore there. They're all quite positive that nobody could have left the island before they got there. There was a big sea on after the storm."

"Couldn't someone have swum ashore?"

"It's over a mile to the coast and there were heavy seas and big breakers inshore. And there were a lot of people, boy scouts and others on the cliffs looking out towards the island and watching."

The A.C. sighed. He said, "What about that gramophone record you found in the house? Couldn't you get hold of anything there that might help?"

Inspector Maine said, "I've been into that. It was supplied by a firm that does a lot of theatrical stuff and film effects. It was sent to U. N. Owen, Esq., c/o Isaac Morris, and was understood to be required for the amateur performance of a hitherto unacted play. The typescript of it was returned with the record."

Legge said, "And what about the subject matter, eh?"

Inspector Maine said gravely, "I'm coming to that, sir." He cleared his throat. "I've investigated those accusations as thoroughly as I can. Starting with the Rogerses who were the first to arrive on the island. They were in service with a Miss Brady who died suddenly. Can't get anything definite out of the doctor who attended her. He says they certainly didn't poison her, or anything like that, but his personal belief is that there *was* some funny business— that she died as the result of neglect on their part. Says it's the sort of thing that's quite impossible to prove.

"Then there is Mr. Justice Wargrave. That's O. K. He was the judge who sentenced Seton. By the way, Seton was guilty—unmistakably guilty. Evidence turned up later after he was hanged which proved that beyond any

158

shadow of doubt. But there was a good deal of comment at the time—nine people out of ten thought Seton was innocent and that the judge's summing up had been vindictive.

"The Claythorne girl, I find, was governess in a family where a death occurred by drowning. However, she doesn't seem to have had anything to do with it, and as a matter of fact she behaved very well, swam out to the rescue and was actually carried out to sea and only just rescued in time."

"Go on," said the A.C. with a sigh.

Maine took a deep breath. "Dr. Armstrong now. Well-known man. Had a consulting room in Harley Street. Absolutely straight and aboveboard in his profession. Haven't been able to trace any record of an illegal operation or anything of that kind. It's true that there *was* a woman called Clees who was operated on by him way back in 1925 at Leithmore, when he was attached to the hospital there. Peritonitis and she died on the operating table. Maybe he wasn't very skillful over the op.—after all he hadn't much experience—but after all clumsiness isn't a criminal offense. There was certainly no motive.

"Then there's Miss Emily Brent. Girl, Beatrice Taylor, was in service with her. Got pregnant, was turned out by her mistress and went and drowned herself. Not a nice business—but again not criminal."

"That," said the A.C., "seems to be the point. U. N. Owen dealt with cases that the law couldn't touch."

Maine went stolidly on with his list. "Young Marston was a fairly reckless car driver—had his license endorsed twice and he ought to have been prohibited from driving, in my opinion. That's all there is to him. The two names John and Lucy Combes were those of two kids he knocked down and killed near Cambridge. Some friends of his gave evidence for him and he was let off with a fine.

"Can't find anything definite about General Macarthur. Fine record—war service—all the rest of it. Arthur Richmond was serving under him in France and was killed in action. No friction of any kind between him and the General. They were close friends as a matter of fact. There were some blunders made about that time—

commanding officers sacrificed men unnecessarily—possibly this was a blunder of that kind."

"Possibly," said the A.C.

"Now, Philip Lombard. Lombard has been mixed up in some very curious shows abroad. He's sailed very near the law once or twice. Got a reputation for daring and for not being overscrupulous. Sort of fellow who might do several murders in some quiet out-of-the-way spot.

"Then we come to Blore." Maine hesitated. "He of course was one of our lot."

The other man stirred. "Blore," said the Assistant Commissioner forcibly, "was a bad hat!"

"You think so, sir?"

The A.C. said, "I always thought so. But he was clever enough to get away with it. It's my opinion that he committed black perjury in the Landor case. I wasn't happy about it at the time. But I couldn't find anything. I put Harris onto it and *he* couldn't find anything, but I'm still of the opinion that there was something to find if we'd known how to set about it. The man wasn't straight."

There was a pause, then Sir Thomas Legge said, "And Isaac Morris is dead, you say? When did he die?"

"I thought you'd soon come to that, sir. Isaac Morris died on the night of August 8th. Took an overdose of sleeping stuff—one of the barbiturates, I understand. There wasn't anything to show where it was accident or suicide."

Legge said slowly, "Care to know what I think, Maine?"

"Perhaps I can guess, sir."

Legge said heavily, "That death of Morris' is a damned sight too opportune!"

Inspector Maine nodded. He said, "I thought you'd say that, sir."

The Assistant Commissioner brought down his fist with a bang on the table. He cried out, "The whole thing's fantastic—impossible. Ten people killed on a bare rock of an island—and we don't know who did it, or why, or how."

Maine coughed. He said, "Well, it's not quite like that, sir. We do know *why*, more or less. Some fanatic with a bee in his bonnet about justice. He was out to get people who were beyond the reach of the law. He picked ten people—whether they were really guilty or not doesn't matter—"

The Commissioner stirred. He said sharply, "Doesn't it? It seems to me—" He stopped. Inspector Maine waited respectfully. With a sigh Legge shook his head. "Carry on," he said. "Just for a minute I felt I'd got somewhere. Got, as it were, the clue to the thing. It's gone now. Go ahead with what you were saying."

Maine went on, "There were ten people to be—executed, let's say. They *were* executed. U. N. Owen accomplished his task. And somehow or other he spirited himself off that island into thin air."

The A.C. said, "First-class vanishing trick. But you know, Maine, there must be an explanation."

Maine said, "You're thinking, sir, that if the man wasn't on the island, he couldn't have left the island, and according to the account of the interested parties he never was on the island. Well, then the only explanation possible is that he was actually one of the ten." The A.C. nodded. Maine said earnestly, "We thought of that, sir. We went into it. Now, to begin with, we're not quite in the dark as to what happened on Indian Island. Vera Claythorne kept a diary, so did Emily Brent. Old Wargrave made some notes—dry legal cryptic stuff, but quite clear. And Blore made notes too. All those accounts tally. The deaths occurred in this order: Marston, Mrs. Rogers, Macarthur, Rogers, Miss Brent, Wargrave. After his death Vera Claythorne's diary states that Armstrong left the house in the night and that Blore and Lombard had gone after him. Blore has one more entry in his notebook. Just two words: 'Armstrong disappeared.'

"Now, sir, it seemed to me, taking everything into account, that we might find here a perfectly good solution. Armstrong was drowned, you remember. Granting that Armstrong was mad, what was to prevent him having killed off all the others and then committed suicide by throwing himself over the cliff, or perhaps while trying to swim to the mainland?

"That was a good solution—but it won't do. No, sir, it won't do. First of all there's the police surgeon's evidence.

He got to the island early on the morning of August 13th. He couldn't say much to help us. All he could say was that all the people had been dead at least thirty-six hours and probably a good deal longer. But he was fairly definite about Armstrong. Said he must have been from eight to ten hours in the water before his body was washed up. That works out at this, that Armstrong must have gone into the sea sometime during the night of the 10th–11th—and I'll explain why. We found the point where the body was washed up—it had been wedged between two rocks and there were bits of cloth, hair, etc., on them. It must have been deposited there at high water on the 11th—that's to say round about 11 o'clock A.M. After that, the storm subsided, and succeeding high-water marks are considerably lower.

"You might say, I suppose, that Armstrong managed to polish off the other three *before* he went into the sea that night. But there's another point and one you can't get over. *Armstrong's body had been dragged above high-water mark.* We found it well above the reach of any tide. And it was laid out straight on the ground—all neat and tidy. So that settles one point definitely. *Someone* was alive on the island after Armstrong was dead."

He paused and then went on. "And that leaves—just what exactly? Here's the position early on the morning of the 11th. Armstrong has 'disappeared' (*drowned*). That leaves us three people. Lombard, Blore and Vera Claythorne. Lombard was shot. His body was down by the sea—near Armstrong's. Vera Claythorne was found hanged in her own bedroom. Blore's body was on the terrace. His head was crushed in by a heavy marble block that it seems reasonable to suppose fell on him from the window above."

The A.C. said sharply, "Whose window?"

"Vera Claythorne's. Now, sir, let's take each of these cases separately. First Philip Lombard. Let's say *he* pushed over that lump of marble onto Blore—then he doped Vera Claythorne and strung her up. Lastly, he went down to the seashore and shot himself. But if so, *who took away the revolver from him?* For that revolver was found up in the house just inside the door at the top of the stairs—Wargrave's room."

The A.C. said, "Any fingerprints on it?"

"Yes, sir, Vera Claythorne's."

"But, man alive, then—"

"I know what you're going to say, sir. That it was Vera Claythorne. That she shot Lombard, took the revolver back to the house, toppled the marble block onto Blore and then—hanged herself. And that's quite all right—up to a point. There's a chair in her bedroom and on the seat of it there are marks of seaweed same as on her shoes. Looks as though she stood on the chair, adjusted the rope round her neck and kicked away the chair.

"But that chair wasn't found kicked over. It was, like all the other chairs, neatly put back against the wall. That was done *after Vera Claythorne's death—by someone else.*

"That leaves us with Blore and if you tell me that after shooting Lombard and inducing Vera Claythorne to hang herself he then went out and pulled down a whacking great block of marble on himself by tying a string to it or something like that—well, I simply don't believe you. Men don't commit suicide that way—and what's more Blore wasn't that kind of man. *We* knew Blore—and he was not the man that you'd ever accuse of a desire for abstract justice."

The Assistant Commissioner said, "I agree."

Inspector Maine said, "And therefore, sir, there must have been *someone* else on the island. Someone who tidied up when the whole business was over. But where was he all the time—and where did he go to? The Sticklehaven people are absolutely certain that no one could have left the island before the rescue boat got there. But in that case—"

He stopped. The Assistant Commissioner said, "In that case—"

He sighed. He shook his head. He leaned forward. "But in that case," he said, *"who killed them?"*

A manuscript document sent to
Scotland Yard by the master of the
Emma Jane, *fishing trawler*

■

From my earliest youth I realized that my nature was a mass of contradictions. I have, to begin with, an incurably romantic imagination. The practice of throwing a bottle into the sea with an important document inside was one that never failed to thrill me when reading adventure stories as a child. It thrills me still—and for that reason I have adopted this course—writing my confession, enclosing it in a bottle, sealing the latter, and casting it into the waves. There is, I suppose, a hundred-to-one chance that my confession may be found—and then (or do I flatter myself?) a hitherto unsolved murder mystery will be explained.

I was born with other traits besides my romantic fancy. I have a definite sadistic delight in seeing or causing death. I remember experiments with wasps—with various garden pests. . . . From an early age I knew very strongly the lust to kill. But side by side with this went a contradictory trait—a strong sense of justice. It is abhorrent to me that an innocent person or creature should suffer or die by an act of mine. I have always felt strongly that right should prevail.

It may be understood—I think a psychologist would understand—that with my mental make-up being what it was, I adopted the law as a profession. The legal profession satisfied nearly all my instincts.

Crime and its punishment have always fascinated me. I enjoy reading every kind of detective story and thriller. I have devised for my own private amusement the most ingenious ways of carrying out a murder.

When in due course I came to preside over a court of law, that other secret instinct of mine was encouraged to develop. To see a wretched criminal squirming in the dock, suffering the tortures of the damned, as his doom came slowly and slowly nearer, was to me an exquisite pleasure. Mind you, I took no pleasure in seeing an *innocent* man there. On at least two occasions I stopped cases where to my mind the accused was palpably innocent, directing the jury that there was no case. Thanks, however, to the fairness and efficiency of our police force, the majority of the accused persons who have come before me to be tried for murder have been guilty.

I will say here that such was the case with the man Edward Seton. His appearance and manner were misleading and he created a good impression on the jury. But not only the evidence, which was clear, though unspectacular, but my own knowledge of criminals told me without any doubt that the man had actually committed the crime with which he was charged, the brutal murder of an elderly woman who trusted him.

I have a reputation as a hanging judge, but that is unfair. I have always been strictly just and scrupulous in my summing up of a case. All I have done is to protect the jury against the emotional effect of emotional appeals by some of our more emotional counsel. I have drawn their attention to the actual evidence.

For some years past I have been aware of a change within myself, a lessening of control—a desire to act instead of to judge. I have wanted—let me admit it frankly—*to commit a murder myself*. I recognized this as the desire of the artist to express himself! I was, or could be, an artist in crime! My imagination, sternly checked by the exigencies of my profession, waxed secretly to colossal force. I must—I must—I *must*—commit a murder! And what is more, it must be no ordinary murder! It must be a fantastical crime—something stupendous—out of the common! In that one respect, I have still, I think, an adolescent's imagination. I wanted something theatrical, impossible! I wanted to kill. . . . Yes, I wanted to kill. . . . But—incongruous as it may seem to some—I was restrained and hampered by my innate sense of justice. The innocent must not suffer.

And then, quite suddenly, the idea came to me—started by a chance remark uttered during casual conversation. It was a doctor to whom I was talking—some ordinary undistinguished G.P. He mentioned casually how often murder must be committed which the law was unable to touch. And he instanced a particular case—that of an old lady, a patient of his who had recently died. He was, he said, himself convinced that her death was due to the withholding of a restorative drug by a married couple who attended on her and who stood to benefit very substantially by her death. That sort of thing, he explained, was quite impossible to prove, but he was nevertheless quite sure of it in his own mind. He added that there were many cases of a similar nature going on all the time—cases of deliberate murder—and all quite untouchable by the law.

That was the beginning of the whole thing. I suddenly saw my way clear. And I determined to commit not one murder, but murder on a grand scale.

A childish rhyme of my infancy came back into my mind—the rhyme of the ten little Indian boys. It had fascinated me as a child of two—the inexorable diminishment—the sense of inevitability. I began, secretly, to collect victims. . . . I will not take up space here by going into details of how this was accomplished. I had a certain routine line of conversation which I employed with nearly everyone I met—and the results I got were really surprising. During the time I was in a nursing home I collected the case of Dr. Armstrong—a violently teetotal sister who attended on me being anxious to prove to me the evils of drink by recounting to me a case many years ago in hospital when a doctor under the influence of alcohol had killed a patient on whom he was operating. A careless question as to where the sister in question had trained, etc., soon gave me the necessary data. I tracked down the doctor and the patient mentioned without difficulty.

A conversation between two old military gossips in my club put me on the track of General Macarthur. A man who had recently returned from the Amazon gave me a devastating résumé of the activities of one Philip Lombard. An indignant *mem sahib* in Majorca recounted the tale of the Puritan Emily Brent and her wretched servant girl. Anthony Marston I selected from a large group of people who had committed similar offenses. His complete callousness and his inability to feel any responsibility for the lives he had taken made him, I considered, a type dangerous to the community and unfit to live. Ex-Inspector Blore came my way quite naturally, some of my professional brethren discussing the Landor case with freedom and vigor. I took a serious view of his offense. The police, as servants of the law, must be of a high order of integrity. For their word is perforce believed by virtue of their profession.

Finally there was the case of Vera Claythorne. It was when I was crossing the Atlantic. At a late hour one night the sole occupants of the smoking room were myself and a good-looking young man called Hugo Hamilton. Hugo Hamilton was unhappy. To assuage that unhappiness he had taken a considerable quantity of drink. He was in the maudlin confidential stage. Without much hope of any result I automatically started my routine conversational gambit. The response was startling. I can remember his words now. He said:

"You're right. Murder isn't what most people think—giving someone a dollop of arsenic—pushing them over a cliff—that sort of stuff." He leaned forward, thrusting his face into mine. He said, "I've known a murderess—known her, I tell you. And what's more I was crazy about her. . . . God help me, sometimes I think I still am. . . . It's hell, I tell you—hell— You see, she did it more or less for me. . . . Not that I ever dreamed. Women are fiends—absolute fiends—you wouldn't think a girl like that —a nice straight jolly girl—you wouldn't think she'd do that, would you? That she'd take a kid out to sea and let it drown—you wouldn't think a *woman* could do a thing like that?"

I said to him, "Are you sure she did do it?"

He said and in saying it he seemed suddenly to sober up, "I'm quite sure. Nobody else ever thought of it. But I knew the moment I looked at her—when I got back—after . . . And she knew I knew. . . . What she didn't realize was that I loved that kid. . . ." He didn't say any more, but it was easy enough for me to trace back the story and reconstruct it.

I needed a tenth victim. I found him in a man named Morris. He was a shady little creature. Amongst other things he was a dope peddler and he was responsible for inducing the daughter of friends of mine to take to drugs. She committed suicide at the age of twenty-one.

During all this time of search my plan had been gradually maturing in my mind. It was now complete and the coping stone to it was an interview I had with a doctor in Harley Street. I have mentioned that I underwent an operation. My interview in Harley Street told me that another operation would be useless. My medical adviser wrapped up the information very prettily, but I am accustomed to getting at the truth of a statement.

I did not tell the doctor of my decision—that my death should not be a slow and protracted one as it would be in the course of nature. No, my death should take place in a blaze of excitement. I would *live* before I died.

And now to the actual mechanics of the crime of Indian Island. To acquire the island, using the man Morris to cover my tracks, was easy enough. He was an expert in that sort of thing. Tabulating the information I had collected about my prospective victims, I was able to concoct a suitable bait for each. None of my plans miscarried. All my guests arrived at Indian Island on the 8th of August. The party included myself.

Morris was already accounted for. He suffered from indigestion. Before leaving London I gave him a capsule to take last thing at night which had, I said, done wonders for my own gastric juices. He accepted it unhesitatingly —the man was a slight hypochondriac. I had no fear that he would leave any compromising documents or memoranda behind. He was not that sort of man.

The order of death upon the island had been subjected by me to special thought and care. There were, I considered, amongst my guests, varying degrees of guilt. Those whose guilt was the lightest should, I decided, pass out first, and not suffer the prolonged mental strain and fear that the more cold-blooded offenders were to suffer. Anthony Marston and Mrs. Rogers died first, the one instantaneously, the other in a peaceful sleep. Marston, I recognized, was a type born without that feeling of moral responsibility which most of us have. He was amoral—pagan. Mrs. Rogers, I had no doubt, had acted very largely under the influence of her husband.

I need not describe closely how those two met their deaths. The police will have been able to work that out quite easily. Potassium cyanide is easily obtained by householders for putting down wasps. I had some in my possession and it was easy to slip it into Marston's almost empty glass during the tense period after the gramophone recital.

I may say that I watched the faces of my guests closely during that indictment and I had no doubt whatever, after my long court experience, that one and all were guilty.

During recent bouts of pain, I had been ordered a sleeping draught—chloral hydrate. It had been easy for me to suppress this until I had a lethal amount in my possession. When Rogers brought up some brandy for his wife, he set it down on a table and in passing that table I put the stuff into the brandy. It was easy, for at that time suspicion had not begun to set in.

General Macarthur met his death quite painlessly. He did not hear me come up behind him. I had, of course, to choose my time for leaving the terrace very carefully, but everything was successful.

As I had anticipated, a search was made of the island and it was discovered that there was no one on it but our seven selves. That at once created an atmosphere of suspicion. According to my plan I should shortly need an ally. I selected Dr. Armstrong for that part. He was a gullible sort of man, he knew me by sight and reputation and it was inconceivable to him that a man of my standing should actually be a murderer! All his suspicions were directed against Lombard and I pretended to concur in these. I hinted to him that I had a scheme by which it might be possible to trap the murderer into incriminating himself.

Though a search had been made of everyone's room, no search had as yet been made of the persons themselves. But that was bound to come soon.

I killed Rogers on the morning of August 10th. He was

chopping sticks for lighting the fire and did not hear me approach. I found the key to the dining-room door in his pocket. He had locked it the night before.

In the confusion attending the finding of Rogers' body I slipped into Lombard's room and abstracted his revolver. I knew that he would have one with him—in fact, I had instructed Morris to suggest as much when he interviewed him.

At breakfast I slipped my last dose of chloral into Miss Brent's coffee when I was refilling her cup. We left her in the dining room. I slipped in there a little while later—she was nearly unconscious and it was easy to inject a strong solution of cyanide into her. The bumblebee business was really rather childish—but somehow, you know, it pleased me. I liked adhering as closely as possible to my nursery rhyme.

Immediately after this what I had already foreseen happened—indeed I believe I suggested it myself. We all submitted to a rigorous search. I had safely hidden away the revolver, and had no more cyanide or chloral in my possession.

It was then that I intimated to Armstrong that we must carry our plan into effect. It was simply this—*I* must appear to be the next victim. That would perhaps rattle the murderer—at any rate once I was supposed to be dead I could move about the house and spy upon the unknown murderer. Armstrong was keen on the idea. We carried it out that evening. A little plaster of red mud on the forehead—the red curtain and the wool and the stage was set. The lights of the candles were very flickering and uncertain and the only person who would examine me closely was Armstrong. It worked perfectly. Miss Claythorne screamed the house down when she found the seaweed which I had thoughtfully arranged in her room. They all rushed up, and I took up my pose of a murdered man.

The effect on them when they found me was all that could be desired. Armstrong acted his part in the most professional manner. They carried me upstairs and laid me on my bed. Nobody worried about me, they were all too deadly scared and terrified of each other.

I had a rendezvous with Armstrong outside the house at a quarter to two. I took him up a little way behind the house on the edge of the cliff. I said that here we could see if anyone else approached us, and we should not be seen from the house as the bedrooms faced the other way. He was still quite unsuspicious—and yet he ought to have been warned— If he had only remembered the words of the nursery rhyme, "A red herring swallowed one. . . ." He took the red herring all right.

It was quite easy. I uttered an exclamation, leant over the cliff, told him to look, wasn't that the mouth of a cave? He leant right over. A quick vigorous push sent him off his balance and splash into the heaving sea below. I returned to the house. It must have been my footfall that Blore heard. A few minutes after I had returned to Armstrong's room I left it, this time making a certain amount of noise so that someone *should* hear me. I heard a door open as I got to the bottom of the stairs. They must have just glimpsed my figure as I went out of the front door. It was a minute or two before they followed me. I had gone straight round the house and in at the dining-room window which I had left open. I shut the window and later I broke the glass. Then I went upstairs and laid myself out again on my bed.

I calculated that they would look closely at any of the corpses, a mere twitch aside of the sheet to satisfy themselves that it was not Armstrong masquerading as a body. This is exactly what occurred.

I forgot to say that I returned the revolver to Lombard's room. It may be of interest to someone to know where it was hidden during the search. There was a big pile of tinned food in the larder. I opened the bottommost of the tins—biscuits I think it contained—bedded in the revolver and replaced the strip of adhesive tape. I calculated, and rightly, that no one would think of working their way through a pile of apparently untouched foodstuffs, especially as all the top tins were soldered. The red curtain I had concealed by laying it flat on the seat of one of the drawing-room chairs under the chintz cover and the wool in the seat cushion, cutting a small hole.

And now came the moment that I had anticipated—

three people who were so frightened of each other that anything might happen—*and one of them had a revolver.* I watched them from the windows of the house. When Blore came up alone I had the big marble block poised ready. *Exit Blore.*

From my window I saw Vera Claythorne shoot Lombard. A daring and resourceful young woman. I always thought she was a match for him and more. As soon as that had happened I set the stage in her bedroom.

It was an interesting psychological experiment. Would the consciousness of her own guilt, the state of nervous tension consequent on having just shot a man, be sufficient, together with the hypnotic suggestion of the surroundings, to cause her to take her own life? I thought it would. I was right. Vera Claythorne hanged herself before my eyes where I stood in the shadow of the wardrobe.

And now for the last stage. I came forward, picked up the chair and set it against the wall. I looked for the revolver and found it at the top of the stairs where the girl had dropped it. I was careful to preserve her fingerprints on it.

And now? I shall finish writing this. I shall enclose it and seal it in a bottle and I shall throw the bottle into the sea. Why? Yes, why? . . . It was my ambition to *invent* a murder mystery that no one could solve. But no artist, I now realize, can be satisfied with art alone. There is a natural craving for recognition which cannot be gainsaid. I have, let me confess it in all humility, a pitiful human wish that someone should know just how clever I have been. . . .

In all this, I have assumed that the mystery of Indian Island will remain unsolved. It may be, of course, that the police will be cleverer than I think. There are, after all, three clues. One: the police are perfectly aware that Edward Seton was guilty. They know, therefore, that one of the ten people on the island was not a murderer in any sense of the word, and it follows, paradoxically, that that person must logically be the murderer. The second clue lies in the seventh verse of the nursery rhyme. Armstrong's death is associated with a "red herring" which he swallowed—or rather which resulted in swallowing him! That is to say that at that stage of the affair some hocus-pocus is clearly indicated—and that Armstrong was deceived by it and sent to his death. That might start a promising line of inquiry. For at that period there are only four persons and of those four I am clearly the only one likely to inspire him with confidence. The third is symbolical. The manner of my death marking me on the forehead. The brand of Cain.

There is, I think, little more to say. After entrusting my bottle and its message to the sea I shall go to my room and lay myself down on the bed. To my eyeglasses is attached what seems a length of fine black cord—but it is elastic cord. I shall lay the weight of my body on the glasses. The cord I shall loop around the door handle and attach it, not too solidly, to the revolver. What I think will happen is this. My hand, protected with a handkerchief, will press the trigger. My hand will fall to my side, the revolver, pulled by the elastic, will recoil to the door, jarred by the door handle it will detach itself from the elastic and fall. The elastic, released, will hang down innocently from the eyeglasses on which my body is lying. A handkerchief lying on the floor will cause no comment whatever. I shall be found, laid neatly on my bed, shot through the forehead in accordance with the record kept by my fellow victims. Times of death cannot be stated with any accuracy by the time our bodies are examined.

When the sea goes down, there will come from the mainland boats and men. And they will find ten dead bodies and an unsolved problem on Indian Island.

(Signed) LAWRENCE WARGRAVE

Agatha Christie is addicting!

Mystery and suspense with
every turn of the page.

_____ 54319	**DEATH COMES AS THE END**	$3.50
_____ 70230	**DESTINATION UNKNOWN**	$3.95
_____ 44723	**EASY TO KILL**	$3.50
_____ 70091	**ENDLESS NIGHT**	$3.95
_____ 60174	**EVIL UNDER THE SUN**	$3.50
_____ 69652	**FUNERALS ARE FATAL**	$3.95
_____ 70231	**HALLOWEEN PARTY**	$3.95
_____ 70263	**HICKORY, DICKORY DEATH**	$3.95
_____ 55701	**MIRROR CRACK'D**	$3.50
_____ 70090	**MRS. McGINTY'S DEAD**	$3.95
_____ 55267	**MURDER IS ANNOUNCED**	$3.50
_____ 70462	**MURDER OF ROGER ACKROYD**	$3.95
_____ 70463	**MURDER ON THE ORIENT EXPRESS**	$3.95
_____ 60221	**MURDER WITH MIRRORS**	$3.50
_____ 70264	**MYSTERY OF THE BLUE TRAIN**	$3.95
_____ 70416	**NEMESIS**	$3.95
_____ 70265	**ORDEAL BY INNOCENCE**	$3.95
_____ 54207	**THE PALE HORSE**	$3.50
_____ 60062	**PASSENGER TO FRANKFURT**	$3.50
_____ 70266	**PERIL AT END HOUSE**	$3.95
_____ 70266	**POCKET FULL OF RYE**	$3.95
_____ 70232	**REMEMBER DEATH**	$3.95
_____ 55222	**TEN LITTLE INDIANS**	$3.50
_____ 69653	**THIRD GIRL**	$3.95
_____ 70233	**TOWARDS ZERO**	$3.95
_____ 55645	**WHAT MRS. McGILLICUDDY SAW**	$3.50

POCKET BOOKS

Simon & Schuster, Mail Order Dept.   AGA
200 Old Tappan Rd., Old Tappan, N.J. 07675

Please send me the books I have checked above. I am enclosing $_____ (please add 75¢ to cover postage and handling for each order. N.Y.S. and N.Y.C. residents please add appropriate sales tax). Send check or money order—no cash or C.O.D.'s please. Allow up to six weeks for delivery. For purchases over $10.00 you may use VISA: card number, expiration date and customer signature must be included.

Name _____

Address _____

City _____ State/Zip _____

VISA Card No. _____ Exp. Date _____

Signature _____ 399-04